Sin and Grace

Book One
of the
Si Tanner Chronicles

Suzanne –
I do hope you
enjoy!

Catherine A Zaude
aug 20, 2007

Sin and Grace

A Historical Novel of the Skagway, Alaska Sporting Wars

BOOK ONE OF THE
SI TANNER CHRONICLES

BASED ON A TRUE STORY

By Catherine Holder Spude

Illustrations by the Author

Lynn Canal Publishing
Skagway, Alaska

ISBN: 0-945284-08-X

Direct inquiries to:
Lynn Canal Publishing
P.O. Box 498, 264 Broadway
Skagway, Alaska 99840-0498

www.skagwaybooks.com

Printed In Canada

TABLE OF CONTENTS

Dedicated to
Virginia Hillery Burfield
1914-2000
Magistrate of Skagway

LIST OF CHARACTERS

 **Tuck Flaharty:** Gold prospector, railroad man, and all-round Sport. He loves a prostitute and will never stop. His dream is to own the Board of Trade Saloon.

 **Essie Miller:** A career woman of the line, brothel worker, and landlady. She loves only one man. Her dream is to share her bed with only that man.

 **Si Tanner:** City magistrate, councilman, mayor, U. S. Marshal. Si is the law in Skagway. He knows the people better than anyone else. Can he get away with playing God, too?

 **Anna Stinebaugh:** Temperance leader, wife of barber J. D. Stinebaugh, owner of the Duchess Resort. Anna will sell her soul to rid Skagway of each and every saloon and prostitute.

 **Kitty Faith:** The Queen of the District, the richest woman in Skagway, and the one person from J. D. Stinebaugh's past who will plague Anna all her life.

Ida Freidinger: Skagway's oldest, most respected madam and Essie's mentor. She'll make or break Essie's fortune.

John W. Troy: Editor of Skagway's only daily newspaper. He thinks he controls the city.

Hans Schneider: Railroad foreman and bounty hunter, he thinks he can take the law into his own hands and satisfy a sick lust. He doesn't count on Si Tanner knowing more than he does.

Chris Wandsted: A simple carpenter who captures the heart of the richest woman in Skagway, answering a twenty-year old prayer.

Tad Hillery: One of the boys who frequents the Board of Trade and plays on the baseball teams, he's a sport that will wait years for his true love.

Jeannette deGruyter: The daughter of a gambler, she can't marry until she's 21, but she'll stay true to Tad. Their daughter will be the future of Skagway.

Lee Guthrie: Owner of the most lavish gambling resort and saloon between Seattle and Dawson during the gold rush days and the richest man in Skagway.

Sam Wall: He replaces John Troy at the helm of The Daily Alaskan. Can he run the city the way his predecessor did?

THE LADIES OF THE W. C. T. U.

Sarah Shorthill: The founder of Alaska's organization in 1899, Skagway's chapter in 1900, and the woman behind the passage of Alaska's temperance bill in 1917.

Grace Zinkan: Married to the Canadian Customs Agent, Gleason V. Zinkan, Anna Stinebaugh's best friend and officer of the organization.

Roberta "Bertie" Yorba: One of the women missionaries at the Peniel Mission.

Victorine "Vicky" Tooley: The other Peniel missionary.

Harriet Pullen: A widow and owner of the Pullen House, the largest, most opulent lodging place in Skagway. Harriet is Skagway's unofficial historian.

Elizabeth Harrison: Sarah Shorthill's daughter, wife of Floyd Harrison, who owns a funeral parlor and furniture store.

MAP OF SKAGWAY, ABOUT 1908

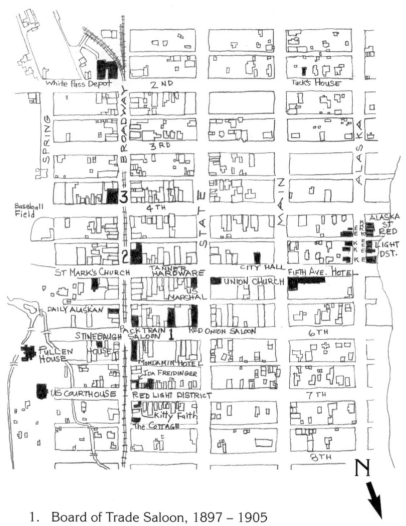

1. Board of Trade Saloon, 1897 – 1905
2. Board of Trade Saloon, 1905 – 1914
3. Board of Trade Saloon, 1914 – 1916
E: Essie's Brothels on Alaska Street, 1912-1917
K: Kitty's Brothels on Alaska Street, 1910-1915

Preface

We think of sports as vigorous outdoor games played with rules and balls and lots of physical combat. Sometimes they're played indoors, too. Boxers don't use a ball, but there's plenty of contact.

At the turn of the century, sports were something in which men engaged, and the sporting world included a lot more than games played with a ball. Important as the men found those athletic competitions, they knew a larger Sporting World. They called their bartenders Sports. Their best pals were Good Sports. Women who lived in that world referred to themselves as Sporting Women.

Today, when we pay a dollar for what they bought with a nickel, we've forgotten about that other Sporting World, outside the games played with balls – I mean the round, rubber ones you hit with a bat or a cue or bounce on a gym floor. We've forgotten because the good women of Skagway – and cities and towns all over the nation – fought a war to shut down the Sporting World and leave the men only their competitions.

Count now the casualties of the Sporting War.

Skaguay 1898

Chapter 1

Headed North

Wednesday, February 16, 1898. Tuck Flaharty followed his brother, Flick, off the gang plank of the S. S. Cleveland. Ed, Fitz and Billy were right on his heels, threatening to trip him up, gawking at the crowd and the wharf and the gray cliff like they had never seen wet, stone cliffs before. Well, sure, Bucyrus, Ohio didn't run to craggy, raw mountains dropping straight into choppy, glacier-fed, ocean inlets. But Tuck thought a man could pretend it was all old hat, instead of walking around with his jaw dropped open.

Flick found the lighter agent, who'd seen a hundred nervous greenhorns like these Ohio boys. "Yeah, yeah, lot number one thirty-four, we been through this ten times, buddy. Seventy-five hundred pounds. Here's your receipt. One of you guys wanta' watch us off-load it?" Flick nodded his head vigorously.

"You guys go on into town," Flick instructed. "Get us a room for the night. Then I want you, Tuck, back here by eight o'clock to relieve me. We'll take it in shifts. Tuck until

1

eleven. Clymer to two. Billy from two to five, then Fitz. We're all here at eight to take the lighter to Dyea. I'll bring you breakfast, Fitz."

Each man groaned at his assigned time, none of them as much as Tuck. Tuck would be missing the prime saloon time. But no one argued with Flick. They all agreed he was captain of this expedition, and he had taken the first watch, when he was probably just as curious about Skagway as the rest of them.

They said their begrudging goodbyes to Flick, as he clambered atop the crates, pistol at his side, wrapped up in four or five layers of sweaters and hats and scarves that Ma and Cad had knit for them, topped off with a brand new Yukon coat trimmed with coyote fur. Someone said it was ten degrees out here. Tuck didn't believe it. They were all too excited to feel the cold. Each of them swung his haversack over his shoulder and followed the stream of men into Skagway.

It was a raw, new town, huddled between soaring gray mountains. Tuck couldn't see their tops. They disappeared into white snow, which disappeared into white clouds. They were surrounded by mountains, enclosed by mountains. Somehow, they had to get over those mountains to find the mountains of gold.

Tuck lowered his bright, blue eyes to the town before him. This was no lazy Midwest farm town on market day. There were more hucksters and street callers than he'd ever seen in one place before. Men strode in a deliberate, determined pace everywhere he looked, the muddy streets thronged with crowds moving constantly up and down, to and fro, in and out of the rough-hewn buildings. Most of the false-fronts weren't even painted, seemingly freshly built. Those that wore colors sang them out brightly, and loud signs proclaimed imaginative names: the Glory Hole, the Falkboulia Barbershop, the Klondyke Trading Company, the Manhattan Wood Yards, the Pill Box Drug Company, E. R. People's Furniture and Funeral House, the Sterilized Milk Depot, the Red Front Stove Factory, the Portland Mitzpah House, the Pioneer Shoemaker, the Manila Cigar Store, and Mademoiselle Lavee's. Tuck paused by the latter's shop, curious, and then found she was a clairvoyant. That wasn't exactly what he had in mind, so he hurried to catch up with Billy and Clymer.

Then there were the saloons. Starting with the Hot Scotch at Second and Broadway, Tuck counted twenty before he lost track. There was the Idaho, the Club, the Merchants, the All Nations, the Monogram, the White Navy and the Al-Ki, the Jewel, the Kentucky House, the Little Club and the First and Last Chance all on Broadway before they even got to Sixth Avenue. Sixth was where the saloon district started, on the corner with the Pack Train. Down the street was the Board of Trade, said to be the grandest place between Seattle and Dawson. Tuck itched to go inside, glimpsing arches of elaborate woodwork and flashing crystal chandeliers, as he listened to the clatter and tinkle of roulette wheels.

"Oh, no you don't," Fitz Clymer grabbed his collar. "Flick said to get us a hotel room. You're not going drinking and gambling and whoring until we've got us some beds and grub, and I'm not letting you outa' my sight until I've handed you over to Flick."

"Ah, Fitz. This is the first we've been to Alaska. We're outa' Bucyrus. Ma's three thousand miles away. Flick is a mile and a half down the road and a captive of that grubstake. Three drinks. No more than two dollars on the poker tables, I swear it. Just one woman. I bet I can do it all before eight. I promise I'll be back at the lighter on time. You have my word on it."

"The hotel. Food. We'll go with you to the saloon. Two drinks. A dollar. At the Pack Train. No women. I'm taking you to Flick."

Tuck grinned, contented. He'd work out the woman on his own after his shift. He'd gotten all he really wanted.

They ended up at the Mondamin Hotel, at the corner of Sixth and Broadway, across the street from the Pack Train, in a room for just the five of them. With one taking watch over the supplies, there would be only the four of them to the one bed. They felt lucky. With the Cleveland and two other vessels offloading on the same day, the town's forty hotels filled up fast. They had dinner at The Mug Restaurant for fifty cents apiece and thought they got taken, but ate up good anyway. Tuck sincerely believed his beefsteak must have walked all the way to Alaska, it was that tough.

Every bit as good as any saloon at home, the Pack Train excited Tuck a good deal more. The cigar smoke hung thick in the air and the men talked loudly of their plans. Most of them relayed their supplies over the White Pass, trying to haul them by horseback over the narrow trail. They talked eagerly of the day when the railroad would be built, but wanted to beat it, because then the country would be flooded with greenhorns, people the experienced men called Cheechakos, who would steal the gold from men like them who had sweated and toiled and earned it the hard way. Tuck and Fitz and Billy and Ed sat quietly and listened, Cheechakos themselves, determined to get their claim to fortune.

Tuck downed his two-bit whiskey and looked around for a black jack game, tired already of the talk about hard work and sweat when the temperature hovered around ten degrees outside. "I'm going to get into that game," he told Fitz, indicating a table to his left. His old pal from Bucyrus eyed him skeptically, and then watched him like a hawk as he changed his dollar into one- and five-cent chips. Tuck snapped the single bill first at Fitz and then at the dealer to make sure both saw it was just one. Fitz smiled and leaned back to finish his whiskey at leisure. He was permitting himself only two as well, and was going to nurse his.

Tuck had the Flaharty luck and managed to keep his dollar – and to get two more – during the evening. He kept one eye on Fitz and Billy, just to make sure he knew their whereabouts, and so was able to find out where the girls tended to be. He wouldn't be heading straight back to the Mondamin when Fitz showed up at the dock at eleven. This was his one night in a town for another five months. He wasn't going to pass up his only chance at a woman until next June.

Tuck sauntered up State Street, avoiding Broadway because he'd been there already, and he thought he might run into Flick, out looking for him. That wouldn't do at all, not until he'd found that woman he needed. The agent back at the dock said to try Paradise Alley, back behind the saloons, but he also said the Red Onion could be a good place to start. The whiskey certainly would be cheaper than in a whore's crib.

Because he'd been counting the streets, Tuck knew when he got to the alley before Sixth. Well, it didn't take any genius to figure it out, even then, what with the women in their petticoats and chemises sitting out by their doorsteps and all those red curtains in the windows of the little houses along the alleyway. Tuck grinned as an extremely plump, brassy-haired harlot pursed her lips at him, crooked her finger in his direction and urged him to step her way. Figuring he'd be the one on top, he thought he'd be safe enough, but he wanted to enjoy himself a little longer than the fifteen minutes she'd allow him, so he chuckled and shook his head.

Rounding the corner of Sixth, he popped into the front door of the Red Onion Saloon, glancing through the crowd quickly to see if Flick or any of the other boys had settled on this place. Nope. No one familiar. Good. He strolled over to the bar and ordered a whiskey, feeling rich because he knew he'd be rich in another few months, as soon as he and the guys staked their claim in the Klondike.

"Hello, Sport," cooed a sweet voice at his shoulder.

Just the sound of the woman exhilarated him. He knew before he even turned to look at her that he'd be inside her before the night ended. He broke into a broad grin as he turned. Yep, even better than expected.

"Buy a girl a drink?"

"You betcha'," Tuck had been reaching for another quarter before she even asked, and he slapped it down on the bar just as she said the word "drink." He didn't need to look at the bartender. The vision of loveliness before him consumed his attention. He could see nothing else.

Tuck sat back and filled his memory with the sight of Essie. He knew she had forever ruined him for good and righteous women. Essie, of the long, dark brown tresses that spilled in thick coils around her bare throat and arms. Essie, with those big, dark brown eyes, that pale, milky skin with

5

not a mar or blemish anywhere, all of it smooth, and silky and perfect. Essie, who would let a man look at as much of that skin as he wanted, let him touch where he wanted, she who let a man do with that lovely body exactly what he wished. He couldn't imagine a good woman taking such an onslaught so good-naturedly. The very thought of her made his loins ache and he just satisfied, not three minutes ago.

"Oh, you're fine, Essie. Let me stay and talk awhile. It's been a long time since I talked to a woman," he begged.

"You know my rate, Cheechako," she smiled, not meaning any harm by calling him a newcomer. "You're paid up through the next fifteen minutes. Then you gotta' plunk down another two dollars. Don't matter what we do with the time."

Tuck scrambled for his pants. He found them on the floor where he'd thrown them about ten minutes ago. "Here," he came up with two silver dollars and dropped them on her naked belly. "Paid up through midnight. Now, let me tell you my story, let me gaze on your beauty, and maybe I'll want you again before you boot me out the door."

Essie giggled, apparently charmed by this young man, in spite of herself. "How do you want me? Back in my corset and petticoat?" She started to get up.

"No, just as you are. We'll be weeks on the trail, then on the Yukon and in the creeks. I won't see anything but hairy shins and beards from now until I'm rich. Let me look at that smooth skin and those lovely breasts of yours."

So she settled herself on the bed, like a Grecian goddess attended by nymphs. Before he could begin quizzing her on her origins, a subject she'd have to dance around, she asked him first.

"Where ya' from, Tuck?"

"Bucyrus, Ohio. Flat as they come. Nothin' but corn fields as far as you can see, if you stand on top of a wagon first, that is. Why here, you climb to the top of a mountain and see nothin' but mountain tops in every direction. Gets a man to wonderin' what's between those mountains, which one of them has the gold hidden under its top.

"You're a poet, Tuck, not a miner. Go back to Bucyrus. Poets don't find any gold here," Essie warned.

6

"I'm not leaving the North until I'm rich, Essie, until I've made my dream. I'm not going back to Ohio to work on the railroad like my daddy did." Tuck twisted his normally impish face into a fierce scowl. It seemed to surprise Essie.

"You're quite serious," she remarked.

"You bet. No long, lazy summer evenings sitting on the front porch watching the neighbors walk by for me. I'm gonna' make gold, play baseball and pool, and bowl, and buy me a saloon and live in it and find me a woman to wake up with everyday and laugh with the boys the rest of the time."

"Sounds fun, Tuck," Essie agreed.

He stretched out beside her on the bed, as naked as she was, caught up in his dream, forgetting he lay beside a ravishing beauty. Then he rolled over on top of her, quick as lightning, pulling her into his arms.

"We're all quite independent now, you know, Essie," he boasted. "Fitz cooks for us most of the time, but I'm getting passing fair at it, too. Either that, or we're all just getting used to our own cooking. I wrote Mama and our sister Cad that we can cook, wash, mend our clothes, etcetera, and the only thing we need wives for is to talk to. All they need do is to be at home at meal times. My brother Flick was furious. He said that Mama would be heartbroken, that she needed us to need good women to take care of us. He told me that if she thought we could take care of ourselves, she'd know this hare-brained scheme of ours was just exactly that, and that

7

we had cheated her of grandchildren forever."

"He's right, Tuck, you should never say such a thing to a mother."

"She knows darn well we need wives for more than just talking to!" Tuck replied indignantly. "I just couldn't say it to her and Cad."

Essie chuckled. Tuck knew that she, being a whore, understood perfectly well what men needed women for.

"Flick said that, too. He told me that wasn't the point. He told me relieving myself of desire with a woman like you wouldn't get me a son. Having a woman cook and clean for me and pamper me would get me sons, and that's what Mama wanted for us. He made me promise not to go telling her such things again. He said it's worse than saying we're staying up here forever."

"You want sons, Tuck?" Essie asked.

He knew it was an idle question, so he ignored it.

"But I might well be staying up here forever, whether Mama wants to believe it or not."

She wiggled beneath him and the important part of him responded. He forgot about talking to this woman about his dreams and getting the gold. He lowered himself a little and did what came naturally. He enjoyed Essie.

Anna Stinebaugh paused at the end of the steamer ramp to clasp her two small sons' hands more securely and look frantically about for Fay, who was only six years old. Oh, good, the child clung to her skirt like Anna had firmly instructed her. The crowd beat at her from every side. Where could James possibly be? All of these harsh, ugly men, with their loud voices, and their cursing, and the smell of liquor and tobacco reeking from their clothes. To what sort of terrible place had she brought her children?

She glanced up into the gray sky, only to have the wind whip one of the black ribbons from her austere felt hat into her face, slapping her with its sodden tail. She scowled at the miserable weather, forgetting to be thankful it wasn't snowing, as she was so sure it could be doing this time of year in Alaska. What had ever possessed her husband to leave Grants Pass, Oregon for a place like this? Anna knew that

8

times were hard in Oregon, that the change to the gold standard in 1893 had taken a terrible toll on the mining districts in the area where they lived, and that the lumber industry had never caught up, but really. A boom town in Alaska. It was no place to take a young family. The latest child was due any week now. But Anna knew if she stayed away any longer – well, there was just no telling what sort of economic scheme James would come up with next.

When Anna had found out about the Opera House, that shameful place in Grants Pass, it was just too much. He claimed he had invested as a silent partner, that it brought good money for the family since long before he met her. How dare he! To force her to agree to leave her home of eight years in the shame of knowing she had been living well because that sinful place existed.

Anna stepped back out of the stream of shoving, swearing, sweating men in their rubber and wool overcoats, their odor rank in the cold Skagway drizzle. She took a large breath to steady herself, and then sent a silent prayer upwards to her Lord to deliver her and her brood safely to her husband's door this evening. When she opened her eyes, she felt calmer, ready to face the almost unending job she had set for herself when she set foot on the S. S. Cottage City – to civilize whatever hellish new town her husband was taking her to. For the good of her children, and for the good of her fellow human beings.

Ah, there he was now. Anna dropped four-year-old Lewis' hand for only a moment, urging him to her side as a mother duck would do, and waved her hand frantically towards her wayward husband as she called out his name.

SIN AND GRACE

PARADISE ALLEY

Chapter Two

Mating Dance

Tuesday, April 2, 1901 (three years and one month later).   This fine, sunny afternoon demanded a stroll uptown, Essie Miller decided.   Melting snow and snippets of green, spring grass dazzled the eyes.   Now that she worked in a regular parlor house for Madam Ida Freidinger, she got out far too seldom, waiting for some man to come along and notice the red curtains in the window.   Time to display the wares. Essie donned one of her prettiest frocks, one not too risque', but with plenty of underskirts.   She applied her rouge and lip paint in a subdued manner (it wouldn't do to run into one of those temperance women) and skipped out Ida's door.   She ducked next door to Minnie's, to see if she wanted to go along.

11

By the time she made it to Broadway and Sixth, she had been joined not only by Minnie, but also by Josie, whom they had picked up at her one-woman brothel along Seventh Avenue, enjoying the purple crocuses by her front door. Oh, their high spirits soared. Essie had returned to Skagway only two weeks ago, working her circuit from Seattle to the gold fields, but the weather had been gray and gloomy, and business slow. With Essie ready for the men, the sun would bring them out. It had been a dull winter in Seattle, and she was prepared for the north's excitement.

The gaily bedecked women only complemented Skagway's flashy streets on this sunny spring day. Four years old and attaining a bit of a polished veneer, it was a still a rough town, huddled between those soaring gray mountains, the green at their feet promising a lush summer to come. Ordinarily a mere human couldn't see their tops because they shoved themselves into a perpetual cloud cover, hiding their snowy heads in the rain and the drizzle, up above that constant wind.

But today was different. That deep, blue sky opened high and endless above, and the white-topped peaks drew the eyes upward, pulling the men north, promising endless riches. The freshly turned garden beds and curtains dancing in open windows cried out, "Stop a little while and partake of Skagway's pleasures before you go on! You'll have lots of money before you come back. Spend a little of it now before you go." Essie and her sisters in sin knew they only added to the temptation.

The saucy tartlets sauntered down the street, past the mammoth, freshly painted side of the Mondamin Hotel, the beast that housed the miners since the first months of the rush. The three sashayed right at the corner and began their promenade past the brightly painted false fronts with their glittering windows, the noise of the player pianos, barkers, and clattering roulette wheels, and through the tobacco smoke pouring from the open doorways of the saloons, cigar stores and barber shops on Sixth Avenue. They joined the bachelors of Skagway, a street only the most brazen of women dared to trod.

In the lee of the Senate Saloon, that place that Essie had

once known as the Red Onion, the three hussies sashayed past four dapper young gentlemen, obviously also out for an afternoon stroll. Well, to say they passed each other understates the matter. The seven circled, an intricate mating dance, hips and shoulders swaying, skirts swirling, hats tipped and whistles called. Nothing was subtle. Essie slipped into full sports competition, suddenly forgetting all her friendly feelings towards her companions. Ida would appreciate having all four gentlemen at her place this evening.

She quickly snapped open the small purse at her waist and drew out four tokens. Each one read "Good for 50 cents at Ida's," twenty-five percent off the standard half hour, a very good deal. The men might brag, and bring more business. She flourished the coin purse, and then slowly pulled her full skirt, with the lace flounces underneath, up and

over an arched and shapely leg. Josie gasped at her brazen behavior. Minnie glanced up and down the street, especially towards Fifth, the direction of Sarah Shorthill's shop and the U. S. Marshal's office. None of them noticed the children beginning to spill out of the school held at the old Union Church across the street.

ESSIE

All four men ogled the leg. They would have been fascinated in her bedroom. Mesmerized that such a display might be attempted in broad daylight on a sidewalk next to a saloon, such an act had never even occurred to them before. Essie did not stop raising the skirt until well past her red garter, at mid-thigh. She rested the hem of the flounces two inches above the hosiery, pale, silky flesh tempting

13

them above the black stockinged leg. She slowly slipped a forefinger under the garter, inviting each man to do the same with a quick glance in his eyes, and then slipped the purse under it. She paused, caressing her naked flesh above her stocking briefly, before dropping the skirt. The four men inhaled in unison, having forgotten to breathe.

Essie glided to each man in turn, pressing against him as she slipped a token into his pocket, then let her hand linger on his upper thigh. "I'm at Ida's, Seventh and Broadway," she cooed. "We open at seven."

"My door is always open," Josie chimed in, attaching herself to the first gentleman as Essie, in her greed, abandoned him to move on to the next one. Essie heard her whisper in the chap's ear, "And I'm cheaper than that hussie." Essie snorted gently, thinking Josie ought to be grateful she could benefit by the warming up Essie had done for her.

Then Essie shrugged her shoulders. She really didn't mind. She knew she'd made an impression. The boys would be by this evening, all four of them. They'd all want another look at that leg and more of that skin, would fancy taking that stocking off. She doubted much else would have to go, just the stockings.

Minnie and Josie had each taken the arm of one of the first two dandies and begun to promenade back up State Street. Essie stood next to the third man, a sassy looking imp with deep, blue eyes and a bushy mustache. He looked familiar, but that didn't shock her. He'd probably been with her before. She went to slip the token in his pocket, but he grinned and took it from her.

The remaining man shot daggers of disgust at him. "Stay away from her, Tuck. I mean it."

"You're not stopping me this time, Flick. This one I'm going with. We're finally rich, and we can afford it. She's mine."

Flick Flaharty turned angrily on his heel and strode back up to Sixth. Tuck pulled Essie close to him and kissed her, long and sensuously. "Hello, Essie," he said when he released her. "If you won't have me until seven, then I'm sticking with you until then. Drinks and dinner, Darlin'?"

"I take it we've met before?" Essie smiled, unsure

whether she wanted to be tied up with this infectious young man during her next three hours.

"Oh, yes, twice now," he replied in an affected Irish brogue. "Now, the second t'was a night to remember." His eyes got a far and distant, glazed look. "At least for me," he chuckled. "I thought the stars had never blazed brighter, nor the air smelled sweeter. But it was summer in Dawson, and you don't see stars that time of year that far north. So it must have been the shimmer of your eyes and the milk of your skin instead of the Milky Way that I saw, and the perfume of your very essence that filled my soul."

Essie smiled in spite of herself. A whore, a good one, but a prostitute, nonetheless, she did not inspire lovesick youths to poetry. "You're full of blarney, Tuck, to sweet-talk a harlot like that."

"Ah, but it's a gift," he replied in his best Irish lilt. "Stay with me, Essie. We'll have some fun."

"I cost four dollars an hour," she warned.

"Done!" He dug a roll of bills out of his pocket. Glancing up and down the street, and then turning his back to the children across State, he counted out seventy dollars. Essie's eyes grew wide. "That will hold me until eight-thirty tomorrow morning. Oh, eight thirty-seven." He flipped her the token.

"For this, you get until nine," Essie grinned, clutching the roll of bills. She slipped the token and the one she meant for his brother back into his pocket. "Keep these for later." Essie slipped her hand into the crook of his arm, and Tuck swung her off towards Sixth Avenue.

Seven year old Lewis Stinebaugh tentatively entered the kitchen. His five-year-old brother, Sammy, followed right behind him. He saw his sister Goldie playing on the floor. "We're home, Mama." The door thwacked shut behind him. He cringed. He knew not to let it bang like that.

"Don't let the door slam, Lewis," Anna reminded him, sternly. "Where's Fay?"

"She had to stay after to help Mrs. Rosenberg with tomorrow's lesson."

"Oh, that's right. I remember now. Well, here are some

cookies and milk. Up to the table with both of you, and then outside for a while. I've lots to do yet, so I want you two to play outside this afternoon."

"Yes, ma'am." The boys knew better than to cross their busy mother. But for the moment, here in the kitchen, they had her captive. He chewed his cookie thoughtfully.

"Mama?" he asked tentatively.

"Hmmm?" Anna replied absently, concentrating on the potato she peeled.

"Sammy and I saw some ladies acting strange by the school this afternoon. One of them pulled her skirt way up past her knee! Why'd she do that?"

"What!" Anna cried, caught completely off guard. She knew the day would come when the boys would ask about those women, and she had wanted to be calm and reasonable when she explained about the women's – and the men's – sins. She had not meant to frighten the boys. Yet here they stood before her, puzzlement on their faces, now combined with fear from her exclamation of horror.

The damage done, she sank to her knees before her sons' chairs and took their hands in hers. She modulated her voice to a calm, quiet register, the model of motherly comfort. "Tell me what you saw, Lewis. Don't leave anything out. I'll try to explain it all." She did her best to contain her fury as Anna Stinebaugh's sons related their version of Essie's and Tuck's mating dance.

* * *

Monday, April 22, 1901 (thirteen days later). Tuck Flaharty rounded the corner of the courthouse, looking for city magistrate Si Tanner. He found the tall, broad-shouldered man on the leeward side of the building, smoking one of his favorite cigars, needing something to clear his head after all that smoke-blowing at the city council meeting inside. Tuck sauntered up to him.

"What just happened, Mr. Tanner?" he asked. "I was there, but I don't understand. Mrs. Shorthill and Mrs. Stinebaugh, they got all upset about Miss Miller showing her stockings where the kids at the school could see them, so they ask the council to close down the alleys? Sure, Jap Alley is right behind the Union Church, where the school is.

16

And Paradise Alley is just across the street. But that school is temporary. The liquor licenses are paying for a new school clear down on Twelfth. The kids will be gone in another few months."

Si shook his head. "Essie reminded the reform women that the business girls exist in Skagway. Those women had been thinking about the saloons so much they forgot about the gals in the alleys. Essie pulling up her skirts made those little boys and girls start asking questions their mommas and papas don't like to answer."

Tuck scowled, trying to think it all out. "But it doesn't make any sense. Those women forced the Japanese and French girls out of a living, and then the council goes and turns Seventh Avenue into an official red light district. How does that get rid of the problem, as the reform women see it?"

"What you boys gonna' do if you don't have the girls to go to, Tuck?" Tanner asked around the puff of cigar smoke he exhaled.

Tuck thought a minute, then grinned. "Well, now, that Fran Stinebaugh. She's mighty fine looking. Guess I'd ask her out. Start courting her."

"She's what, sixteen years old? How many young ladies like her are in town?" Tanner raised one of his big, bushy eyebrows.

"Hmmm, that's the problem, isn't it?" Tuck admitted. "There's Jeannette deGruyter and, uh, Hazel Cleveland and Lillie Donaldson, and maybe half a dozen more, the businessmen's daughters."

"And how many men working on the railroad right now, all bachelors and all feeling pretty lonely?" Si asked, stroking his equally bushy mustache. Someone comparing the two men would have been hard put to say which one had the messiest bunch of hair above his lip. That didn't mean either one of them had even one card short of a full deck.

"Oh, gotta' be fifty, sixty of us, at least." Tuck shook his head.

"You think J. D. Stinebaugh wants five or six of you courting his sixteen-year old daughter all at the same time, putting pressure on her to put up? You willing to share her attentions with five other men like you are some woman over on Seventh Avenue?" Si pointed out.

Tuck shook his head. He could see where there might be the sort of problem that even Anna Stinebaugh could comprehend.

"You understand why some folks call it 'The Necessary Evil?' They don't see anyway around it. They know they need you railroad boys here in town, or there wouldn't be a town. They know you gotta' have some female companionship, and they don't want you chasing after their daughters. So they find a place they can put the business women where they can pretend the girls don't exist."

Si leaned back against the courthouse and took another puff of his cigar. "When a girl like Essie makes a fuss and calls it to everyone's attention, well, then someone has to pay. You pick on the most obvious, the ones that can't fight back. In this case, it's the Japanese women, because their only champions are Frank Keelar, a big blow-hard, and Lee Guthrie who's powerful and well-connected, but conveniently out of town at the moment. Both of them own the lots the Japanese women rent. But Lee also happens to own land on Seventh Avenue and will make a killing renting to whores up there. Frank's pretty much already decided to leave Skagway anyway, so he just has to swallow his losses."

"I still don't understand all of it, Mr. Tanner," Tuck said, clearly puzzled. "I thought women like Anna Stinebaugh and Sarah Shorthill wanted to get rid of the working women altogether. What's the good of running the girls out of the alleys? Seems to me it will only get better for them up on Seventh, not worse."

Si grinned. "You're thinking like a working man, Mr. Flaharty, not a businessman or a reformer. You see, those reform women, they think they've just driven the Japanese whores out of town. They don't realize they've sent all the other working girls to a protected place, where they can operate their business without any trouble from now on. That's the deal Mr. Keelar just cut with the madams. Yeah, they may have gotten rid of the crib women and the saloon girls, but Anna Stinebaugh and Sarah Shorthill just did one giant favor for business women like Ida Freidinger and Kitty

Faith, not to mention landlords J. D. Stinebaugh, Lee Guthrie and Phil Snyder."

"How's that?" Tuck wanted to know.

"The madams and the landlords now own a limited commodity, property that will only go up in value, in a business the rest of us will do a great deal to protect. Like I said, can't run a railroad town without whores, can we?"

Tuck grinned, beginning to understand.

"Yep, the only thing Frank Keelar's mourning tonight is his own shortsightedness in not buying property on Seventh Avenue years ago. He'll never get any now." Si shook his head, sadly.

"I hear you got a friend or two in the demimonde," Si continued, piercing Tuck with his sharp eyes as he took another puff on that cigar.

Tuck nodded his head, thinking about Essie.

"She's smart to be with Ida. If she stays there, she'll be in good shape, you know that, don't you Tuck?" Si warned.

Again Tuck nodded. He couldn't fool the magistrate. He'd heard a lot about this man. Si Tanner knew more than anyone in town about everyone. Obviously, he knew who Essie had been with when she showed the school children her leg.

"Reason we in the law profession don't much care for the crib women, the saloon girls, and the ones working on their own, is because they're problems. They get drunk, call attention to themselves, let the kids and the decent women know they're around. You know what I mean?"

Tuck nodded.

"But when the women work in the parlor houses, the madams can control them. Now that we have a district, we can set up rules with the madams, who will keep their girls straight, quiet, out of trouble. They'll stay indoors during the day, won't drink, or use opium, won't end up in John Troy's newspaper. Women like Anna Stinebaugh won't hear about them and will soon forget they even exist. Then you can go on spending your money the way you want, my boy, the little kids won't be asking uncomfortable questions at home, and the landowners on Seventh Avenue can continue to rake in their outrageous rents. Everyone's happy." Si took another big puff of that cigar he was smoking.

"I guess," Tuck allowed. "Seems to me, though, that things just got a bit more expensive for us working guys, building in another layer of overhead like that."

Si laughed. "You've got that right, Sport. But, at least you still have your amusements. For now."

Si tapped the ash off the end of his cigar. Tuck made a move to leave, but the magistrate had another thing or two he wanted to say. "Speaking of amusements, I hear you want to start up a baseball team. Any truth to that?"

Tuck's face lit up like a lantern. "You bet. You like the ball games?"

"I've organized teams since I was sixteen. We need more games around here. You think you can get some of those railroad bum friends of yours to put up a team against, say, the guys at the wharves?"

"Who'd manage them?" Tuck wanted to know.

"I heard Shea wanted to get a team going. He's been asking around the saloons."

Tuck grinned. The bartender at the Board of Trade, huh? Yeah, he hung out with Billy Blackmer, one of the mechanics, and Harry Schofield, a wharfinger. Okay. Didn't know they liked baseball, but the marshal would know if anyone did.

"Thanks Mr. Tanner. I'll go see Shea."

Tuck sauntered away with a lot on his mind, mostly baseball. If he was gonna' stay in Skagway – and he had a good mind to do just that – he'd sure as hell need to have a baseball team to play with. As he walked off towards the Board of Trade to get to know this Chris Shea guy, he forgot he needed to warn Essie about staying away from Si Tanner.

Chapter Three

Bachelor Life

Saturday, June 20, 1903 (two years later). Tuck swung the bat with all his might, connecting with the ball squarely, just like he knew he would. He couldn't always hit Chris' fast balls, but when he saw this one coming, he knew he'd do it. He let out a whoop of joy and bounded off around the bases, dancing as he went, not in a great hurry. A home run, he brought in two men with him. He laughed as Chris threw down his cap in exasperation.

Flick pounded him on the back after the game. The Monkey Wrenches had beat Chris Shea's team, the Eccentrics, once again. These rag-tag baseball games – John Troy, editor of The Daily Alaskan, insisted on calling them "ragtime games" – created a hell of a lot of fun. They made working for the railroad again bearable. Tuck looked around for Chris, wanting to rub the victory into his face. He saw the short, muscular, dark-haired, clean-shaven man talking to that little slip of a girl, Helen Eckert, the preacher's daughter. Why a bartender would go sniffing after a preacher's girl, Tuck had no idea. He decided to leave him alone for a while. That tease Helen never let Chris walk her home. Chris would be around later. Tuck walked over to where Bob Stilts had his keg of beer instead. Bob, the bartender at the Mascot, always brought some beer to share.

Just as Tuck predicted, it didn't take long for Chris to show up. He flicked Tuck's hat off onto the ground. "That's for getting mine all covered with dirt."

"I saw you throw yours down on purpose."

"That's two games now you've hit my best fast ball. I can't help throwing my hat down after you do something like that."

"It's Tuck's luck. It has nothing to do with talent." Flick appeared beside them, never far from his brother.

"Hi, Harry," Chris greeted Flick, calling him by the name their Mama gave him. Flick had decided to become more respectable, to forego the family nickname here in Skagway. Tuck would have none of that nonsense. He could not tolerate anyone calling him Frederick, or Fred, or even Freddy.

"You pitched a good game, Chris. You lost by only those three runs that Tuck picked up on his unreliable Flaharty luck."

They all knew it to be true and grinned. "Come down to the Board of Trade. Drinks are on me." Traditionally, the captain of the losing team bought a round for the winners. Chris clapped one arm around Tuck and another around his good pal Billy Blackmer, Tuck's catcher, and steered them both towards Broadway.

In the saloon, Chris drew the last of the drafts for his own team, then one for himself and sauntered to the end of the bar where Tuck perched on the single stool Lee Guthrie allowed. Billy lurked in the shadows nearby, but Tuck ignored him. Chris winked at Billy and indulged Tuck, who'd been admiring the ornate, gleaming woodwork and crystal chandeliers. The Board of Trade, a high class resort, was not the sort of place he usually went. The guys all trooped out to the main room, to cluster around the black jack tables, studiously avoiding the roulette wheels. They'd drink their one beer, and then drift off to the Mascot or the Pack Train, somewhere more welcoming to the laboring crowd than the fancy Board of Trade. Being Lee's best bartender, though, Chris got his beer for half price. He'd buy the guys his round at the saloon where he worked.

"You know I'm gonna' own this place some day, don't you?" Tuck observed, a little too casually.

Chris turned the left side of his mouth up in a half smile at Tuck's usual opening. "Lee might have something to say about that."

Tuck waved the observation aside as if it made for no consequence. "Only I'll make it a lot friendlier. All the guys will want to come here. It will be busy and noisy, and will have lots of good music."

"Well, I do have to admit the Board of Trade seems all too quiet these days. The businessmen, engineers and high class travelers that come in here like a subdued atmosphere, just the sound of the roulette wheel spinning and business conversation at the tables," Chris observed, neutrally. "But when will you have time to run a saloon, Tuck? Handball in the spring, baseball in the summer, bowling in the winter. Oh, yeah, Essie in the fall. I can barely manage baseball in the summer, and I'm just a bartender on a night shift. Believe me, I'm relieved when the season's over, and I can get some sleep again."

"At the rate you're going with that pretty little preacher's daughter, you won't be getting any sleep in the daytime, either," Tuck winked.

Chris grinned. "Her papa's got her locked up tighter than Henry's wives in the Tower of London. I'm lucky to have ten words with her at the games. I have to go to Kitty's on my day off when my needs exceed what my heart desires."

Tuck saw the longing on his friend's face, and for a moment envied the man his devotion to a single woman. Then he thought of Essie and realized he had developed his own sort of devotion. When Essie came to Skagway, he went to no one else. He never thought of the other men with whom she lay. When he was with Essie, it was just the two of them, just a man and a woman, binding themselves in an act of joy. With Essie it was better than with any other woman. With Essie, he lost himself completely. With Essie he was all man, completely a man, had not given away his fortune, was not once again a lowly laborer working on a railroad.

Tuck looked up as Wil Cleveland came in the door, having walked his sister home. Tad Hillery motioned him over to the table that he and a couple of other guys claimed. Tuck remembered that Wil liked to visit the women of Seventh Avenue, too. He'd seen him at Ida's once or twice, when he'd been waiting for Essie.

Essie. Now that he had Essie in his head, he couldn't get her out. She'd come back to Skagway early this year and seemed to be staying longer. Tuck slugged down the rest of his beer.

"I gotta' go, Chris." Tuck nodded to Billy, finally acknowledging him as the catcher replaced him at the stool.

Chris raised his eyebrows, not really surprised at Tuck's sudden leave-taking. Tuck's mercurial moods never really took him aback. He smiled as Tuck headed for the door, pretty sure he knew what had precipitated the man's sudden change in plans. He wished his own heartaches could be cured so simply. He turned to Billy and asked his old friend how he was doing.

Tuck entered Ida's deceptively large parlor, given the narrow hallway from the modest door on Broadway. Ida, dressed severely in black taffeta with old-fashioned mutton chop sleeves, rustled her way across the room to greet him.

"Why, Mr. Flaharty. It's always a pleasure to see you," she simpered. "I'll get you a beer. I'm sure Miss Miller can join you sometime soon."

Ida knew him well, knew what and who he wanted. He flirted with the unattached blond that came out of the corner to circle him, matching her clever remarks quip for quip. He had great fun, but it was just a warm-up for Essie. Millie didn't know that. Being new, Tuck bet she thought she had this imp with the bushy mustache and twinkling blue eyes for herself. When he heard the footsteps in the hallway, the man leaving through the front door, the softer rustle of skirts coming through the portiere, he turned in pleasure to catch Essie up in his arms. Millie assumed a pretty pout.

"He's mine, Essie. I had him first," she sulked.

"That's where you're wrong, Millie," Essie returned, not

looking her way. She and Tuck had eyes only for each other. "Tuck's always been mine, haven't you, Lover."

In answer, he covered her mouth with his, kissing her thoroughly, in a way even a whore would savor. Millie groaned in envy. Tuck slapped almost two days' wages down on the small table, then swung Essie up in his arms and carried her off to her room without a backward glance at Minnie or Ida. It wouldn't even get him three hours with her, but what time he had would be worth it.

"You must have won tonight, Tuck, my boy," Essie observed when he lay still at her side, muscles finally soft, his breathing still fast, but slowing in her ear.

"How'd you know, Darlin'?" he mumbled into her hair.

"You always have an extra juice, a special flair when you win, as if you're still driving that bat into the ball," she chuckled.

Tuck smiled. "Ummm. That's what it feels like. That extra push, the special umph that pays off." His eyes glazed over. "Just talking about it makes me feel it again."

He snuggled in closer to her, running a hand over her naked breast. "You shouldn't talk about such things, Darlin'," he warned. "You'll rush me. I still have two and a half hours." He idly caressed her arm. "Three times. I wanted three times with you tonight, so I have to rest a little in between."

Essie smiled in return and stretched luxuriously. Times like now, with a man like Tuck Flaharty, she enjoyed this job. He made her feel good, and she always had fun with him. He made her forget about the work, made her think it could be something else. For a little while, she could pretend it was. That first time he stayed all night, when she woke with Tuck beside her, she wondered what it would be like to live as the good women in town did, to wake each morning with the same man in bed with her, holding her like he really cared, not like he wanted only her body, but like he wanted her heart as well.

She wished he had not gone home to Bucyrus, Ohio and given all his money to his parents and then come back to Alaska to work for the White Pass railroad at two dollars a day. He told her the North was in his blood, that if he had to work for a railroad, at least let it be one in Alaska. He told her Minnie Owens had married Jimmie Johnson and had a bouncing baby boy by the time he got back to Bucyrus, and that he couldn't stay away from Essie. He told her he slaved at the railroad to become a baggage man so he could afford to see her more than once every two weeks. He said he despaired when she left in the summer to go to Dawson or the Tanana or wherever the men went, and in the winter to go to Seattle. He claimed he lived for spring and fall, when she came to Ida's. Flick wouldn't let him leave Skagway, not to run after a whore. She begged him to stay here in Skagway, save his money, wait for her. Someday he would get his saloon, if he'd only save his money.

Essie tried not to think about Tuck with other women, but she knew when she was gone, he went to them. Ironic that a whore would be jealous of other whores. She didn't think he begrudged her what she did for a living. It made her treasure him all the more. She wouldn't take his money from him, if Ida didn't make her. Essie thought of the savings account she had in the Canadian Bank of Commerce here in Skagway. She put only Tuck's money in that special account. All of Tuck's money went there, starting with that first forty-five dollars, including the tips. It would go for something that would be only hers and Tuck's.

Essie turned to Tuck, responding to his caresses. "I love you, Darlin'," he whispered in her ear. "I can't live without you."

Essie returned his kiss with heart-felt passion. A whore could never admit of loving a customer, not aloud. Tuck knew that. But he knew how she felt, and the fact that she would admit it, even with the return of his passion, fired his loins. He wondered if he could manage four times.

Ida

Chapter Four

Betrayal

Wednesday, July 1, 1903 (eleven days later). Dark and handsome, Hans Schneider had a way with women. Most of the female clerks and waitresses in the shops and restaurants in Skagway dimpled when he strode into their places, lifted his hat, flashed that smile at them, and asked for whatever he came in to get with just the mere suggestion of lechery in his voice. He knew it sent delicious thrills up their spines. All of them wondered what it would be like to feel those muscular arms around their waists, those full lips on their mouths, those strong thighs pressed against their skirts. He would leave corsets heaving in his wake, ladies needing to sit down to catch their breaths, wishing they hadn't laced up quite so tightly that morning.

He might have been a very good catch, at least from the standpoint of the daughters of Skagway, even with the rather

27

modest jobs he seemed to prefer. Lately he had taken the position as a job foreman on the railroad. He seemed a natural leader and could make men do what they needed to get the job done. The women in town didn't know how he did it. Men did. Not many approved, but they kept their opinions to themselves. The management at the White Pass and Yukon Route thought he worked out just fine.

The town's papas discouraged his attentions when he came to call at the door. Mr. Hans Schneider, unhappily, had two major failings. First, Hans could consume great quantities of liquor and, oh, how he loved his liquor. It was his good fortune that his friends tolerated his withdrawn behavior when he became drunk, largely for the sake of his generosity. He treated all his friends to whiskey when he drank, and let them match him glass for glass, at his expense. Schneider's brooding gaze and rude manners could easily be ignored for such lugubrious rewards.

Secondly, the town fathers knew where Mr. Schneider spent most of his evenings, and it wasn't at the ball games, with most of the young men. When he wasn't in the saloons, getting drunk, then he was in the company of women, and the ladies with whom he associated were not ladies. While he knocked on the doors of the businessmen's homes from time to time, he had long ago given up the idea of any real courtship, for he wanted results far too quickly. Hans had lately fallen to seeking an unending sequence of brides among the women of Seventh Avenue.

Essie knew all these facts about Hans. She played his bride this evening. She knew he liked her because she played the spry, sassy, glitzy part he found so attractive. She'd learned to tease him unmercifully, and then, just when he thought he'd go mad with desire, she'd be there for him, a little fireball of spunk and plump flesh. As always, she was just what he wanted tonight.

She was being that perky tease, not letting him touch her, just making him look. He reached again for her, but she slid from his fingers too easily. All that smooth, white flesh, still covered up by that corset and those stockings. She knew he needed to see more of her, feel more of her, and then bury himself in all of her silky softness. But since she wouldn't let him grab her, he grabbed the bottle of whiskey on the dresser instead and poured himself another drink.

"C'mon, Honey. I'm needing you real soon now, and I'd like to hold those sweet peaches of yours just a little before I do." Essie just giggled and danced away from him.

She looked Schneider in the eye and realized she didn't know him as well as she might. Suddenly she wondered if she should have let him bring the entire bottle of whiskey into the room with them. Or whether she should have strung him out so long. A good whore knows how to gauge a man's mood, knows just the right time to let him have his way. Essie doubted that she'd had enough experience with this type of man yet. She watched his eyes and understood all of her wrong decisions the moment Schneider hit his mean point.

He sprang at her suddenly, a mixture of raw desire and rage replacing the smile on his face. He laid her flat on her back, his right hand urgently stripping his remaining clothes from his body. As his pants fell to the floor, his hand emerged from a pocket holding a switchblade. He pressed the button on the handle and the blade snapped open. Essie felt panic race through her body.

Essie's heart thundered at the sight of the knife. She had never heard of a man turning violent with one of the girls on Seventh Avenue before. It just didn't happen in Skagway. She opened her mouth to scream, but he slapped his palm over it and growled at her to keep her trap shut, or he'd cut her. Because that's what she thought he intended to do to begin with, she took a breath to steady herself, confused. She watched, horrified, as he lowered the tip to the cleavage between her breasts, and then began to methodically cut the laces on her corset.

The look of mad desire never left his eyes, but a grim smile replaced the scowl of rage that had twisted Schneider's mouth. When he had cut all of the laces, he pulled the corset apart and stared at her naked breasts. It seemed like such a simple thing, and if Essie had only shown them to him three minutes earlier, she would not be lying there wondering if she would feel a blade in her ribs next. He tossed the knife to his fallen pants, and then handled her breasts, taking one into his mouth, to suck long and hard. It hurt, but she lived, and she didn't bleed anywhere. In another moment, he was in her and pumping, and then he was done, heavy and limp on top of her, as if he were the one who was dead.

Essie the whore had never been treated like that before. She was a fun harlot and the men who came to her came to have a good time. What had just happened was not a good time. She took a lung full of air and screamed. Then she pitched Hans Schneider off her bed. She grabbed up a kimono and shimmied into it faster than she had ever shimmied out of it. Clutching her severed corset to her breast, she took one last horrified look at her attacker and fled to the safety of her madam's room.

* * *

Saturday, September 26, 1903 (three months later). U. S. Deputy Marshal John Snook ushered Mrs. Ida Freidinger into U. S. Commissioner J. J. Rogers' office. Town magistrate Si Tanner accompanied him. Si smiled knowingly. When the deputy left the room, he settled against the door to listen in. Si learned everything that happened in this town. He wasn't going to let this event pass without his knowledge. The judge and the madam ignored him. Si would keep his mouth shut. He was the most reliable man in Skagway. Si Tanner deserved to know what deal they cut.

Judge Rogers nodded to the chair beside his desk. Ida looked at it a moment, considering whether she wanted to play any games, then decided better. She walked to the chair and sat in it, without a flounce, a sway, or so much as a little flirt. She did allow herself half a smile.

"Ida," the judge stated, flatly.

"J. J.," she replied.

Having acknowledged each other, the two did not seem to know where to go next. Finally, Rogers sighed and tossed his pencil onto the desk. "Why are you doing this, Ida?"

She turned her eyes from her lap to meet his. "I'm getting tired of this, J. J. Your boss in Juneau says he's turning us over to the cities. So now I gotta' be nice to Si Tanner. I like being nice to Si." She flicked her eyes over to the magistrate, smiling slightly. "He's tall and strong and handsome and has some integrity. I can trust the man. He brings me into his court just a month ago, and I hand over twenty dollars, and he tells me that if I come in nice and sweet every three months with my twenty dollars, I won't get any more trouble from you or him or any of the coppers around town. That was the deal." She fluttered her eyes at Si, then at J. J.

"Judge Brown, he said it was all over between you and me, and I believed him. Now, here I am, back in your courtroom again, and you asking me for more money. Me and a dozen other business women from Seventh Avenue. I believe all of us had the same chat with Mr. Tanner just last month." Ida glanced at Si again, and turned back to Mr. Rogers. "Now maybe all of them are going to pay Si twenty dollars and you twenty dollars every three months, but I don't think I'm going to." Ida fluttered her eyes again. "That's why I entered a plea of not guilty. That's what this is all about."

"You know you're guilty, Ida."

"That's not the point, J. J."

Rogers picked up his pencil and tapped it against the corner of his desk. "I've got my orders, sweetheart. This isn't up to me."

"Then I guess it will be a trial, won't it," Ida answered him.

Si smiled to himself. He knew Rogers didn't want a trial. Most of the men in Skagway would let her go free. Public opinion would go with the demimonde this time, thanks to John Troy. Ida probably wanted to plant a big, sweet kiss on that man for all the kind things he'd been saying about the women on Seventh Avenue lately. Disguised in his usual rhetoric of home rule, he actually fought to keep the federal courts out of the business of collecting fines from Skagway's prostitutes. He and the good men at City Hall wanted all of those revenues for themselves. Well, more power to them if they kept the fines to a sweet eighty dollars a year. The deputy and Mr. Rogers had a nasty habit of fining her from fifty to a hundred every time they dragged the prostitutes into federal court, usually without warning.

"Mr. Troy would love the spectacle of poor Mrs. Freidinger in court, wouldn't he?" Ida suggested.

Si grinned, thinking how the newspaper editor might turn that particular story into another tirade for home rule. He had once called her one of Skagway's better endowed land owners. I wonder if he would remember that time, he reflected. Wouldn't do to recall a time when the almost ninety percent male populous loved the whores and thought well of them. Those days were long gone.

Rogers squirmed. Si knew he didn't like to think of what John Troy would do with the story. The newspaper editor made far too much controversy of this little territorial spat over who got to keep the fines from the prostitutes as it was. Trust Troy to turn a simple little trial of a four-dollar whore's fine into this month's big story.

J. J. shook his head, closed his eyes, and massaged his forehead. "What do you have in mind, Ida?"

Ida Freidinger smiled. Si predicted that J. J. would see this her way.

"I understand Mr. Schneider's trial is coming up next month, and it's due to be here in Skagway."

"You understand correctly, Mrs. Freidinger. If I remember correctly, you have been subpoenaed as a witness for the prosecution." J. J. acknowledged.

"Now, rumor has it that Mr. Schneider's attorney has asked for a continuance until the next court session, which would take the trial to Juneau, where he would not have nearly so many friends. That's true, isn't it?"

Judge Rogers scowled. Si knew he didn't like the fact that Ida understood so much about what was going on in this town, more than the judge did.

"Now why would he do that?" J. J. wanted to know.

Ida shrugged, not privy to the minds of lawyers.

"So what does this have to do with you pleading guilty to yesterday's charges?" the judge wanted to know.

"A prosecuting witness can turn into a defense witness pretty easily, if she has sufficient incentive. In fact, seeing as Miss Miller is one of my girls, there may not be a need for a trial at all. Either way, everyone comes out feeling better about the whole thing."

Except Miss Miller, Si thought.

"And what makes you think I am at all interested in the outcome of Mr. Schneider's case?" demanded J. J. Rogers. Si knew he was bluffing. The two of them played poker on

Wednesday nights, and Si understood all of J. J.'s tactics.

"I just suspect that you would prefer that both cases stay out of Mr. Troy's newspaper at this time," Ida suggested coyly. "Besides, most of you gentlemen would rather pretend that the highest performing foreman on the railroad for six months in a row is a man above reproach. I have noticed that his weekly debaucheries at both the saloons and the places along Seventh Avenue remain unmentioned in Mr. Troy's newspaper. If all of you are so anxious to keep Mr. Schneider at work and out of jail, then I suppose you can find a reason to help me."

J. J. frowned. Si could see him searching for other alternatives, but he couldn't come up with one. He knew she had him. "Alright. I understand the stove in the courtroom does not work properly. We will not hold court for the next several days. Your paperwork will become lost by the time it is fixed. You had better deliver on Mr. Schneider's testimony, or I shall find the paperwork, believe me. And we can always find excuses to press charges for selling liquor without a license or other, similar accusations," he reminded her.

Ida smiled. She stood and offered him her hand. "I always enjoy doing business with you, Mr. Rogers," she cooed.

The judge took the offered hand and brought it to his lips, smiling. She could be charming. Dangerous, but charming. He led Mrs. Freidinger to his door as Si opened it for them. J. J. called Deputy Snook to have him escort her to the clerk.

Only after he shut the door again did J. J. look at Si.

"The woman's smart," he acknowledged.

"She runs a business she has to protect," Tanner pointed out. "This town needs her kind of business, and it needs their revenues. We're going to get them, and we're going to keep them. Troy's right. The general treasury doesn't even let Alaska keep the money. We can fix our streets, pay the electric bill for our street lights, our city doctor's fees, and the night watchman's salary with the prostitutes' fines. Give it up, J. J."

"As soon as Judge Brown gives the word, I will. You know that."

The city magistrate grunted.

"I think I'll take a little trip down to Juneau. Judge Brown owes me one for backing down on the saloon protest. You watch. You won't be hearing from the D. A. again."

J. J. Rogers smiled. "If Si Tanner says something will happen, it will. The man who rounded up the Soapy Smith gang, then held off the town lynch mob can make miracles occur."

Si smiled his sardonic half-smile. "I had help back in '98. You know that. Soapy Smith, that old con man, he deserved to die. Frank Reid shot him fair and square."

J. J. raised his eyebrows, but didn't argue. The folks in the know recognized that Reid didn't fire the fatal bullet and that Si's rifle was the only one within shooting range with a matching caliber bullet. Si glared at him, daring him to take up the old debate, but J. J. wisely kept silent.

"The days of Soapy Smith and anarchy in Skagway are over," Si stated in a steely voice. "I'm not the deputy marshal any more, but I am the city judge, and I will see that law and order reside in this fair city. It's my turf now, J. J., fair and square. This town is finally mine, and I'm going to see that it stays that way. That includes keeping the whores in line."

With that, Si stepped forward, dragging the door open with him. He turned abruptly and stalked into the corridor, leaving the U. S. Commissioner remembering who really ran Skagway. And it wasn't John Troy or the U. S. Marshal.

Chapter Five

The Deal

Monday, December 14, 1903 (two months later). Si Tanner looked up from his crowded desk to find city marshal Charlie Moore standing at his doorway. Next to him stood a windblown young strumpet. What was her name? Oh, yes. Essie Miller.

"Another one here to pay her fine, Judge," Moore announced.

Essie jerked her arm away from the grasp of the marshal, fixed him with a withering glare, and marched into Si's office without a backward glance. She shoved the door in Charlie's face.

"Now Miss Miller, you really should be a bit more courteous to the chief of police around here. It wouldn't do to get on his bad side, you know that," Si warned her.

Essie snorted. "Charlie came to get me. He didn't need to do that. I know when I'm due in here, and I got three more days. Now you're gonna' add another two dollars to my costs. I don't like it, Mr. Tanner. It's not right."

"Charlie's doing a round-up at the moment, Miss Miller. All you gals are paying the same thing. I'm waiving the marshal's costs. It's just part of the fight the city is having with Juneau right now. I know you ladies are caught in the middle, but it's about to be cleared up."

Essie eyed him suspiciously. She scowled, but then she let her mouth relax. "Oh, all right. If you say it's gonna' stop, I gotta' believe it, Mr. Tanner. It's just that, well, you know John Snook, the U. S. Marshal, arrested me just last week for selling liquor without a license 'cuz Ida wasn't here, and she left the place for me to run while she was gone. Now it's on my record. I had to come up with a hundred dollars. Now you want me to pay twenty. Ida will make it good for me, but I can't go back to Seattle until she evens up with me. When's this all gonna' end? A girl can't make a decent living in Skagway anymore, what with you and the federal folks arresting us every time we turn around."

"That's the last of it, Essie. Judge Brown, down in Juneau, assured me that they will not touch you women again. They want you to know that they can do the liquor license fining, but I really don't think they'll try it unless any of you make a big ruckus. You tell the others that. The rest of the time, you come in real regular, every three months, pay me your twenty bucks, and J. J. will leave you alone."

Essie snorted, a not very ladylike sound. She dug out her purse, this time from a bag that hung from her waist, tied beneath her coat. She knew better than to hike her skirts up for Si Tanner. All of the women knew he could not be seduced. He loved his wife, Juliette, with a passion, and seemed to be oblivious to any woman's charms.

Tanner had pulled a big, leather-bound red account book off the shelf behind him. It looked exactly like a half dozen others. Some of them were labeled with words like TAXES, DEEDS, and ELECTIONS. The one he opened on his desk had no heading. Essie watched him write down the date, a case number, her name, and "keeping a house of ill-fame,"

$20.00 plus $2.60 costs. Well, okay, he didn't add in Charlie Moore's costs. It could have been worse.

Essie handed over her money, and Si wrote out a receipt. "Thank you, Miss Miller," he said, graciously. "Why, do you know that, in the last month you ladies have brought in three hundred dollars? At four times a year, the city council knows you generate more than a thousand dollars. Judge Brown promised us the gamblers next. Between the Board of Trade and the Pack Train, we have twenty house-operated gaming tables in Skagway. That'll be four hundred every three months." The city magistrate shook his head again at the city profits from vice.

"I just hope that means we have some protection from those reform women," Essie retorted.

"Oh, it does. The city council understands that you women and the gamblers pay for essentials we could not afford unless we raised the property taxes. Any city councilman that tried to do that would be committing political suicide. No, you're quite safe, just as long as you all stay quietly in the district, don't make yourselves too obvious, and pay your fines on time."

"How about that John Troy, with his newspaper? He hasn't been very quiet about us in the last few months. Why he's been writing about Frankie Belmont, her place, The Cottage, and all of us girls two or three times a week since last September."

"And you should be glad of it, too. With him spouting off about home rule – Alaskans getting to make decisions about what's good for Alaska instead of people in Washington doing it – we were able to move the court fines here to Skagway. Now Charlie brings you to me, not U. S. Marshal Snook taking you into J. J. Rogers. He has decided that it's his duty to keep the temperance women out of the politics of this fair city. He thinks he, as chairman of the nominating committee for the Citizen's Party, should have more control than someone like Sarah Shorthill or Anna Stinebaugh."

"But John Troy does run this town," Essie protested. "He chooses the city council every year. The voting men elect whoever he endorses. The only thing people think about is what he writes about in his paper. And you have to admit, no man can write like Mr. Troy can. Much as I dislike the man, he sure makes me laugh." And Essie did just that, thinking about all the jokes Troy had been making about George Rice selling off the Pack Train building the other day.

"What are you going to bid on the Pack Train corner? That seems to be the method of salutation in Skagway at the present time." Just as if every person in town would want to be stuck with Lee Guthrie's eight thousand dollar judgment against it. If you weren't careful, Troy could charm even a whore with his slippery language.

"Well, you know we have Mr. Troy to thank for Sarah Shorthill leaving us, don't you?" he asked.

Essie's eyes grew wider. She knew the leader of the W. C. T. U. had moved to Ketchikan. She also knew the Women's Christian Temperance Union no longer held weekly meetings in Skagway. She hadn't connected the two events with John Troy.

"You remember the city council meeting when Frank Keelar told the town that one of the men whose wife led the temperance movement supported her with rents from 'disreputable places?'"

Essie laughed at the memory. "Of course. The joke still entertains strangers in Skagway, and draws a lot of customers to J. D. Stinebaugh's resort, the Duchess."

"The fact that Mr. Troy repeated that accusation in the newspaper did a great deal to discredit the W. C. T. U., and Mrs. Stinebaugh in particular. Do you remember the saloon protest of the previous September?"

Essie grinned. "I remember Sarah Shorthill, Anna Stinebaugh and their friends got Judge Brown to review the liquor licenses of the four saloons closest to the Presbyterian Church."

"Whose was closest? Do you remember that?" Si asked.

"The Reception Saloon was right across the street, at the corner of Fifth and State." Essie smiled.

"What's at that corner today?" Si smirked.

"Tanner's Byke and Hardware Store."

"And did I have to buy the Reception from the owner in September 1900, when Judge Brown shut it down?"

Essie laughed. "No, sir. You already owned the building.

In fact, you had been ignoring the law that said saloons had to be at least four hundred feet from a church in order to get a liquor license, ever since August of 1899. Being U. S. Deputy Marshal here in Skagway, no one had thought to question your integrity and right to own a saloon across the street from a church."

Si continued to grin. "So, the W. C. T. U. shuts down the U. S. Deputy Marshal's saloon, the one that belongs to the man who cleaned out the town of Skagway back in July 1898. John Troy made sure everyone knew those liquor licenses, if they had come to the city, would have paid for a new school for the children. The W. C. T. U., by protesting the licenses, kept the school from being built. Therefore, the children had to stay at the old Union Church, next to Jap Alley."

Essie hadn't seen all of the connections before. She was beginning to enjoy this conversation with the city magistrate.

"Next the temperance ladies get the city council to move the girls who keep the town's virgin daughters safe from the rapacious men who work on the railroad. Off they go to Seventh Avenue. Then, it turns out that one of its members enjoys a comfortable way of life because her husband owns the Duchess gentlemen's resort, smack dab in the middle of Seventh Avenue. Not four months later, the organization falls apart because the women of Skagway stop attending their meetings."

Si leaned back in his chair, waiting for Essie to understand all of the connections.

"So, you mean that Mr. Troy drove Sarah Shorthill from Skagway, by making it sound like the reason the school couldn't be built was because the four saloons were shut down? And then the move to Seventh Avenue was to profit the Stinebaughs?"

Si just nodded.

Essie whistled.

"Did you notice what Mr. Troy did when Sarah Shorthill left Skagway last February?" he asked.

Essie shook her head.

"Well, you know Mrs. Shorthill is a very progressive woman. She always liked to be referred to as Mrs. S. E.

Shorthill, using her own initials, not her husband's. Mr. Troy merely noted that the Ladies Aid Society of the Methodist Church gave her a going away party as she left town. He did not mention her activities with the Skagway W. C. T. U., or that she then headed up the Alaska branch of the W. C. T. U., only that she was a Sunday school teacher here in Skagway. He referred to her as Mrs. Thomas Shorthill."

Essie giggled.

"When I asked him about it, he told me that the ladies at the church gave him that information. He said he could not disappoint the ladies. He also maintained that he had convinced the respectable women of their folly in trying to get themselves involved in a man's world, in politics where they had no business."

Essie smiled once more at her protector as she stood to take her leave. She felt a great deal better about giving him her twenty-two dollars and sixty cents. She could trust Si Tanner. He'd look out for Ida, her and the girls at Ida's place. She experienced some pride in knowing the streets would be lighted at night, a watchman would parade the town's sidewalks after the marshal went to bed, checking her door as well as those of the merchants on Broadway, and that the streets would have no potholes because she paid her fine. After all, Skagway was her town, too.

"Thank you, Mr. Tanner," Essie blushed. "You'll see me in ninety days, without fail."

Anna Stinebaugh emerged from the water closet, having vomited into her wash basin for the second time that morning. Sure, this phase of the pregnancy would be over soon. She thought it would be easier this time, but this child seemed bent on being a trial to her.

God seemed to be testing her in many ways these days. First, J. D. with that horrible business of his on Seventh Avenue, then John Troy's attack with the school funds, saying that the saloons near the churches needed to stay open or they wouldn't be able to afford to build the public school. He implied the W. C. T. U.'s protest against issuing those four liquor licenses would prevent the town from building the public school, which was sheer nonsense. But so many people believed him.

Next Frank Keelar behaved so abominably in the city council meeting, pointing out that one of the reform women, meaning her, Anna, was supported by rents from the disreputable women. The gossip had started, and within a week, everyone knew about J. D. and the Duchess, if they hadn't figured it out long ago. Then the ladies all abandoned the W. C. T. U., unable to bear the criticism that John Troy hurled at them.

Sarah said it would work out. She said that progress would be slow. She said that they had accomplished much here in Skagway. They had districted the prostitutes, had gotten them out of the back alleys and saloons. It was time to be quiet for a while, let the men get complacent, let them think they had won. She said it was part of the strategy. Sarah said it was time she moved on, to help other towns. She said that Anna was strong enough to continue here in Skagway without her.

"Rest awhile," Sarah told her. "Let Mattie Keelar get the ladies interested in social clubs. Work on J. D. and make him sell the Duchess. Give the ladies time to forget about that horrible place. Then you should join those silly social clubs. Start one or two yourself. Make them inclusive ones, where all can participate and work together, not exclusive ones like Mattie's that women compete to join. A sewing bee, maybe, where there's plenty of time to talk. Then, when they are ready, we will start the W. C. T. U. anew in Skagway. You still have allies here, my daughter Elizabeth, women like Bertie and Vickie at the Peniel Mission, and Harriet Pullen. They will help you. And this time, we will cleanse the city. I promise you that. I did not say we would do it in three short years. I told you it would take decades. But we will do it, Anna."

Anna straightened, feeling better, now that she had purged herself of both stomach contents and guilt. Sarah was right. She would rest while taking care of this child. She would let J. D. and John Troy and Si Tanner and the other men of this town think they had won. For a while. Next time the good women would do things differently, and next time, they would force the change.

SIN AND GRACE

Tuck and Flick's House

Chapter Six

The Nightmare

Tuesday, September 6, 1904 (nine months later). Essie tried to open her eyes and thought better of it when she heard the clang of the metal door slamming shut. The thin pillow under her cheek barely cushioned her pounding head and wouldn't stop the room from spinning. Better just to lie on this narrow cot and ride it out.

She didn't mean to sneak that bottle of whiskey up to her room. Ida forbade that sort of thing. Essie knew the reasons. Getting drunk cut down on the work a girl could do. Sure, men expected her to drink, and they thought they were paying for her to sip at whiskey or champagne when all she drank was cold, diluted tea or sparkling apple juice. But tonight Marty Collins brought that bottle of Jesse-Moore Hunt whiskey and left it behind. He never came back for it, and Essie thought he wouldn't miss just one jigger full. Next thing she knew, it was three or four, and then she lost count.

Essie turned over on the cot, almost falling off, but catching herself before she landed on the scratched, hardwood floor. It looked like someone had taken rocks to it and scratched deep gouges across the grain. Boredom, she guessed. Essie, now, she hurt too much to be bored.

Buck up, girl, she told herself. You've been lower than this before. At least you've got a madam this time. Used to be, when I had to work out of the cribs, I was on my own. Twenty dollars fine, plus costs in those days could be three or four days' earnings. Barely less than working it off in the jail. At Ida's I can make that in a day and a half, easy, less with tips. Wish Ida would let us keep all of our tips like Kitty Faith does with her girls. Wish Kitty had a place for me.

Essie dared to open her eyes. Kitty would never want Essie at her place. Kitty knew trouble when she saw it. Only Ida had the patience to let Essie come back year after year.

Essie knew she had a tendency to break the rules. She also knew Ida had a soft spot in her heart for her wayward charge. Ida had told her once that Essie looked like her oldest daughter, with that thick, dark hair spilling all over her shoulders in random coils and that generous mouth. As grim as Ida could be, Essie had also caught her smiling when she teased the men in the parlor and pumped them up with her ribald jokes. She never saw Ida smile at any of the other girls that way. No, even though the madam could be harsh, she still took care of her favorites.

Except with that man Schneider.

Ida had tried to explain it all to her, about getting rid of the federal fines and making it so that only city marshal Charlie Moore and Judge Tanner had anything to do with them. Ida said if she just had to deal with the local authorities, they could keep those temperance people away from the district, keep them from meddling where they had no business. With the D. A. and the federal judge and their Juneau grand juries, women often ended up in jail. For months at a time. Is that what Essie wanted? To spend her summer in jail?

Hell, no. Essie didn't even want to spend the night in jail. She knew Ida had reasons for her rules. She knew her madam had cause to lie about what happened when Hans Schneider came to her that night a year ago. But it still felt like a betrayal. Ida paid for the safety of the district with

Essie's humiliation.

No one else seemed to care much. Sure, Ida took more precautions, screened her clients better. The other girls gave her their sympathy. For awhile. Then they seemed to forget about it. The next season, it was a whole new crowd and no one else knew the story.

She didn't tell Tuck, but he seemed to sense her need for his obvious affection. He responded tenderly, just what she needed without knowing it. When had she become so attached to Tuck?

She wished she could remember their first time. He said it was here in Skagway, back in '98, at the height of the boom. There had been so many men, how could she remember all those faces? Then again, how could she forget that bushy mustache, those twinkling blue eyes, that reddish-blond hair and that mischievous set of those hips and tousled head? He said they'd been together in Dawson, too. For her, their third time had been their first, on that April day two years back, with the sun shining so fine, when she had hitched up her skirts and shown him her leg, him and his Ohio buddies and all the school children across the street. It had seemed a mistake later. Now it didn't. Now they had a district and rules, and if you played by those rules, no one bothered you.

"Tuck, where are you?" Essie whispered. She hadn't seen him for three weeks. Sure, he'd been promoted to baggageman. But if he wanted to spend the whole night with her, sleep with her, it meant she could only have him once a month. Ida and her damn rules, wouldn't let her have a night off to spend with a friend. Rumor had it that Kitty gave her girls one day every two weeks to do whatever they wanted. One day outside their time of month, that is, during the middle of their cycles.

Essie heard the front door of the jail house slam shut and the screech of jailer John Burns' chair as he rose to greet whoever had walked in the door. She listened half-heartedly, but couldn't catch the words. Apparently only one man, the two engaged in a low-pitched conversation.

I used to have a dream, Essie thought. My own place, not a crib, but a nice place with two or three bedrooms and a parlor and a couple of girls working for me. I could take nights off, not work all the time. I know enough now, I could do it. Sure, I'd have to charge less, to compete with Ida and Kitty. But Belle Schooler, she's getting old, almost fifty now. She sold her place to that madam up in Fairbanks and is just renting it now. When she leaves, Skagway will need another madam.

"But I need the money. I gotta' keep working. I don't have time to yearn for the same man in my bed each morning," Essie whispered aloud.

There, she said it. She took a deep breath, hoping it would clear her head.

"I can't afford to be getting drunk," she said, louder.

"Rules are rules. They're there for your own good," Ida said. "Don't drink on the job. Keep to the time limits. Clean him before he touches you. Don't forget to use the vaginal sponges, and change them every hour. Change the towels and linens between customers. Don't tell the men your real name or your real story."

Don't fall in love.

Well, Ida knew Essie sometimes broke the rules. Not all of them, but some of them.

Essie turned her back to the jail bars and tried to get some sleep.

Essie swayed to her feet when she heard city jailer John Burns call her name. "Miss Miller. Seems you've got a friend after all. Your fine's been paid. You're free to go."

Burns stepped aside as Essie staggered passed him. She heard him draw in a quick breath so he could hold it before she got to him. She knew the smell of cheap whiskey preceded her down the hallway. How could a woman get in that condition, she could almost hear him mutter, even a whore? Burns grunted. She bet they thought we have to stay drunk to stand the work. Well, it was true only part of the time.

Essie looked around blearily when she got to the cramped little office outside the cells. Burns handed her the purse she took with her the previous evening and gave her a paper to sign. She scrawled her signature, after checking the contents of the little coin purse. She guessed everything was there. She couldn't remember, but it made sense to make a show of it anyway.

Then Tuck stood beside her, taking her arm. She leaned into him, glad to have him there. Before she could help herself, her eyes swam with tears. She buried her face in Tuck's shoulder so Burns couldn't see.

"I'm so sorry, Tuck," she sobbed. "I didn't do it on purpose."

"I know, Darlin'," he soothed her, hugging her to him, glaring at Burns, daring him to tell a soul who had come to her rescue. Burns shrugged, as if to ask why he should care about some guy off the railroad tracks. The jailer turned his back and went to his jail cells.

"Let's get you outa' here." Tuck pulled a cloak around Essie's shoulders and led her out the door. He started towards Broadway, towards Ida's place.

"Don't take me back to Ida," Essie protested. "She'll make me go back to work. I can't go back to work tonight, Tuck."

Tuck stood under Skagway's black velvet sky, with the woman of his heart sobbing in his arms, gazing at stars so bright they made the snow-covered mountains shimmer. Essie knew he weighed his brother's wrath at finding a whore in his home against her need for peace for only one night. He turned her towards Second Avenue and the modest bachelor house he kept with Flick.

Tuck had left the porch light on when Wil had rousted him from bed two hours earlier, and he'd left the door unlocked. He hushed Essie before bundling her into the small parlor. She had enough sense left to pay attention, although she relied on him to steer her through the crowded furniture. Tuck sent a silent prayer of thanks to his Lord for Flick's tidiness and for the fact that he'd not had enough time to leave his usual trail of odds and ends lying about the floor. They made it from the front door to Tuck's bedroom without incident.

There Tuck undressed Essie, for once doing it mechanically, simply to get the job done, to relieve her of things that would wrinkle under bed clothes, and then look unbecoming in the street the next day. He did it for her comfort, not his pleasure, leaving her in her camisole and a petticoat. He tucked her into his bed, and then shed his own clothes to his underwear before dousing the light. Tuck's small bed was built for one person, and he briefly considered the sofa in the parlor. But Flick might find him there and wonder why he didn't sleep in his room. Better to stay here. Tuck slid into the bed with Essie, pulling her to him, molding himself around her, his front to her back, spoon-like. She already snored gently. He sighed in contentment, hoping his brother would stay ignorant of his guest, wanting nothing more than the simple joy of holding Essie in his own bed.

The next morning, Essie woke in a man's arms. It took only a few heartbeats before she knew they belonged to Tuck. The facts that she wore her camisole and petticoat and she slept in the strange room confused her. The light reddish hair on his arms was familiar, the feel of them, strong and yet gentle, the particular way his hand cupped her breast. No other man did it just that way. She caught the smell of him, pungent and male. This man was Tuck, and she wanted him. How could a whore want a man so?

She turned in his arms to find him also clothed in undershirt and shorts. The narrow bed threatened to pitch him off, and he tightened his grip on her as he teetered on the edge, shifting them both closer to the wall.

"Darlin'," he whispered into her throat.

Essie slid her hand under his undershirt to feel the muscles along his waist. She thought no further than that, but he stopped her hand. "I can't afford you, my Love. You took all my cash last night."

Essie smiled up at him. "It seems I owe you for my fine, then." Her hand moved lower.

He grinned back at her. "You've been in my bed for far more than two and a half hours, Essie. I believe I'm running a tab already."

Essie's lips met Tuck's to still his protest. Her morning-after breath could have knocked out a horse, but Tuck drank it in like nectar. "I'm not at Ida's. You do not owe her a dime

48

for any of this. I'm in your debt." Suddenly, Essie's breath came more rapidly, and she knew shame to be talking of money and debts. She just wanted to be with this man.

The range of emotions that passed through Tuck made his head spin. Ordinarily a simple man with simple needs, he felt far too confused to deal with this complex situation. His brother, a commonsensical man who would not tolerate a whore in his house, slept on the other side of a very thin wall. Tuck lay on a narrow, squeaky bed with the love of his life, a woman who offered herself freely to him for the first time. It would be the first that he knew she was his, that she came willingly for love and not for greed or money. This woman, whom he ached for constantly, whom he would never be rich enough to have always, wanted him without condition or price. And Flick was sure to hear of it.

Tuck covered her mouth with his, lingering over her tongue, as bad as it tasted. "I'll cook you some breakfast, Love, and we'll have a talk with Flick. When he's gone, I'll let you make good your offer, and then I'll take you back to Ida." His eyes grew soft and serious. He saw something in Essie's eyes he'd never dared hope to see before, and knew without doubt that few men would ever see the like in a woman of her kind. Tuck Flaharty knew to the core of his being that Essie loved him and would do so until the day she died. It gave him the strength he needed for the talk he and Flick would have.

SIN AND GRACE

Tuck's Board of Trade

Chapter Seven

The Dream

Tuesday, November 14, 1905 (a year later). Tuck drew another beer, handed it to George Carson, and wiped down Chris Shea's bar in the Pack Train Saloon. Chris had bought it about a year ago, leaving the Board of Trade when Lee Guthrie sold out. This was the life Tuck wanted. He earned no more money as a bartender than he did as a baggage man, but he enjoyed himself a great deal more. And working for his pal Chris was a damn sight better than slaving for the White Pass.

When he and Flick quit working for the railroad and took off to Fairbanks last March, they hoped to find something better than Skagway. Of course they didn't, but when they got back, Tuck knew he wouldn't go back to the railroad. Flick did. Flick was steady, and Flick was in a rut. Tuck knew the time had come to change. That was what this new century was all about anyway, change. Just because Dad had worked for the railroad and married a good woman and had five kids didn't mean that's what he and Flick had to do.

51

He'd give up his father's dream. Tuck, now, he was going to buy the Board of Trade, sleep with Essie, and live in a man's world the rest of his life. He'd been saying that for a long time. He still meant it.

Men crowded around the Pack Train's two pool tables, in the middle of the nightly pool tournament. Tuck could have been a contender for the title, but as bartender he had to watch. It was just as well. He saved his money this way, saved it for the Board of Trade. He watched Wil Cleveland, because he had the best chance tonight. Tuck had bet a dollar on him. Wil had sunk four balls and was setting up his fifth. He had a chance of sinking all nine. Tad Hillery, Wil's opponent, did not look happy.

Tuck grabbed three mugs of beer in each hand and lugged them all to the crowd around the table. He gathered up the dimes as he distributed beer, men clapping him on the shoulder for being so foresighted. Tuck hadn't been at the job long, but he had patronized saloons since he was sixteen. He knew what to do by instinct.

Tuck made two more trips before he served all the spectators. A rowdy bunch, not only Tad and Wil stood to make money by tonight's game. Everyone had a stake. And it wasn't just tonight, but the standing for the week and how the winner might come out at the end of the tournament, whenever that might be. The rules were complicated. The men knew them by heart. The game constituted part of their souls, whether they handled the cue or not. Pool was an integral part of the saloon, a sport that made them all sports.

Wil sank the eight ball into a corner pocket, without Tad getting to pick up his cue. A third of the crowd cheered, the rest groaned. Wil gave them an upset. The men who won their bets magnanimously bought beer for those who lost. Little money traded hands, except for the dimes for the beer that went into Tuck's apron pocket, and the ten he picked up winning the odds betting on Wil.

Wil and Tad came over to the bar once Tuck had everyone settled with at least a brew or two. He drew out two more and set them on the bar for the contestants.

"But I tell you, Wil, ole' Doc deGruyter won't let her marry me until she's twenty-one. Him being an old gamblin' man and all, you'd think he'd be more liberal."

Tuck laughed. "You'd think so! Essie told me Kitty Faith rented a room from him when she first came to Skagway. He wasn't too particular in those days!"

The mere thought of Madam Faith living in stuffy old Doc deGruyter's home sent the boys into spasms of laughter. Some time passed before Tad's predicament sobered him again. "But Doc said I gotta' wait at least one more year. I don't know if I can. She's all I can think about. I'm going crazy needing her." Tad's face took on an agony of desire.

Wil laughed. "Go to Ida's or Kitty's or one of the cheaper women on the row. That's what they're there for."

Stay away from Essie, Tuck almost said, and then remembered how she needed the money, too. He kept his mouth shut. These men were his friends. They knew about Essie, and they knew to stay away from his woman.

"It won't work. That's not what I want." Tad turned to Tuck, unhappy with the answer. "What do you do, Tuck, when Essie's in Fairbanks or Seattle?"

Tuck grinned, happy to be on the giving end of advice. He seldom had anything good to offer, but always a joke or two. "I just 'tuck' him in and tell him to behave 'til she's back."

It doesn't take much to make men who've been drinking laugh. That's what made Tuck so popular, his silly humor and indomitable good cheer.

"Don't know if I could last a year, though," Tuck admitted. "Baseball in the summer and bowling in the winter, that's me. Lots of good, active sports. Wears a man out so he's not thinking about that all the time. Then come to the Pack Train, play some pool, get drunk, go sleep it off, go to work the next day. Could work for a year, I suppose. Don't forget the Board of Trade, though, once its mine," he reminded them.

The two men grinned back at Tuck. He hit the answer square, they knew. Sports and the saloon addressed the emptiness a woman left in them. Work hard, play hard, drink hard, stick with their pals, and they could forget a man's needs if they couldn't make do with a whore, when denied the woman of their dreams.

Tuck thought it ironic. He remembered Minnie Owens, back in Bucyrus. Had she let him in her skirts, he wouldn't be here in this saloon. He'd be in Ohio, working on that railroad, with a plump wife, home-cooked meals, sex every night and four or five kids by now. He'd be too busy for saloons.

From the look in his eyes, Tuck knew Tad Hillery thought of Jeannette deGruyter once again, that wispy, brown hair and those mellow blue eyes. From the way he talked, those eyes made him melt every time he thought of her.

Tad changed the subject. "Willard wired from Fairbanks. He's got a good job in a bank up there. He says they need a clerk, and they want me."

Tuck and Wil sobered. The Hillery clan usually stuck together, but times were getting harder in Skagway. If Tad's older brother, Willard, called him, Tad was leaving. Like Flick and Tuck, it was hard to separate Willard and Tad.

"I've told Jeannette that I'll come back for her in a year. She says she'll wait. I trust her." Tad buried his face in his mug.

"She'll wait," Tuck assured him. He remembered how Jeannette behaved at the baseball games, her eyes never leaving Tad. Wil nodded in agreement. They each thought they knew love when he saw it, and it was there with Tad and Jeannette.

Tuck glanced away from the boys while his eyes misted up, unaccountably. He suddenly found himself wishing he could count on the same kind of life these men were looking at. He'd seen the way Tad and Jeannette looked at each other, Chris and Helen, Wil Cleveland's cousin Gladys and her beau Herman Kirmse. He had Essie. But not the way these men would have their women.

"Speaking of Willy," Wil brightened. "I heard those stuffed shirts earlier this month chose him to be a delegate to the convention down in Seattle, that one that will choose our delegate to Alaska. Now that's something. One of us young bucks with those old fellers." Wil whistled.

"Yeah, Jack McCabe was at the meeting, too. It's like it's a new day here in Skagway. Chris Shea's getting interested in politics, acting like he might run for city council. Men like

McCabe, who work for the railroad, showing up at meetings run by John Troy. My brother's going off to a convention in Seattle with Troy and Dr. Keller, the dentist. Skagway isn't the gold rush town it used to be. It's becoming respectable. And something else, I don't know what. We average guys seem to have a lot more say, if men like Chris Shea, who listen to us, can just wrestle that power from men like John Troy," Tad shot back.

"Chris can't do it by himself, you know," Tuck pointed out. "He'll have to have votes, and he won't get those unless the guys in this saloon and the other saloons will elect him. We gotta' spread the word."

"They'll do it for Chris. We'll all do it for Chris. You know that," Tad assured him. Both Tad and Wil had been on Chris Shea's Eccentrics baseball team for the past two summers. The two men would do anything for Chris. Even Tuck, who played opposite Chris, loved the man.

"Speak of the devil," Tuck observed as Jack McCabe wandered up to the bar.

Jack banged down his empty mug and his dime, clearly indicating his need for another one. "Been reading much, lately, gentlemen?"

The men laughed. "The good Reverend Glenk is downright optimistic, isn't he?" Tuck chuckled. "Have you each chosen your branch of study? I'm thinking brunettes for mine. But if you'd rather have that particular subject, Tad, I could take bowling or handball."

"Now me, I've always been partial to poker, you know that, Tuck," McCabe interjected. "Although I have a little lady on the side over on Second Avenue that might just distract me some from time to time. I could do some studying up on women from Louisiana, if the Reverend wanted someone who could lead a discussion on that subject."

The men all knew they possessed great wit. The conversation continued at some length in the same vein. Reverend Glenk at the Methodist Church would find few new members for his reading club among the men in this saloon. That he wished to divert this very group of men from the evils of the saloon constituted his main purpose in setting up the club. They would have none of it.

So the evening went. Tuck loved his life in the saloon, gambling with these men, listening to talk about women, comparing how he felt about his own woman to how they felt about theirs, talking about their love of sports, the sports of all kinds. They got their news of the day here, whether they read Troy's paper or not. The men decided whether John Troy knew what he was talking about in this place. The men elected the next city councilmen and groomed the next mayor in the Skagway saloons. The heart of Skagway beat in the Pack Train, especially now that Chris Shea owned it. Tuck loved being in the middle of the action.

Now, he rubbed down Chris' bar, enjoying the gleam of it, while he waited for the next man to walk up with an empty mug to be refilled. He spotted Chris at the corner table, in earnest conversation with Lee Guthrie. Chris met his eye and nodded. Tuck grinned back. Lee would be leaving for San Francisco soon, and then Tuck would have Chris to himself again.

At that moment, Guthrie stood, pulled on his coat and slapped Chris on the back. Shea stood back and watched the richest man in Skagway leave his humble, working man's saloon. Between his teeth, he clenched the expensive cigar with which Guthrie had gifted him and sauntered over to the single stool at the end of the bar. He carried the bottle of Old Valley whiskey that he and Lee had been sharing. It had its cork seated securely in the top. Only a finger's width of the amber liquid still lay at the bottom of Chris' tumbler.

Chris smiled at Tuck shining the bar. "So you like the job. I can tell when a man's happy behind a bar. He caresses it like it's a woman's back. Just like you're doing. Just like I do, every chance I get."

Tuck grinned. That's almost what it felt like, that smooth, polished wood. He thought of the beautiful bar at the Board of Trade. Just like he had once thought of Essie, he wondered if it would ever be his. Yes, it would belong to him, he knew it, as surely as Essie now belonged to him. Others might stand behind that bar and caress it, but he would possess it, he was sure of it.

"This bar belongs to you, Chris. I do appreciate you

letting me be a man here." He spread his arms wide and drew his hands slowly towards each other along the polished wood surface, enjoying the imagery. "But you know I won't stay. The next time the Board of Trade comes up for sale, she's mine."

Chris savored his cigar, letting the smoke escape his mouth, then curl past his nostrils. Tuck suspected it was a very expensive cigar, one Chris only enjoyed with Lee. He envied them their friendship.

"If you say so, Tuck. Lee loves that place, that's why he bought it back. He won't let it go to just anyone. He wouldn't let me have it."

"He knew you needed the Pack Train, Chris." Even as simple a man as Tuck could see that. Chris could tend bar in a place like the Board of Trade, but the day he stood behind the bar at the Pack Train as its owner, all of Skagway would understand the perfect match had been found. Tuck suspected that Lee Guthrie knew it all along. That's why he priced the Board of Trade out of Chris' reach. Tuck lusted after fine, romantic, exciting worlds. Chris Shea sometimes didn't know what he wanted until he found it, then recognized at once what was a perfect fit, what he was born to do. The Pack Train, its working class men, its glossy bar and big phonograph and four blackjack tables was exactly why Chris Shea was put on earth. The Pack Train was all part of God's plan for him.

Just like Essie Miller and the Board of Trade comprised part of God's plan for Tuck.

The two of them leaned on the solid bar in companionable silence for a few moments. "So, Chris. You gonna' bowl with me this season?" Tuck ventured.

"You'd lose the cup," Chris predicted.

"That's not why I do it, you know that," his bartender protested.

"Stick with Si. He's a much better bowler," Chris advised.

"He's also stuffy and bosses me around too much. You wouldn't tell me how to roll the ball or keep score. C'mon, Chris. We'll have fun." Tuck practically got down on his knees and begged.

Chris laughed. "I'll come and watch. But I won't deny

you the pleasure of winning. And I won't deny my wife the pleasure of my company, nor myself the pleasures of hers. Surely a man like you can understand a sentiment so simply stated."

Tuck cursed, envying a man so happily married. But then again, he noticed that all his year-round sports companions were bachelors – Si Tanner excluded. Oh, well. He supposed he should be grateful that Chris still played baseball with him.

"Hey, barkeep! What does a man need to do to get a beer around here?" Both Tuck and Chris startled out of their reveries. Tuck hustled to the tap, muttering his apology. As he glanced back at Chris, he saw his boss smiling. He knew Chris couldn't picture Tuck at the Board of Trade. But then, Tuck hadn't imagined Chris owning the Pack Train, not at first, or married to that preacher's daughter, Helen Eckert. Stranger things had happened.

The Scales

Chapter Eight

Lost Innocence

Saturday, May 12, 1906 (eight months later). Wil Cleveland slid up to the bar behind Ezra Kurtz. He waited, somewhat impatiently, for Tuck to fill Ezra's mug, to make a silly joke and send the man on his way. Ezra slapped his thigh, chortling, as he left with the mug.

Tuck pulled a clean mug from the back bar and tipped it under the tap.

"No, Tuck. None for me. I just need a word with you." Wil glanced up and down the bar. Chris Shea sat at the end of the bar, fiddling with an account book. He didn't look up.

Wil leaned in close anyway. "It's Essie. She's in jail again. Indecent exposure this time. Ten dollar fine. I think she's still drunk."

Tuck closed his eyes. These episodes happened all too frequently any more. He personally didn't mind them. He'd take her home, let her sleep it off, she'd be grateful, and he'd get his money's worth and then some. After that first time, Flick would only glare at them. He hated Essie with a passion equal to his love for Tuck, but because of the love for his brother, kept his mouth shut around her. Essie despised Flick equally, but for her love of Tuck, forgave him and tried to stay out of Flick's sight. They danced an uneasy step.

Tuck just detested the fact that Essie could not control the liquor, that she would do this to herself. A simple man, he didn't understand her. He vowed he'd get it out of her this time.

Tuck unwrapped the apron from his waist as he strode towards the end of the bar. "I've got to go, Chris. Essie – ."

"I heard," he said as he looked up. "I'll cover for you. But you gotta' stop her, Tuck. Tanner and Troy go after the trouble-makers. Don't forget what they did to Frankie Belmont, to Minnie Wallace, Rose Arnold and Ruth Brown. They run women like Essie out of town. If she doesn't clean up her act, Anna Stinebaugh will hear about her. If Anna and the Peniel Missionaries start making trouble again, we're all going to pay, and it won't just be people like Essie. It will be the gambling tables, and maybe even our saloons. You tell Essie to keep a lid on her drinking, Tuck."

Tuck grabbed up his coat as he tossed the apron to Chris. He'd soaked in every word, and they shook him to his core. He remembered, finally, his long-ago talk with Judge Tanner. He hurried out the door, scared for Essie for the first time since he had known her.

* * *

Sunday, May 13, 1906 (the next morning). The larger bed filled most of his room, leaving little space for his dresser and a chair to toss off his clothes. He couldn't stand between an open drawer and the bed. It didn't matter. The double bed held both Tuck and Essie easily, and the bedsprings didn't squeak, at least not so badly. Flick could pretend he didn't know when Essie lay with his brother.

Tuck leaned on his elbow, watching Essie sleep, her lips slightly parted, her jaw relaxed in slumber. Her hair lay across his pillow in wild abandon, strands in her face. He wanted to clear it from her eyes, but didn't touch her for fear of waking her. What could he to do to keep from losing her?

Essie opened her eyes to look squarely into his, seeing nothing but his love, mistaking it for his lust. She reached for him, responding as she always did to those blue, Irish eyes. He did not break from her kiss, and where that led, for a long time. They enjoyed each other a very great deal.

When Tuck's heart finally had resumed its normal steady beat, and he could move again, he enfolded Essie into his arms and settled her head on his shoulder.

"Burns told me the night watchman found you in the street wearing only your corset and a petticoat," he accused her gently. "I had to go to Ida's for some clothing for you. She demanded I bring you back immediately. I think she knows that you get out of jail earlier than you let on when I pay your fine. I think she wanted me to leave a deposit for the clothes, equal to a night's pay for you." He chuckled. "I didn't cooperate."

Essie gasped, horrified at the thought. Ida would do something like that, alright.

Then, instead of comforting her, Tuck told her what Chris had said. He feared she would cry, beg his forgiveness, promise never to do such a thing again. He didn't know if that's what he wanted. He knew he wouldn't like these clandestine nights to end. He wanted her to keep needing him to come and rescue her. But he didn't want Si Tanner, city marshal Charlie Moore and John Troy to run her out of town.

Essie didn't cry. She lay there, not moving, not saying anything, her eyes wide, thinking. She also needed Tuck to rescue her from time to time. What would she do if she couldn't run away to him when it got too hard to take?

"Why do you do it, Essie?" he asked her, when she didn't do or say anything.

"Why did you come back to Alaska, Tuck? Why didn't

you stay in Bucyrus, with your fortune and the home-grown Ohio women who would have given you children and cooked your meals and made you fat and very happy instead of getting you out of bed to go pay their jail fines?" She turned the question back on him.

Tuck stared at her for a long moment, and then his eyes glazed over.

"I suppose I did have that dream once. But I lost it. Did I ever tell you about Palm Sunday, back in '98?" he asked.

"I know you helped dig those men out of the avalanche on the Chilkoot Trail," Essie replied.

"I was only twenty-four when we came north, the five of us, from Bucyrus. You know how the Chilkoot Pass was, you've been over it, Essie. Steps were cut in the snow over the pass. They forced the men – and an occasional intrepid woman like you – to stream single-file up the forty-five degree slope to the pass. Every twenty feet or so, a side passage let the weary stand aside to rest. Sixty people lined the golden stairs from its base at the Scales to the Summit of the Chilkoot Pass when the worst happened at noon that day. The heavy blanket of snow on the surrounding peaks lost its grip and came crashing down. The people on the golden stairs could only watch in horror as the bowl below them became filled with snow."

Essie covered her mouth with her hand, her eyes went round with horror. She had heard this tale before, from dozens of men who had seen it. It never ceased to appall her.

"Even three miles away in Sheep Camp, we heard the crashing of the avalanche. We had heard the sound all night, and thought it to be thunder, although the Sourdoughs said thunderstorms were rare as hens' teeth on the Alaskan coast. I knew, especially, that we wouldn't get thunder when it was snowing like that." Tuck looked at his hands, but he didn't see them.

"That morning, though, there was no doubt what we heard, no confusion over thunder or cannons in the distance. We grabbed ropes and shovels and water and food and anything else we thought might be useful and ran up the trail. Fitz, our cook, followed with the horse and harness and extra canvas as soon as he could get the kitchen under minimal control."

"Nothing could have prepared us for what we saw. At least forty feet of snow filled the valley, burying everything in its wake. I found Mr. Mahon, a man whose outfit we had hauled to the summit the day before. We were trying to make extra money on the way, and packed for others, you see. He was dazed, barely able to stand. Flick located a log for him sit on and left him with me. I guess he wanted to spare me the hard work," Tuck admitted with a wry smile on his face

"Mahon said he was the last one on the rope. He saw it coming, and a guy named Sullivan tossed out the rope. The avalanche threw Mahon up, then buried him, then threw him up again. He stared at me in disbelief. It left the poor guy only half covered with snow, only waist deep. He got out and followed the rope, digging out men until he found one dead. He told me he saved six men, but not the seventh. There were ten of them on that rope. Then he put his head in his hands and wept." Tuck's eyes glistened just remembering the man coming to grips with what had happened.

"I didn't know what to do. I sat there, my hands in my lap, feeling helpless. I had to go help the others dig out people. I couldn't stay there with that grief-stricken man. Feeling the coward, I stood, shuffled my feet around and begged my excuse. Then I fled to the safety of the work, to the oblivion of the sweat, to the mindlessness of moving the tons of snow."

Tuck looked up from the useless hands on his lap and brought his gaze to the present. "At only twenty four years of age, I lost the innocence of Bucyrus that day, lost it in the agonized faces of the loved ones who huddled over the cold bodies of brothers and childhood friends. I watched those same men leave their dead kin to help dig in the avalanche field. The sight of a bit of clothing brought hope that a trace of life might linger, that I might save another person. But so often, I was disappointed. Then I became toughened to the frozen face of death, to the horrified grimace at the realization that no more air could come into the frozen tomb, to the peaceful, sleeplike countenance of those who closed their eyes and accepted what had happened, hoping to waken to a place much better."

Tuck looked at the wall between his room and that of his brother, as if he could see through it. "I never would have made it without Flick at my side, urging me forward. Once, when I found my fourth frozen body, I just stood and stared and couldn't go on. Flick took the shovel from me and made me sit. He brought me hot tea and sat with me, the heat from his body warming my side, reminding me that other people lived and needed the help. Flick put his arm around my shoulder and told me that the five of us still lived, Ma and Pa and Cad were home safe, and others still lived under the snow. 'Buck up, Tuck,' he said. 'We gotta' keep goin'. I never forgot the message."

His eyes came back to Essie, and she met them squarely. "Palm Sunday, April 3, 1898, lasted years. I felt like an old man when Fitz dished out his beans and biscuits that night. Flick allowed us each a half cup of whiskey. We sat silent through the meal. We wrote letters home, then Billy and Fitz left for Dyea to send them out, so Ma and Pa would know we made it. I laid down on my bedroll that night, closed my eyes, shut my mind, and slept like the dead."

He reached for Essie's hands, then. "When I woke the next morning, I just lay there and listened to the chatter of active men around me. I knew how quickly it could all go away, Essie, how short life could be. I knew right then I had to live each day like it was my last, enjoy each moment, because there was no guarantee there would be any tomorrow. Sure, I would work for that gold, but hanging onto a dream that would take twenty years to build? I couldn't do that, Essie."

She felt the tenseness that had built in his body turn to eagerness as his eyes lit up.

"Alaska got in my blood, Essie, probably every time a mosquito bit into me, a little at a time. This is a man's country. All those mosquitoes drink men's blood. Sure, Flick and I would go back to Bucyrus from time to time, but I found I couldn't stay in that slow, tamed world for long. I felt held back by the old ways of the women who wanted to bind me to a place no longer mine. I had tasted something different, a life of laughter at the silliest nonsense, playing jokes, finding joy in just being alive. I found that saloons weren't dens of evil, but of companionship, a place where a man could drink of gladness and pour out his soul if he so chose. I found that I did not have to lose my love of sports, but that plenty of like-minded men shared my passions of physical activity. And I found a whole world of women willing to fulfill the needs I had of them."

"And then, wonder of wonders, I found you, and I've not needed a whole world, but just one woman and a steady job, a dream and something to hold on to. Now I can't leave Alaska."

Essie lay next to her lover, quietly, staring into space. She loved him so. But why did he have to dump all of this on her? They would make her leave, and she would take his dream with her. It would be her fault that he lost yet another dream.

Tuck propped himself up on his elbow. She looked at his face and saw his eyes soaking up her face.

"Why do you do it, Essie?" he asked her again. She hadn't answered his question.

"Why do I do what, Tuck?" she asked back. "Why do I get drunk? Why do I take off my clothes and let men look at me? Why do I screw men for money? What question are you asking me? Don't you know that all men want to know the answers to those questions? And don't you know that we never tell?" Her eyes blazed with anger that he had betrayed her so, that he had become so ordinary, just like every other man. She pushed him aside so she could get out of the bed and get dressed.

When she glanced back at him, she saw that Tuck was devastated. She turned from him quickly, unable to look at his face.

"Essie!" he cried, the hurt in his voice so raw he could hardly gasp out her name. The sound stopped her, her back to him, her camisole falling into place.

"Essie," he cried again. "Help me understand. Change the question to something you can answer, and tell me what you will, but tell me something. Don't leave me here wondering why I love you, and why I can't have you, and why they will take you away from me. What can I do to save you from them?"

At last he asked a question she could answer for him. She turned back to him, kneeling on the bed, her hand on his jaw. "Oh, my Love. You can do nothing to save me. This I have to do myself."

"But I want to be there for you. I have to be there for you, Essie," he pleaded.

"You are. You always will be, Tuck," she smiled. "I won't go away."

"You always go away," he observed, truthfully. "Every summer and winter, I suffer without you. I'm only happy in the spring and fall. I'd die if you never came back."

"I'll stop the binges, Tuck. Is that what you want to hear? I'll follow all of Ida's rules and be a good girl and not cause any more trouble." She sat on the bed beside him, looking away from him, her lip trembling. She bit on it to stop it, and a tear fell down her cheek. "And I'll have to wait for you to save up enough money to make it past my gatekeeper, for a couple of precious hours, and I'll not wake in your arms in the morning."

Tuck pulled her to him, crushed to hear his own fears confirmed. "Why do you work for her, Essie? Why don't you just leave? Other women work for themselves. Start your own business," he urged.

Essie thought of Josie, in her little one-room crib, tied to a usurious landlord who demanded rent whether she had customers or not. Josie out hustling twenty-four hours a day, never knowing when the next man would come to her door, not working regular hours, not resting when she was sick. Essie had done that before. She didn't think she could do it again. She wouldn't do it ever again.

"You don't know what a woman gets for working in a brothel, Tuck. Ida earns her fifty percent. I'd only be able to charge half on my own. A man wants a nice parlor and a madam and a choice."

"Not this man." Tuck grinned, pulling her close, nuzzling the underside of her jaw.

"Ah, but you wouldn't be a paying customer, so you wouldn't count," she admonished him, grinning back. He already had her day-dreaming. Her eyes widened, suddenly remembering something.

"Belle Schooler's gone. I told myself once that I'd get a nice little parlor house when she left. Then, well, I found out you'd come and get me when I got drunk, and I forgot. But you're right. Maybe I could do this," she thought aloud.

"I'll ask Chris if Lee has any houses for rent," Tuck urged. "I've got some money set aside. You can have that if you need it," he offered.

"That's your Board of Trade money!" she protested. She climbed to her knees and put her fingers across his mouth. "No, I have money. We have money," and she told him about the savings account. "But I don't think I'll need it. We don't need to rush into this yet, Lover. Let's find out if Lee or someone else on Seventh Avenue has a place they'll rent for the rest of the season. A nice place," she cautioned. "I'll settle my debts with Ida with what I make in the meantime, and I'll stay off the booze."

She took a steadying breath, her eyes suddenly aflame with hope. Had she really forgotten her dream? Beyond putting that money aside, had she failed to remember what it was for? Had she lost sight of what the freedom of her own business would mean?

"Tuck, when I'm free, I'll give myself days off and find myself at your door, and we'll get drunk together and wake together in your bed away from the stink of other men."

"And when I own the Board of Trade, you'll be Madam Essie, and have your own brothel," he grinned. "No, you'll have a whole string of brothels and you'll be Queen of Seventh Avenue. You'll never work again, but just collect your fifty percent from each of the girls who work for you."

Essie laughed at the dream he built for her. She'd never thought beyond having those days off, those days when she could wake in Tuck's arms without a headache. An almost stray thought occurred to her. If I'm a madam, Tuck would be the only one. She tried to shove the thought away, it seemed so outrageous, so impossible. But it stayed in her head, like an impossible vision that wouldn't disappear now that it had set itself there.

"We'll have a bedroom on the back of the second floor of the biggest place, just you and me, and no one else will ever go there," she dared dream. "And I'll wake in your arms every afternoon, because, both being night people, we'll sleep during the day."

Tuck pulled her to him, excited by the fantasy. Anything seemed possible in this new twentieth century. A railroad worker's son could own a saloon, and a woman could have her own business. And they could live happily ever after, if they just put their minds and heart to it.

"Let's make a promise, then," he said. "A promise that Tuck will own the Board of Trade, and Essie will be Queen of the District."

Essie smiled, melting into Tuck's embrace. She could never resist his blarney. "I promise. Tuck's Board of Trade and Queen of the District."

Chapter Nine

Closed Up

Friday, November 9, 1906 (seven months later). Tuck stared at Lee Guthrie's back as he walked out of the Pack Train saloon. He couldn't believe what he had just overheard. Surely someone must be joking. He glanced at Chris, but his boss just sat at the table next to the big front windows staring up at the twin Dewey Peaks. A lot of them did that when looking for Divine intervention. Tuck had a feeling that's what it might take this time.

He carried a fresh cup of coffee over to Chris, thinking maybe he needed it. He'd been over there with Guthrie a long time.

"Did I hear right? City council shut down gambling in this town?" he asked, still not believing it.

Chris just nodded his head. "Thanks," he said, taking the cup of coffee and shoving the empty cup that sat in front of him out of the way. He nudged the chair where Guthrie had been sitting, indicating Tuck should have a seat. Being morning, only a couple of customers sat at a table on the other side of the room, nursing mugs of beer that Tuck had just filled. Chris knew he'd dash off if anyone else came in.

"Lee shut down the Board of Trade last week because the White Pass railroad told all of its employees they couldn't gamble. If a manager caught any man gambling in a saloon, he was out a job, on the spot. It's the reform people's way of helping them increase their earnings," Chris commented, a grim tone to his voice.

"Whose earnings?" Tuck asked, not sure he was following the logic.

Chris chuckled. "Both, believe it or not. You see, the businessmen convinced the railroad that if the workers weren't wasting their money gambling, then they'd have more to spend in the businesses here in town, without the railroad having to raise wages. Railroad wins because it doesn't have to increase pay. Business wins because the customer has more disposable income. Working man wins, because he's got more money to spend. Only ones who lose out are Lee Guthrie and Chris Shea, who run gaming tables in their saloons."

"And Tuck Flaharty, who's gonna' buy the Board of Trade." Tuck threw down the towel he'd been carrying.

"Well, who knows, Tuck. This might just be the straw that breaks Lee Guthrie's back. He might be looking for a buyer now that he's lost the mainstay of his operation. Those roulette tables and Faro boards of his are legendary in the Southeast. With his place closed down for the winter, the city had nothing to lose by shutting me down. My forty dollars worth of fines this winter wouldn't do the city any good at all. Without even Lee in town, the Pack Train's helpless to fight them off."

"I don't understand," Tuck protested. "What are they running scared of? A bunch of women who meet for sewing bees? What can they do?"

Even Tuck and Chris had heard about Anna Stinebaugh's sewing circle. Once a week a whole bunch of women got together in one of Harriet Pullen's big parlors at the Pullen House and sat around sewing together. Women couldn't keep their mouths shut while they were pulling thread or knitting. They talked. Martin Itjen said he had walked past that parlor one day when he'd been asked to run an errand for Mr. Berdoe, the general manager for White Pass. He said those women were talking about sin in the city, how there were too many saloons and drunken men in the streets, and what were they gonna' do about it. The men in the Pack Train had just laughed, painting pictures of Harriet Pullen and the Peniel Missionaries chasing drunks down in the street with their knitting needles.

Chris shook his head. "It appears it's something bigger than Anna Stinebaugh and her sewing circle. Do you remember how Judge Wickersham shut down all the saloons in Valdez last month?"

Tuck nodded his head. "Yeah. He said the reform people deserved it, complaining about the gambling in the saloons. When he did that, he cut off all the revenue for the public schools, because the liquor licenses are the only source of money for the schools. The folks in town are panicking, trying to figure out how to get their schools reopened."

"Whatda'ya' wanna' bet that the saloons reopen without gambling?" Chris asked.

Tuck shook his head, not having considered that alternative.

"Then, a couple of weeks ago, down in Ketchikan, Judge Gunnison hauled all of the saloon owners into federal court. That hasn't happened in four, five years around here, not since Judge Brown turned the authority to fine over to the cities."

Tuck stared at Chris, aghast at the notion the federal courts were getting involved in a local issue. Wickersham, the Second District Judge from Fairbanks, making dictates in Valdez, then Gunnison, the First District Judge messing around in Ketchikan. He thought he could see where this might be headed.

"Yep," Chris nodded, as he watched the light dawn in Tuck's eyes. "What's the usual federal fine for gambling, Tuck?"

Tuck had been in the business long enough now to know, right off the top of his head.

71

"Hundred bucks." A good gambler working the tables for Chris could bring that in in about two weeks. It wasn't chicken feed, but something a saloon owner could swallow and go right back to gambling if he had to.

"Lowest fine Gunnison assessed was three hundred. Highest was eight hundred. He told the men that if they tried to reopen their places, he'd have them arrested again, and he'd fine them double next time. He was sending word out to the other district judges with their names and the same warning. Said he'd be doing the same thing in every other town in the Southeast."

Tuck let out one long, low whistle.

"So I'm looking at it this way," Chris explained after he took a sip of his coffee. "City Hall is saving me a heap of money, instead of costing me. Lee just advised me to stock up with some better liquors, upgrade my bar a bit, advertise to the businessmen so I can absorb his business. And you, Tuck, I suggest you start looking at your financial situation, if you're all that serious about owning the Board of Trade. It may be up for sale, real soon."

Tuck grinned at that. "You want those fancy men in your saloon?"

"I do if I'm going to get them to vote for me," Chris said into his cup of coffee.

That just about knocked Tuck out of his chair. "What are you talking about, Chris? You gonna' run for councilman again? Didn't you learn your lesson last April?"

Chris grinned at him, tapping the end of his cigar into the ashtray in the middle of the table. "That was just practice, and you know it. I was a last-minute candidate and lost by only twelve votes. This time, I'm gonna' win. I'm putting together a strong party, full of popular guys that will take the entire vote. We're going to show John Troy who really runs this town, and then we'll take it away from him. All I have to do is get the working men out voting, something they've never done before. Once that's happened, the people who live in this town will have some say about what goes on, instead of a handful of businessmen and their busy-body wives sitting around gabbing in a sewing circle."

Tuck returned the grin, suddenly understanding, and not

feeling at all unhappy about how things were changing. Lee Guthrie leaving town, giving up on the Board of Trade? Now that was a pleasant thought, all the way around. And he knew that gambling wouldn't end, not with Chris in charge of Skagway.

Wil Cleveland walked in the door, off the night shift at the railroad. Tuck dashed off to the bar to pour the man a beer and to hear the latest news from up the line.

That afternoon, Anna Stinebaugh watched Harriet Pullen push the tea cart into her large parlor at the south end of the Pullen House. The matron of the hotel seated herself in an elegant, straight back reception chair, and began to pour the tea into lovely pink and green decorated china cups, touched off with highlights of gold, the very latest in fashion. Anna didn't doubt that every woman in the room, herself included, would want something like them for Christmas. She hardened her heart and turned her mind to the real subject of this gathering.

Thanking Harriet for the refreshments, she launched immediately into their purpose for getting together. "As you all know by now, we have good reason to celebrate, ladies." Anna beamed with joy in the moment. "The city council responded to our husbands' requests to prosecute the gamblers. We have eradicated one more sin from our town."

At that moment, Harriet's baker walked into the parlor with a large layer cake. On the top stood a figure of Victory, and sprays of evergreen surrounded the coconut-sprinkled concoction. The ladies all ooh-ed and ah-ed as the woman proudly lowered the heavy confection to a round table and stepped back so all of the guests could admire it. A round of applause began.

Elizabeth Harrison, Sarah Shorthill's daughter, moved to Anna's side as the ladies crowded up to the table to get a closer look.

"I wish Mother could be here to celebrate with us," Elizabeth said.

"She would enjoy the moment," Anna agreed.

"One more of those evil men have gone," Elizabeth gloated.

"Oh, no. Lee Guthrie isn't beaten yet. He's just gone off to lick his wounds," Anna warned. "But he's taken a terrible blow, and he will not recover, not entirely. Our next target is his properties on Seventh Avenue. Yes, Mr. Guthrie is the most dangerous man right now, but by taking care of the District, we will take several of them at the same time."

Elizabeth turned away from the cake, which she had been trying to see over Lena Wurzbacker's shoulder. "Oh? And how will we do that?"

"Get your cake, and I'll tell you the way your mother explained it to me," Anna replied.

* * *

Tuesday, April 2, 1907 (five months later). Tuck grabbed up six beer mugs, three in each hand, and carried them over to the table where Martin Conway, Michael McLean, Jim Nettles, Dan McKay, Clarence DeSerisy, Luke McGrath, and Chris Shea celebrated the complete victory of the Labor Party at the day's city election. Luke worked as a blacksmith for the railroad, but had been a laborer before that. Clarence was a railroad foreman. Mike was one of Will Remick's blacksmiths and Jim ran a tinsmithing business with Cort Ford. Only three of the men around the table could be considered businessmen. Conway managed Behrend's Dry Goods store, and McKay ran Frye-Bruhn's Butcher Shop. And Chris, of course, was part owner of the Pack Train. Tuck had seen ample evidence in John Troy's newspapers over the past three weeks indicating he thought a saloon owner would make a very poor city representative.

Two of the men had also been on the Citizen's Party ticket, which meant only they had John Troy's endorsements this year. For the first time since Skagway had run a legitimate city council, 1901, Troy had not determined who sat in City Hall. As Tuck passed out the mugs, he thought about the dirty campaign Troy had run, starting three weeks ago. His usual tactic had been to come up with some unsubstantiated allegations about the opposing candidates the day before the election, something bad enough to convince just enough voters to cast their ballots for the Citizens' Party, whom Troy ran as head of the nominating committee. It usually worked. Whoever John Troy picked to run Skagway, did so.

This year, in mid-March, Troy started telling all of Skagway that Chris Shea was leading an effort to reinstall gambling in Skagway. Despite the fact that Chris and his fellow candidates denied the allegation every chance they got, and went on to describe their fair taxes and public utilities platform, Troy wouldn't let the subject drop. Chris just laughed and said he was going to let Troy do his campaigning for him.

Sure enough, the working men turned out in droves. What Troy didn't realize was that by totally forgetting to mention the winter-long labor strike in his newspaper, he'd just killed himself with the working man. The railroad workers, laborers and wharf rats voted for their favorite saloon owner, the guys they worked with, and for the men they saw in their everyday businesses downtown, not the managers upstairs.

Tuck swung by the table with another double handful of beers, meaning to leave one off for Chris, who he'd had to by-pass on the last round, only having strength enough to carry those six. As he drew level with his boss, he realized city marshal Charlie Moore had him under questioning. Chris took the beer with an amused grin and indicated that Tuck should give the marshal one, too.

"Now you know I can't have one of those right now, Chris," Charlie protested. Tuck noticed that he took it anyway.

"You're just about done with your shift, marshal, and Henry Friedenthal will be coming on duty real soon. One of the first things I'm gonna' do is see that Henry gets a raise in pay for being night watchman, so don't worry about a thing. He knows it. Just stay and have two or three beers, on the house. You heard me, Tuck, let the marshal have what he wants."

Charlie stood there, wavering, but then he gave in and took a big swallow of the Red Star beer that Chris kept on tap. Yep, he thought it was pretty good. So he took another.

"And I suppose you think that now you're on the city council, I'm supposed to just ignore those gaming tables you got going over there, Chris," the marshal pointed out.

"You hear anyone complaining?" Chris asked.

"Well, no," Charlie admitted.

"You think one of those temperance women's going to come in here and say something?" Chris asked.

"Pretty unlikely," Charlie confessed.

"You see any of my men working that table?" Chris asked.

Charlie squinted at the men around the table and had to admit that none of them looked like Shea's usual bartenders. 'Course one of them was John Woods, who had worked for Lee Guthrie on a pretty steady basis ever since 1902, and often as a gambler. Didn't mean he was gambling for Chris Shea.

"Woods working for you?" Charlie asked.

"Hell, no. He's Guthrie's man. Just came in for a friendly game of cards. Nothin' wrong with the men playing cards in a saloon as long as the house isn't involved," Chris pointed out.

Tuck wondered if lying to a lawman carried a specific penalty. He hoped not. He sure didn't like to see a city councilman starting his political career off by telling such a big fib. He knew that Woods would be in the Pack Train playing cards every night, all night long for the foreseeable future. Just as John Quinn had moved up to the Board of Trade to do the same thing, now that Lee was back in town.

As Charlie tipped up his mug to take another big swig, Chris winked at Tuck, then turned back to the rest of the city council. They'd taken back their town and staved off the temperance folks, at least for a while.

Tuck took off to spread the beers around some. He caught sight of Tad Hillery and brightened considerably. He hadn't seen Tad since his wedding day, last December. The man must be happy, to be staying out of the saloons. He carried the free beer over.

* * *

Wednesday, April 3, 1907 (the next day). Anna Stinebaugh stared at the newspaper headline. "Labor Ticket Wins Easy Victory." She shut her eyes and steadied herself against the door frame, waiting for the dizziness to pass. When she felt able, she went into the front parlor and sat down to read the article. Three of the men weren't even married, she realized. Three might as well be common laborers working for the railroad. And that saloon man! How could it have all happened?

Shea. He had a wife. Harriet and most of the other women wouldn't have anything to do with her. Her father had been a preacher in town, back during the gold rush. When she fell from grace and married the saloon owner, all the women snubbed her, hoping to make her ashamed and bring her back to the fold. All it had done is driven her farther away. Now she went to Catholic mass with her husband. Anna fanned herself with the newspaper. She had had very little luck getting the Catholic women to join with her cause. No, she doubted she could count upon Helen Shea to help them shut down the saloons and eradicate sin from Skagway.

Anna would not let this victory of the sinful element defeat her. She fell to her knees and began to pray.

Sin and Grace

Chapter Ten

Tuck's Board Of Trade

Saturday, June 1, 1907 (two months later). Tuck stood behind his bar, drawing beer and laughing, not paying much attention to the heads he was leaving in the mugs. George slapped him on the shoulder and told him to move aside, he was wasting the stuff.

"Chris told me you would make a good bartender, so what the hell you doin' this for?" he grumbled.

Tuck ducked his head, pretending to be ashamed. They all knew he just wasn't paying attention. He was far too excited to be able to work behind the bar on the opening night of Flaharty and Woodburn's Board of Trade.

Tuck started to grab up six mugs of beer to take them out into the crowd, but his new partner, George Woodburn, laid a hand on his arm and nodded off towards a corner table. "Man over there's been waiting for you. Go talk to him."

Tuck followed George's eyes and saw Chris Shea sitting in the corner, saluting him with an empty beer mug. Tuck

79

grabbed up two full ones sitting on the counter and took off for Chris' table.

"So you finally did it," Chris grinned as Tuck approached.

"Told you I would. You never believed me."

"Sure I did, especially of late. Soon as the gambling fines disappeared and it went underground, I knew the Board of Trade was yours. Lee didn't have the stomach for it anymore. With the railroad officials having to set a good example for the working men, and the businessmen afraid to stand up to a roulette wheel or a faro table for fear someone might tell their wives, Lee's main source of income started drying up. He couldn't make it all on fancy brands of liquor and champagne. I told you he advised me to up the quality of my stock over the winter. With Lee closed down and my political campaigning, a lot of the businessmen ended up at the Pack Train."

Tuck nodded. Working at Chris' place over the winter, he remembered seeing them there.

"Yeah. I couldn't believe your big advertisements in the newspaper. 'Headquarters for Mining and Commercial Men. Strictly First Class.' Far cry from the old Pack Train we all used to know."

Chris scowled, like he had a bad taste in his mouth. "Yeah, well, I had to do it, if I was going to save this town from itself. With Troy ignoring the railroad strike, putting all of the wrong people in the city council, not paying any attention to the things that really need to be done around here, and so many of the businessmen listening to those reform women, I had to do something. Getting their husbands into my saloon and out of their parlors was just the beginning. Cutting their taxes will be the next step. The men will think I'm the best thing that happened to Skagway and will stop listening to their women folk. You wait and see."

Tuck held up his beer to toast the sentiment. The two men touched mugs and took a healthy swallow.

"So, you're going to have to take the overflow, Tuck. The working men, they'll start to think I'm getting too big for my britches over at the Pack Train and they'll want something more familiar. It better be you."

Tuck grinned. "You bet, buddy. Tuck's Board of Trade."

It will be everyone's favorite place in town."

"Why'd you go in with Woodburn? I never would have guessed him," Chris observed, watching the man behind the bar.

"George thought the place was his. You know he'd been tending bar for Lee almost as long as you had. Took your place, I think."

Chris nodded.

"When I heard the place was for sale, I rushed right over. There was George, making Lee an offer. We got into a bidding war. Pretty soon, neither one of us could afford it, so we decided to buy it together. Guthrie just laughed at the two of us, said we'd be out of business before the year was out." Tuck snorted, showing what he thought of Lee Guthrie.

Chris laughed. "No, Lee had it planned that way. He knew you both wanted it, and he knew you'd both make a success of the place. That's why he moved it over here, to the Burkhard Building. It'll do a lot better for you here on Broadway, closer to the depot and the men working at the railroad yards and wharves. Business is moving away from Sixth Avenue. You'd just die at the old location."

"Yeah," Tuck agreed. "But I did love that woodwork. Sure wish I still had that."

The way Chris's eyes glazed over, Tuck could tell he was seeing it, too, the dark wood, the filigrees, and the sun shining through the clerestories. "Yeah, I know what you mean." He slapped the table. "But a saloon's the men in it, Flaharty, not the glass and woodwork. You'll make this place something special, too."

He rose to leave.

"No, wait, I got something for you." Tuck stood and dashed back to the end of his counter, where the cigar stand stood. He reached inside and drew out a box of Margarites, Chris' favorites.

"This one's on Essie," he said as he handed it to Chris. "She made me promise next time you came in to buy you whatever you wanted. She said if you came by her place, you'd get a lot more, but she said she knew you would never accept her offer."

Chris' eyes twinkled. The legendary faithfulness of Chris

Shea to his wife, Helen, demanded that the proprietor of the Pack Train stay away from Essie's place. The sports knew about his old days with Kitty Faith, but he had not been with her since the preacher's daughter had turned her blue green eyes on Lee Guthrie's bartender and started attending all of the Eccentrics' ball games. Kitty had rarely taken a man, making Chris that much more unusual. Some said she hadn't been with any man on a steady basis since. With Kitty now the acknowledged Queen of Seventh Avenue, getting Chris Shea inside Essie's doorway would be quite a coup. They all knew it would never happen.

"Essie owes me nothing," Chris disclaimed. "She should make the offer to Phil Abrahams. He's the one who saved Seventh Avenue at that council meeting last month."

"Tell me what happened, Chris, for Essie's sake. She wants to know." Tuck leaned forward, mouth open, hanging Chris' on every word, needing to tell the whole story to Essie.

Chris leaned back, taking out one of the cigars to light it before launching into his story. "The good Reverend Glenk comes into the meeting with his petition to move the district, signed by ninety eight men and thirty ladies, none of whom own property on Seventh Avenue. Curiously, some who own property on Eighth Avenue east of Broadway, including Lyle Speer, had signed the petition. Rumor has it that the latter would dearly love to see the district moved to his part of town." Chris puffed his cigar.

"Mrs. Grace Zinkan, a new friend of Anna Stinebaugh's, included her name among those on the petition. She and Mrs. Stinebaugh have organized a number of social gatherings lately, featuring inspirational talks of the spiritual nature," Chris observed, almost as an aside. "I recognized the names of a number of other ladies who have been associated with Mrs. Stinebaugh's sewing and social clubs."

"And Mrs. Stinebaugh herself?"

"Missing from the petition. As Phil so ably pointed out, she and Mrs. Shorthill concurred with the location of the Seventh Avenue restricted district in 1901. It would seem hypocritical to protest its location now," Chris pointed out.

"So she just works behind the scenes."

"So it would seem," the mayor speculated.

"And what else did Mr. Abrahams point out?" Tuck wanted to know.

"Oh, how unfair moving the district would be to both the property owners on Seventh Avenue and to those who would become neighbors of displaced madams. He also observed that, being a real estate attorney, he had some familiarity with property owners in Skagway, and he recognized very few on the petition. He suggested they did not understand the problems attendant upon moving the district."

Both Tuck and Chris grinned.

"But he saved the best for last. When the Reverend Harrison suggested the complete lack of necessity for a restricted district, Phil pointed out that the revenues from the prostitutes' fines paid for the electricity for the street lights and the night watchman's salary last year. It clinched the argument. I tabled the petition without action, when Clarence had wanted to bury it in committee."

"Well, Essie expresses her gratefulness," Tuck acknowledged.

"Tell Essie that she is welcome, and suggest she vote for me if Anna Stinebaugh ever gets her the vote." Chris grinned at the irony. He knew women would not vote as a block.

But he sobered quickly.

"What's the matter, Chris?" Tuck didn't like the look on his friend's face.

Chris looked down and grimaced. "We're not really clear of problems with Mrs. Stinebaugh and her followers, you know. I used to think of John Troy as my worst enemy in Skagway. Of late I have had my doubts." He met Tuck's eyes. "Anna Stinebaugh hasn't been stopped, only delayed. Do not sneer at those women and their social clubs. We must be very careful, Tuck. Tell Essie not to let her guard down for a minute."

Tuck narrowed his eyes and nodded his head. He agreed wholeheartedly.

Grace Zinkan set her tea cup down on Anna's coffee table.

"They are having a very big celebration downtown tonight, Anna," she pointed out.

83

"At least we have forced out Mr. Guthrie," Anna pointed out. "He is a pioneer, one of the first here. As I understand it, he came with Frank Clancy, backed by the Clancy Brothers. They run that big gambling syndicate in Seattle, Victoria and Dawson. We are well rid of him."

Grace nodded. "Yes, Gleason told me. The customs agents have long had problems with Guthrie and the Clancys in Dawson. This may help them shut down that operation."

The women sipped their tea. Anna toyed with one of the sugar cookies she had laid out on her plate.

"But I am so disappointed that the Reverend Glenk couldn't get that petition past the city council," she went on.

Anna scowled into her tea.

"I told him it was entirely the wrong time to bring it up. This new council is not at all inclined to take on this particular battle. The Reverend has no aptitude for political strategy, and he will not listen to me. Unfortunately, he had started circulating the petition in early March, and thought he had to save face, presenting it simply because so many people had signed it. We will have to wait another year, that's all. Wait until that saloon keeper has made a fool of himself, and the bumbling idiots from the railroad have shown how little education they have. The men in this town will come around and vote the right way next year, and we can move the district at that time. We get the district out of the ownership of landlords who have a financial interest in it, and we reduce its influence to nothing."

"What about the owners in a new district?" Grace asked.

"Assuming there is a new district," Anna pointed out, "it will probably belong to two or three women. Landladies, I hear they call themselves. How much political power do they have?"

Grace smiled broadly, thinking she knew. Both she and Anna really had very little idea of the number of influential men in Skagway who talked to the landladies of Seventh Avenue.

Chapter Eleven

For Love of the Child

Tuesday, June 25, 1907 (almost three weeks later). Anna Stinebaugh entered the fog-shrouded cemetery, clutching her nosegay tightly. Eight days it had been since her little girl had left her, gasping for breath, raging with fever, tears constantly leaking down the sides of her face. She hoped the child rested in peace now, as she played among the angels. Anna knew that she had plenty of other little angels with whom to play. She wondered why God took so many little ones, and then chastened herself for such a blasphemous thought. Probably because their mothers question Him so, she realized.

Under the tall trees, the mist almost ceased to fall, becoming only an occasional large drip that had gathered on a branch overhead. The world fell quiet except for the sound of those drips, here a mile from town. Anna couldn't even hear the noise from the railroad shops, the nearest place with any sort of activity. The men there worked hard as she drove the surrey through. A few interrupted their labor and tipped their hats. A couple had grinned broadly. She wondered why. It didn't matter. They probably shared a private joke at her expense, told at some saloon. She didn't care. Only craven men would taunt her at this time with little Florence lying in her coffin in the ground.

Anna sank to her knees and laid the flowers on the freshly turned earth above her child's grave. She clasped her hands together at her breast, and with tears streaming down her face, gave herself over to her grief. She tried to be so strong at home, with J. D. and the other children. They needed her strength, needed her to keep them going, to help them get on with living.

Fay, a young woman now, glided through the rooms like a ghost, pale and unspeaking, astonished that the lively child could be running about one day, bed-ridden the next, dead in a week. Fay had just confronted this part of womanhood, the anguish of that emptiness once occupied by a child. Would it make the pain easier for her oldest daughter to learn this lesson with a sister before becoming a mother? Anna didn't know. She only understood that she needed to be a comfort for her older daughter instead of weeping about the house.

And James offered no help either, sitting about in the evening, staring off into space, refusing to speak, as if talking would rupture a carefully built dam he had constructed to wall in all of his feelings. Anna wanted to shout at him to take the boys and play with them, not teach them to have stiff upper lips and pretend little Florence had never lived. For now, the family tiptoed softly about, afraid to say a word to one another, coming to Mother one by one to cry, but none of them saying anything. Anna, as always, simply stood strong for them, refusing to shed a tear in their presence.

Anna knew she had to grieve, too, and took this hour or two alone as hers. Here, in this quiet place, she spent the time remembering her little girl, chastising herself over and over again with everything she should have done to prevent the suffering that child had endured, dreaming what might have been had Anna only been more vigilant, a better mother, less selfish, been away at her meetings less.

So lost had Anna become in her suffering that when the hand fell on her shoulder, she cried out in alarm. She had not heard or seen another person in the cemetery. She tried to rise, but couldn't, her middle-aged knees and growing girth a betrayal. Essie Miller reached down and helped her to her feet.

"I'm sorry for startling you, Mrs. Stinebaugh," Essie said, quietly. "I only meant to sooth a mother's pain."

"What do you know of a mother's pain?" Anna asked cruelly, not knowing who she questioned in her grief and bitterness. She rarely behaved in so uncaring a manner.

At first Essie thought Anna had identified her and struck out in her hatred, but then she saw no recognition in her eyes, only sorrow and misery. "I lost my darling child, too. I still feel the pain, the hardest thing I have ever had to bear. A mother never recovers from the loss, is never the same again. No one can understand unless she, too, suffered such anguish."

Anna Stinebaugh's eyes swam with tears. She found herself in the stranger's arms, crying as she had not done since Florence had fallen ill. No, crying as she had never done before, great wracking sobs that shook her whole body. She could not have borne such pain had there not been someone to hold her while the agony shuddered throughout her.

Anna didn't know how long the two women clung to one another under the wet leaves with the great drops of rain falling from time to time about them. Finally her convulsions stilled and the sobs died away. Essie pulled a handkerchief from her waist and wiped Anna's tears, t'sking gently, and then turned away while Anna blew her nose. Anna tucked the bit of linen and lace into a pocket, meaning to discover where to return it after it had been laundered.

"I come here once in a while to visit my own daughter," Essie explained into the growing silence. She climbed to her feet, helping Anna, and then brushed the matted leaves from her coat. "My Lulu lies over there." She indicated a simple headboard set apart under the tall, gloomy trees. "She was only a little more than two months old. She cried for three days. I longed to take her place. I bathed and nursed and sang songs and comforted and held, but I could do nothing in the end but cry along with her. And then, I cried alone."

"But what about your husband?"

Essie met Anna's eyes levelly. "I had no husband." Then, she looked away. "I have since done better about avoiding such situations in the first place."

Husbands or children? Anna thought, and then realized how quickly she leapt to judgment. This woman had just helped her more than anyone, with all their well-meaning platitudes and words meant to comfort. One moment later, Anna had classed her with a prostitute, husbandless and knowing how to avoid having a child.

"I thought I knew all the ladies in Skagway," Anna began anew, "yet I don't recognize you. Do you live here? Are you just passing through?"

"No. I live here in Skagway. I have for almost ten years. I believe you do know me, Mrs. Stinebaugh. I'm surprised you don't recognize me, for I know you. Perhaps I made a mistake in speaking to you."

Essie looked around in obvious confusion. "I really must take my leave of you." With that, she turned to hurry down the path towards the road to town.

As the woman turned, Anna gasped. She had rarely seen Essie's face squarely, and never close up. She had always stolen glimpses from a distance. Skagway was not that large a place, and everyone knew who everyone else was. She recognized the woman from the furtive turn and swish of skirts as she hurried away, not the calm, comforting woman who had held Anna in her arms and swept a chaotic world of misery into a place that could be contained.

"Miss Miller!" Anna called after her. "Please don't go."

Essie didn't stop. Anna didn't call again. She didn't know what it was she could have said. But she felt shaken to her core.

Essie settled into the comfortable settee in Ida's personal room at the back of her parlor house on Seventh Avenue. She shivered, still chilled as much by her encounter with

Anna Stinebaugh as she was by the rain on this cloudy day. Ida's motherly housekeeper, Sarah, brought them a tray of tea, t'sking at Essie as if she were still one of the girls and had been out in the rain too long. Ida shooed her away, aware that Essie had come for some good reason and didn't need Sarah puttering around.

"I went out to see Lulu this afternoon," Essie admitted, when the plump, white-haired woman left the room.

Ida nodded, encouraging her to continue.

"Anna Stinebaugh was in the cemetery. You know that her youngest died just this week."

"Ah, yes. Tonsillitis, if I recall. It was in several issues of the newspaper, Mr. and Mrs. Stinebaugh being so prominent here in Skagway." Ida managed to hold back the sniff of disdain that Essie felt sure she wanted to add to the statement.

"I felt sorry for her and offered some comfort." Essie went on to describe their meeting. Tears dropped from her eyes.

"At first I felt grateful that she hadn't recognized me, then it made me mad that she did. She doesn't understand us. All she wants to do is ruin our way of life. How could she and I have a normal conversation about anything?" Essie asked.

"It sounds like you did, until you knew who each other were," Ida pointed out.

"I knew who she was from the moment I saw her. I simply treated her as another grieving mother."

"Why didn't you stay and talk some more?" Ida wanted to know.

"She would have lectured me about not having married the child's father, about not even knowing who the father was, about earning my living the way I do. She has no understanding of our lives, what we suffer and why we do what we do. I didn't want to even start arguing with her." Essie stared at the flowers on the wallpaper on the other side of the room, not seeing them. "I would have found myself explaining Tuck to her. What I have with Tuck is far too complicated to talk about with a woman like Anna Stinebaugh."

"Tuck? What about Tuck?" Ida asked.

"How much I love him. How much I wanted him to be the father of that child. How much I dream, sometimes, that he and that baby and I..." another tear dripped down her face.

"You never told him about the child, did you?" Ida demanded, aghast at the very idea.

Essie shook her head. "Of course not. The baby probably wasn't his anyway. But knowing Tuck, he might have claimed her anyway. He's that way. Like Chris Shea, taking his daughter, Nellie, from that woman down in San Francisco and bringing her up here to raise, alone, until he married that preacher's daughter. Who would have thought a saloon man could do that? I'll bet Tuck would have taken Lulu."

"He loves you that much?"

Essie stopped examining the wallflowers and turned her liquid brown eyes on her mentor. "Oh, yes, Ida, he loves me a very great deal. But it isn't just that. It would be in his nature to hope the very best, and then believe it with all his heart. Even if the girl looked like Hans Schneider, he wouldn't have seen it. He'd love her because she was mine."

The two women sipped their tea, each lost in thoughts of the nature of love.

"You say you used to go to church, Ida. I have always heard that Christians speak much of love. Yet, these women seem to want to impoverish us. Is that love? Do they think we need only redemption, that it can put food on our tables and clothes on our backs, care for us in our old age?"

"I don't think that they care what happens to us personally, Essie. They will make of us the casualties of their war, discarded into graves, if necessary. I suppose they believe we can wear sack cloth and beg for food from their poor houses and die early deaths in the cold somewhere. They believe us to be irredeemable, after all. We have earned whatever punishment God chooses to visit on us." Ida sounded uncharacteristically bitter.

"And that is their kind of love?" Essie asked.

"I've never understood Christian love," Ida admitted. "It seems to encompass such a wide variety of people that it becomes tremendously diluted. They speak of loving their neighbors in the same breath as they talk of loving a child. I don't know if the women of the W. C. T. U. love their husbands with the same passion that they love their cause. I believe that they think us incapable of love."

"Anna Stinebaugh thinks I don't know love?" Essie fumed. "She thinks she knows about love, but she and her women can't even persuade their men to stay out of a saloon! The man I love would do anything for me, would follow me from Dawson to Seattle and beyond at the cost of never having a business of his own. I have to beg him every summer and winter to stay in Skagway and wait for me. He'd give up his saloon and his livelihood on my mere whim, at any moment, if I asked him. I couldn't imagine even hinting to Tuck that I'd want him to give up his dream, something he's planned for his entire life. It keeps him alive. I understand what that saloon means to him. For his love, I'd never ask him to leave his saloon. Yet Anna Stinebaugh plagued J. D. for eight years until he gave up the Duchess."

"And this saloon keeper of yours. You believe he loves you that much in return?" Ida asked, curious now.

Essie and Ida had always been close, closer than a mother and daughter. Their quarrel when she had left and started her own modest business had come to nothing, Ida giving her support as if she were the daughter she'd never been able to raise. Essie could see no reason to keep anything from her old madam. "He does. He has loved me longer than I've loved him. He taught me to love a man when my stepfather and stepbrothers had destroyed all hope of that by making me a mother, then ripping the child from my womb." She had not made such an admission even to Tuck.

Ida nodded at the story she had known for many years.

"Then why does he refuse to make you his wife?"

Essie sat on Ida's couch in silence, shaken, and sorry she had answered the question. Ida had a way of getting to the heart of the matter. The query touched a tender place in her heart, making her eyes fall to her hands in confusion.

"He's never asked, and I've never insisted. We make no demands on one another's love. We trust implicitly in one another, give wholly, share all, save nothing back. That's all that's needed. We have no need for a legal document or church blessing to tell us how we must behave towards one another," Essie answered, without waiver. She still did not meet Ida's eyes.

"So you believe," Ida passed judgment.

Essie did glare at her mentor then. "What purpose does marriage serve, Ida? I believe it provides a stable home for children. Once Lulu died, I made sure there would never be children from the union of Tuck and myself. That's not the purpose of our relationship, you know that. We have loved each other long and well, but we both knew children would never thrive in the way we have chosen to live. With no children, there's no need for useless contracts and pledges."

Ida and Essie both knew that the good women of the W. C. T. U. would pay a great deal to know what the women of Alaska Street knew. Respectable women called them the "devices of the prostitutes," those things that Ida had taught Essie to use to prevent children, although they weren't all devices. Yes, Essie knew there would be no children. In turn, she could teach any woman who wanted to know, what to do.

"Still..." Ida suggested.

"Ida, your own experience tells you how little a marriage certificate means. A husband and six children. What did that get you?" Essie accused her.

The two women glared at one another for a moment or two, sparks flying. Then, Ida laughed. "Oh, how I do miss having you around here, my dear girl. I'm glad you have your man, whether he marries you or not. At least he seems devoted to you, and that's what's important."

Essie grinned then, unable to stay angry with her Skagway mentor. "Oh, I do love Tuck. Because of him, I'll stay here in Skagway, and I'll beat out Anna Stinebaugh and her frumpy old biddies, just you wait and see."

Ida laughed again and grabbed up Essie to give her a big hug. "Of course you will, my darling. Of course you will."

George   Tuck Essie   Si   Glen

Chapter Twelve

Closing Doors

September 25, 1907 (three months later). "Damn that Sarah Shorthill! The woman doesn't even live here any more. What right has she got closing us down?" Tuck demanded. He stalked the empty saloon, chairs turned upside down on table tops, balls racked neatly in their triangles on the pool tables, all the cue sticks lined in their racks. The Board of Trade had cleaned up neat as a pin, wood gleaming in the sunlight from the windows above the curtains, not a speck of dust anywhere. That wouldn't be true when he figured a way out of this mess.

"She has no business in a man's world, shutting down a man's livelihood. We stay out of her clubs and her churches. She and her friends should stay out of our saloons and Seventh Avenue," he raged. Tuck hadn't owned the Board of Trade six months before the queen of Alaskan reformers, Sarah Shorthill, had challenged his liquor license.

His friends gathered at the bar, drinking his free beer, free because he couldn't sell it to them without that license. Flick and Essie, both there, of course, studiously avoided each

93

other, Flick uneasy with the situation, Essie pretending he stood in some other room. Chris perched on his stool, smoking a Margarite cigar. Chris seemed to think the stool was his right, as it was. George Woodburn, Tuck's partner, stalked the floor with his co-owner, too agitated for the beer, downing whiskey instead. Wil Cleveland and Tad Hillery moped nearby, clearly disconsolate, wondering where they would go drinking now. They glanced at Chris, remembering the Pack Train sat only a block away.

Si Tanner leaned back against the bar. "We'll figure a way out, Tuck. We can't let those women get away with this. They win this round, they'll start another. Nothing breeds movement like success, and we need to stop their movement. We've done it before."

"I don't like it," interjected Sam Wall, the new editor of The Daily Alaskan. He had replaced John Troy when the latter left Skagway the first of July. Chris drove him from town. After a big political fight with the power company in June, Troy suddenly put two and two together. He finally realized that Chris Shea and the ordinary working men ran Skagway. The editor of the newspaper sold his mouthpiece and left town when he understood he could no longer call the issues and tell the men of Skagway what to do. He gave up when the balance of power tipped, and he lost control. Sam now sat behind the powerful oak desk, but he hadn't yet tried to flex any political muscle. Tuck and Si bet he didn't even know he could.

Si turned on Sam "You might not like it, Mr. Wall, but it's business to us. Those women shut gambling down in this town last fall. It brought the city almost a thousand dollars a year in revenues. The saloon men paid for all the labor maintaining the streets and the city clerk's salary with that money. The whores pay for the street lights and the health officer's salary. White Pass and Moore's Wharf loses laborers because the fun in town is drying up. If you have no subscriptions, do you have a newspaper, Mr. Wall?"

The room fell quiet except for Tuck's and George's pacing.

Chris turned his half smile on Tuck. "Calm down, Sport. Father Turnell doesn't care about the Board of Trade being within four hundred feet of his church, nor do any of his parishioners. This will die down in a few weeks. Business slows in the winter. Lee had to shut his doors during the last two winters anyway. Apply for your license next spring. We'll put our heads together and come up with something else to keep those women occupied. They'll forget about you by then."

"In the meantime, Mr. Wall," Si instructed the newspaper editor, "I suggest you point out that most of the citizens of this city do not agree with the complaint against the Board of Trade. It might help weaken the ladies' resolve. An unsympathetic city editor squelched them last time around."

Wall frowned. "I'm not sure I want to be cast in the same role as John Troy. I've heard about my predecessor's ruthless brand of city politics. It's not my style." Not an Alaskan, Sam Wall didn't love Skagway. "Unlike some people I probably don't need to name, I came to this place with some inborn ethics. I wonder how many men in this room have them."

Chris bridled at the insinuation, shaking out his shoulders and looking at the ceiling while he noticeably worked at checking his sometimes fiery temper. After a couple of long moments, he said, "You know the public sentiment favors the Board of Trade. It's honest enough to print the truth, Sam. If you want, you can put it on tomorrow's gossip page, not as an editorial, and not as your opinion."

The editor met Chris' eyes squarely for a few moments, and then nodded at his suggestion.

As Flick, the last man to leave, glared at Essie and shut the door behind him, she moved along the front of the bar to put her arms around Tuck. "You know I'll help you out," she murmured into his shoulder.

He stroked her hair, shaking his head. "I don't want the Queen's money, Essie. That stays in the bank. We'll get by, George and I. Heck, this will give me time to bowl this winter." He grinned, just thinking about slamming a heavy ball into those pins, imagining them as straight-laced matrons marching on his saloon. He shared his vision with Essie, and she laughed with him. He swung her around, and then up onto his bar, burying his head in her skirts, his hand creeping up a leg. As usual, she wore no underwear. Suddenly, he remembered Chris' comparison of a polished bar to a woman's bare back. He had his woman on his bar. He couldn't pass up this opportunity. He grabbed his stool and sated his sudden lust on his woman on the bar in Tuck's Board of Trade Saloon.

Two blocks away, the Ladies' Aid Society met in the Presbyterian Church. Juliette Tanner, Si's wife, took charge this evening. She had asked Lena Wurzbacker to read the lesson, and she had picked a most instructive paper entitled "Duties to Ourselves."

Grace Zinkan, the Canadian Customs official's new wife, led the discussion that followed the reading. "So, although we have all been taught to be selfless, to think of our families and our husbands first, we do them a disservice not to care for ourselves. If we let our intellects and our purpose wither, then we become useless to those we love."

Harriet Draper, the photographer's wife, interjected, "Men are weak and think only of themselves when it comes to matters of morality. We women must keep the family, our husbands included, pure, chaste, and free from the evils of drink and drugs and degradation. A man cannot do it without our help."

Grace took up where Harriet left off. "If we sacrifice all just for them, administer always to only to our men and our children, thinking never for our needs to be with our own kind, with our friends who will bolster our courage and give us strength for the fight, we will never be able to help our loved ones. We will never be able to help the other women who toil in misery because they have men who spend all their money in saloons. We won't be able to help the women who have too many children to care for because they don't know how to stop having them. It will be impossible to assist the women who must sell their bodies to support their children because their husbands have died and left them nothing. Women get paid so little in this men's world. If we stay home, selflessly giving only to our husbands and our children, we will never break the bonds that force us all to be chattels."

Harriet took up the chant they had heard time and time

again, with each discussion, until they all had it memorized. "Is it your husband who spends the family's money in the saloon, making decisions for the community where women have no voice? Is it you who has had one more child, beloved as she was, one more than you could care for?" Harriet looked at Anna Stinebaugh as she asked the question, knowing how difficult Anna's life with little Florence had been, how sad they all felt when the sickly child died of tonsillitis early last summer. Anna stared at her lap, tears falling unabated into her hands.

"Yes," Anna admitted. "Today poor women are forced to have large families they cannot support, weak, sickly children, because they do not have enough food to go around. Their mothers would gladly have stopped with four children instead of six, had they only had the knowledge. But that law, that Comstock law makes it impossible for physicians to share information on how to prevent children. Only prostitutes know the ways, have the understanding of the creams, solutions, teas, and, devices they need to avert a child. With the vote, women could change that law, and doctors could do the research needed to develop safe, effective birth control."

Anna thought of Essie Miller and the small child that lay in Skagway's cemetery. Even the device of the prostitute had been insufficient to prevent that life. Essie had not begrudged that one. Anna could not speak of Essie, but she could not stop thinking of her either. Anna knew the power that birth control would give womankind. It seemed a sin to reject God's decision of when a life should come into the world. Yet for a woman to choose, especially after the fourth or fifth child, when she grew old and tired and ill so much of the time...to be able to say no to more children, when to have more would be to invite death.... It seemed the greatest cause of all.

"Will it be you who must work at a poorly paid job if your husband dies unprepared, leaving you no property and no means of living into a comfortable old age? What if you have no sons to care for you?" Harriett asked the group.

Anna took up the refrain, her voice shaking with emotion. "I have been selfish all my life, yet I found a good – albeit stubborn – man to share it. He indulges me somehow. I persevered, and he finally listened to me. A year ago, I convinced him to sell that dreadful place on Seventh Avenue. Grace and Harriet are right. We must nurture our social beings, leave our children with our daughters, our neighbors, or their fathers. We have this duty to ourselves, first and foremost, and to our children, ultimately, and to the salvation of their fathers and to all mothers like us."

She took a great breath. "We must be selfish enough to stay devoted to the cause."

Anna's eyes shone with fervor. She knew the strength of her truth. Sarah Shorthill had been so prophetic. She looked around at the ladies who surrounded her, and her pride in them swelled in her throat. They were so strong already, and they were getting stronger. It would not be much longer before they could once again take on City Hall.

Chapter Thirteen

Shut Down

Wednesday, April 7, 1909 (a year and a half later). Tuck woke with Essie on his shoulder, happy to have her there, even though his shoulder felt dead. So he could rub it to life again, he eased it out from under her head, succeeding in not waking her. He grimaced at the needles of pain as he felt the blood begin to flow into his arm again.

He lay in the quiet house, listening for the muted sounds of residential life outside his home. He couldn't hear much on this weekday afternoon, with the wind blowing. He could tell, by the lack of a slash of sunshine across his bed, that the day was overcast, a typical Skagway day.

He didn't expect to hear Flick in the house. His brother had been gone for two years now, since he had married Ellen, the Swedish girl who had come to town and charmed him with her gentle accent and quiet ways. Ellen, in all her generosity, accepted Essie and made Flick behave better in her presence. She even entertained the love of Tuck's life, although not with others invited, of course. But with just the four of them together, Flick would sometimes unbend, say a civil word, meet Essie's eyes and even smile. Flick could see Tuck's happiness. He had never been able to deny that. As the years passed, he couldn't sustain his dislike for Essie.

Tuck slipped from the bed to use the water closet, and then snuggled back under the covers, beginning to want Essie to wake. Now that she belonged to him, now that she gave herself freely, she slept nude with him, wholly accessible. Ordinarily he would not impose on her sleep, being a night worker himself and knowing the preciousness of her day sleep. But he would have to leave her in bed by herself if he stayed here another minute, either that or wake her with his need. Damn Essie's sleep. She'd have to get it tomorrow.

He molded his body to hers, cupping her breasts, sucking at an ear, bringing her to wakefulness with his hunger. She laughed with the joy of it, not begrudging the loss of sleep. She enjoyed the feel of him until her urgency could keep her quiet no longer. "If you don't let me go, Tuck, I'll pee all over you," she laughed. He released her long enough to let her dash to the water closet.

When she came back, they satisfied their lust on one another with much laughter and squeaking of bed springs and banging on the wall. How good not to worry about busy ears through thin walls. They drowsed afterwards, but could not recapture their sleep and finally roused for the beginning of their day.

Tuck fried eggs and bacon for their breakfast at four-thirty in the afternoon. His coffee tasted not so bad, nor as good as he wanted. He still had not developed the trick of settling the grounds before pouring it.

"So Chris still sits on the council," Essie observed, glancing at the newspaper. Tuck knew she'd heard the news last night, as he had, after the election.

Tuck nodded, swallowing his mouthful of eggs and toast. "Both he and Si. But just barely, and only the two of them. The Citizens Party made a come-back." He shook his head.

Essie glared out the window at the bleak, snow-covered peaks above the hedge in Tuck's backyard. "It's because of Sam Wall. It was too much to hope he'd be Progressive. He couldn't remain neutral. If he had even just stayed the middle course, it would have been fine. But Wall's worse than Troy. He went on a one-man crusade to get Chris out of the mayor's seat."

"It worked," Tuck agreed. "Howard Ashley is now mayor. Chris has one friend left on the council. At the best, he and Tanner can block petitions and motions. They can no longer develop and control the issues, at least not until the next election. Chris can just barely hold his ground for this year."

"And in the meantime, Anna Stinebaugh and Grace Zinkan continue their good works in town," Essie sniffed, swallowing a great gulp of Tuck's barely drinkable coffee.

"Drinking troughs for horses and dogs, a reading room for the men to provide alternative entertainment for those nasty saloons and brothels." She smiled broadly, trying to imagine Tuck and his customers choosing to read a book over drinking a beer, and then romping with her in bed.

"Oh, you forgot fixing the road to the cemetery, and building the rest rooms for tourists at Kirmse's curios store," Tuck added. "When they aren't bowling in the lane next to mine at the Elks Hall. Curse them! I can't even escape them in my favorite pleasures! Except with you, of course." He flashed an evil grin her way.

Essie smiled, remembering the first time Tuck had seen Anna Stinebaugh bowling. He had stomped and raved for an hour, sputtering about women entering men's sports. It had taken all her wiles to get him off the subject.

"Oh, they're quite the little hostesses, now that they have reorganized the W. C. T. U." His words sounded mild enough, but his lively, blue eyes blazed with hatred he rarely showed.

"Yes, they have studiously courted Sam Wall. Mrs. Stinebaugh will not repeat the mistake she made in 1901.

She has won over the editor of The Daily Alaskan. He sees them as angels of mercy. The women can do no wrong." Tuck's gaiety of earlier had fled. "Whereas 'Christopher Columbus Shea'," Wall's favorite name for Chris, "can do nothing right for Skagway. We have a set-up for disaster here. When it happens, Chris won't be able to help us."

Essie flounced around the table at him. "Why, you're downright cheerful today, my boy. Chris has always pulled through for us, and he will again." She stood behind his chair and nestled his head between her breasts, as she leaned over to kiss his mouth. "In fact, I'd like you to ask him a little favor for us."

"Hmmm?" Tuck mumbled, transfixed by his captor.

Essie circled round him, her hands never leaving his hair, depositing herself on his lap. He adjusted her comfortably, fondling a breast in the process.

"As sole owner of The Board of Trade, you can help me expand my operation," Essie began.

"Mmmm," he muttered his agreement.

"I've discovered another petition circulating to move the district."

Tuck startled, understanding the implications immediately. Without full support of the council, Chris would have more difficulty tabling the petition this go-round.

"I'm not so sure we're anxious to stop the movement this time," Essie pointed out.

Tuck's eyes widened. What Essie suggested constituted heresy. To give Anna Stinebaugh and the women of the W. C. T. U. hope of success in anything they did represented suicide. He would point that out to her, but first he would hear her out. Essie often had good ideas.

"I've been trying to buy a place on Seventh Avenue since I decided to stay here in Skagway full time, for over a year now."

Tuck nodded. He had blessed the day she had told him she was staying, when November turned to December and she was still in Skagway, still coming to his house and waking in his bed on Wednesday afternoons. She had spent Christmas with him, exchanging gifts, the best Christmas he'd had since he'd come north.

"No one wants to sell. Kitty and Ida have the place locked up tight. Lee Guthrie and Phil Snyder, the only two landlords, won't sell either. I can't break in. The only way I'll make my dream happen and stay here in Skagway full time, Tuck, is to make them move the district."

Tuck saw it, then, crystal clear. He had the Board of Trade. The dream was half theirs. Essie wasn't Queen yet, and he needed to do his part to make that happen.

"Whadda' I need to do, Darlin'?"

"Lyle Speer wants to move Frankie Belmont's old place, 'The Cottage,' over to Eighth Avenue. We have enough to buy it, Tuck. That place was the fanciest whore-house Skagway ever had. I've been in it and seen it. It's still all decked out, wood wainscoting, flocked wall paper, red velvet portieres and crystal chandeliers intact, just waiting for the customers to come pouring back in. If Chris lets this one through, Tuck, I'm on my way to being Queen."

"We let Anna win this round?"

"Depends on how you're looking at it, doesn't it, Tuck. I don't think this will be a loser for you and me," she pointed out.

Something about this felt wrong to Tuck, but he couldn't put his finger on it. Everything Essie said made sense. He tightened his grip on the woman he loved. "I'll talk to Chris as soon as I can find him," he promised. Then he kissed her thoroughly.

* * *

Tuesday, June 8, 1909 (two months later). Lee Guthrie walked into the Board of Trade and straight up to Tuck's bar. Tuck gave him a friendly grin, but Lee didn't return it. "You don't read newspapers, huh, boy?"

Tuck never liked Lee's propensity for calling him "Boy," but he usually just ignored it. Malice gleamed in Guthrie's eyes tonight, and he looked like he wanted to pick a fight. Not in the mood to be needled, the "boy" irritated Tuck and made him prickly.

"Not today. Should I have?"

"Yes. You should have. Could you give me some of your best whiskey?" Lee softened his voice, so he must have decided to drop the belligerent tone. He pushed a silver dollar onto the bar, more than enough to pay for whatever Tuck would have. Tuck splashed half a tumbler full of an expensive brand, took his dollar and returned him fifty cents. Steadying himself with a deep breath, Guthrie tried again. "Perhaps you could join me, Mr. Flaharty. I have some business that concerns a mutual friend. I think you will be interested."

Tuck, intrigued, removed his apron. He remembered yesterday's city council meeting to talk about the red light district. Why hadn't he checked the newspaper? Why hadn't anyone told him about it, for that matter? Actually, he'd only just gotten to the saloon, running a bit late. He hadn't had time to talk to anyone, other than a pleasantry or two. He motioned to John Wise, working some tables, to take over at the bar, and then followed Lee to the corner table.

Lee took two cigars out of his breast pocket and offered one to Tuck. He had never accorded Tuck the honor before. Tuck had smelled these cigars, partaken of them vicariously as he would bring Lee and Chris their whiskey during their private talks at the Pack Train. The king of cigars, Tuck had never thought to have one for himself. He didn't even know its name. He didn't think he wanted to know, because then he would always want to buy one. Better to let it remain unattainable.

Lee lit a match and held it for Tuck, just as he often did for Chris. The owner of the Board of Trade waited while Guthrie lit his own and puffed it to life. As Tuck sampled his, he realized the cigar tasted even better than it smelled. No wonder Chris' face took on that look of ecstasy when he inhaled this cigar. Tuck could only nod his appreciation.

"Chris and Si went to Kitty's a week ago. I guess you knew that," Lee began.

Tuck bobbed his head. Chris had told him, curtly, without emotion. He said Kitty had let them sit behind a curtain, and they had heard Speer offer The Cottage to the madams. He confirmed that Lyle would sell them either The Cottage or any of at least seven other properties on Eighth Avenue, should the council agree to disband Seventh Avenue. Speer bragged that he had four councilmen in his pocket, that it was a done deal. If one of the ladies would make him an offer, she would own the swankiest brothel in Skagway.

Tuck sat frozen at the table, his bowels curdling. He already knew that Speer had turned on Essie. He thought he could shop for a better offer. Fear gripped his heart. Something else had happened. What was Lee going to tell him?

"I had asked Chris to find out what Speer had in mind, because I didn't want to lose my rents on Seventh Avenue. They're just about the only thing keeping me here in Skagway, them and what little influence I have in City Hall."

Lee looked down at the table, ashamed to meet Tuck's eyes. "Chris had it all worked out. He and Si and the ladies planned to tell the council a story of greed by one sleazy saloon keeper, how the whole scheme to move the district came down to one sporting man who was about to lose his bar. They thought they could convince the council how foolish it was to move the district for the sake of one man's profit."

He looked at Tuck in apology. "After hearing the way Speer went after Kitty to buy The Cottage, Chris knew it wouldn't work for Essie anyway."

Tuck nodded as Lee continued. He and Essie had talked about that, after the meeting. They agreed there was nothing Chris could do for them.

"Then they got caught. Henry Phillips, Wall's pressman at the newspaper, waited in one of Kitty's rooms, listening, too. He saw Chris and Si, could counter any special twist the four of them might want to put on the story. Did he tell you about that?"

Tuck shook his head. His gut got icier. He hadn't

thought about how hard this would be for Chris, the consummate family man, with a preacher's daughter for a wife, a teenage daughter, and an elderly mother at home.

Lee swallowed some of the whiskey and tugged on the cigar, as if to fortify himself before continuing. "Chris Shea is perhaps the best friend I have," he admitted. "I did not know what the man would do for me until today." He looked Tuck in the eye. "Perhaps you didn't know either."

Tuck shuddered, not wanting to hear what came next.

"Chris Shea, in his promise to both of us, knowing he committed political suicide, went before the city council last night and argued desperately for two hours to keep the Seventh Avenue district alive and in its current location. He told not only the city council, but the entire public assembled in the council chambers where he was when he learned how Lyle Speer would profit from the sale or rent of his properties to the madams and whores displaced from a district disbanded by the people who signed that petition."

Lee shook his head, swallowing hard. "He knew as he did so that he humiliated a wife he loves above all else in this world and a daughter who he still strives mightily to make love him. He knew as he made his public confession to bring your woman and me a few more dollars that he would have to take his family and leave Skagway and his political career here behind him."

Lee Guthrie suddenly stood. He leaned across the table, grabbed Tuck by the collar, pulled him to his feet and hissed in his face. "You know how much Chris Shea loves Skagway. You know how he loves the politics. You know how much he loves his family."

As he released Tuck's collar, Lee shoved Tuck back, only an inch or two, his rage barely contained. "Now, do you know how much he loves the two of us?"

With that, Lee Guthrie turned on his heel and strode from the Board of Trade.

Tuck Flaharty stared after him, shaken to his core. He wondered if he'd ever see Chris again. For that matter, would he ever see Lee Guthrie again?

***

Tuesday, June 22, 1909 (two weeks later). Tuck looked

up at the next customer to see Si Tanner standing at his bar. He was a welcome sight, but neither man smiled. Si tipped his hat in acknowledgment, and Tuck picked up a mug with a lift of his eyebrow. Si slid over a dime, and Tuck drew a beer for him. As the magistrate turned city councilman nodded his thanks, he thrust the latest newspaper across the bar. "Page four," he said.

It held a short article about yesterday's council meeting. Skagway no longer had a recognized red light district. The council would entertain suggestions on where to designate a new district, but it would not be Seventh Avenue, nor any place so close to downtown. They would agree only to a place amenable to both affected and nearby property owners. Si Tanner had made a desperate move to save his own political career. He had made a motion to completely ban the prostitutes from Skagway. No one had seconded the motion. Tuck hoped certain voters would remember that gesture next election day.

Sam Wall mentioned that Chris Shea did not attend the meeting. Of course Chris was absent. He would soon be on his way to Seward, Alaska, to take up his new duties as game warden for the Kenai District. One of Governor Hoggatt's last acts before leaving office had been to appoint Chris to the job. Tuck had gotten to see him, just the one last time. Their good-byes had been joking, with promises to visit. Each knew the assurances to be empty. The last favor had been called in. When they clasped each other in farewell, their mutual grips said everything their words had not. Tuck would never find another fastball so satisfying to hit.

Tuck would stand on Moore's Wharf to watch the S. S. Georgia leave with Chris and his family for Juneau on the first of July. In the capital city, the Sheas would catch the Northwestern for Seward. He wondered about the whereabouts of Anna Stinebaugh and if she understood the victory she had won this day. If John Troy had been in Skagway, he would have joyfully explained it to her.

Anna Stinebaugh smoothed down her copy of The Daily Alaskan with great pride and began to snip out the article to send to Sarah Shorthill. Our latest victory, she thought. We take another step towards emancipation for the women of this city. The change continues. See, she mused, we even change Mr. Josias M. Tanner. He proposes closing the district altogether. Anna did not believe in his sincerity, but if others did, Mr. Tanner might just have to live up to his promises. If nothing else, Si Tanner kept his word.

Anna smiled. With John Troy, Lee Guthrie and Chris Shea gone, she had only Mr. Tanner yet to worry about. Three down and one to go. With the powerful men gone, the change would be complete.

Alaska Street Red Light District

Alaska Street

Methodist Church

Fifth Avenue

Fifth Avenue Hotel

Chapter Fourteen

Resurrection

Sunday, December 25, 1910 (a year and a half later). Essie woke on Christmas morning with Tuck in her bed. No, this was their bed, for this was their bedroom. She would allow no other man in either one. It was the largest bedroom at the back of the second floor, away from the noise and bustle that would go on in a normal parlor house of this size. The largest house of its kind in Skagway, Essie would be opening it on December 31 with a grand New Year's Eve party. She promised the bachelors of the town that it would be a wonderful way to see the New Year in, this final fillip on the resurrection of the district.

Right now, though, she and Tuck had the whole house to themselves. It was still in pieces, only half the furnishings had arrived, the curtains only half hung, the portieres not yet in place. But she had a Christmas tree, and her girls would start showing up this week. They would help with the rest of the work. She knew it would all be done by New Year's Eve.

Tuck had been helping, of course, all along. Even Flick

and his wife Ellen had been over with hammer and needle and thread. Essie blinked back the tears, still overwhelmed at their generosity. She knew they came for love of Tuck, not because of any affection for her, but it also meant they had accepted her as a part of his life.

Essie toyed with the idea of stirring Tuck to his easily aroused passion, but then decided they had all day. She was hungry, not just for his touch, but also for some food. She'd go downstairs and make coffee before he got to it and made his usual mess. Her breakfasts weren't much better than his, but her coffee definitely was. As soon as this place was a paying proposition, she'd get Jane to cook for them all, if she could steal her back from Ida. Ida didn't pay her enough as it was.

Essie had always been more generous than her old madam, and it was beginning to pay off. She let the girls keep their tips, so now they came to Essie first to see if she had work for them. Essie had had no trouble filling her new place, even though this was a poor time of year to be starting off. She was bringing in four girls, but only for a month. She'd just keep two until spring, and then bring three more back for a full house in the spring.

Essie slipped out of the bed, letting Tuck sleep. She dressed only for warmth, a camisole and petticoat, some stockings and a shawl. There would be plenty of time for clothes later.

Tuck later found her in the kitchen, drinking her good coffee, getting ready to make him a big breakfast with pancakes and bacon and eggs. He caught her up, covering her with whiskery kisses as she squealed and wiggled in protest. Only partly dressed himself, in a robe with skinny, hairy legs sticking out underneath, he was rumpled and as dear to her as a child's worn-out Teddy bear.

It was only when she set the plates of food on the table that she spied the small, gold-wrapped gift. He studiously ignored it, so she did, too, or at least she tried to. It sat in the middle of the table, teasing her. The present stopped all conversation at a meal usually filled with jokes and banter. Tuck grinned, knowing why she didn't talk, waiting for her to ask what it was. She kept her tongue, wondering when he would offer it to her, playing the game, drawing out both their pleasure with the anticipation.

When the last sweet mouthful of pancake and syrup had been washed down with the strong, rich coffee, and Tuck had carried the empty dishes to the sink and refilled their cups, he sat comfortably in his chair. They both looked at the little gold box with the saucy red satin ribbon.

"Open it," he finally commanded.

She pounced on it like a cat on a mouse, afraid it would escape after sitting there taunting her throughout the meal. Her eyes looked like a child's after Santa's visit.

The gold paper crumpled from a deep blue velvet box, and she knew it was jewelry. Tuck had never given her jewelry before, always flowers or chocolates or perfume or some frippery of clothing. Both had agreed to remain frugal to obtain their dreams, his saloon and her parlor house.

Essie stared at the box, suddenly afraid. They had never talked marriage. She hadn't dared to think of it, didn't know what she wanted, didn't know what it would mean. She wanted to put the box down and not have to think about this, not now, not here, not today.

Tuck saw her hesitation and could stand the strain no more. Like the boy he always was, he reached for the box and took it from her. He opened it, then turning it, displayed the sparkling diamond eardrops for her, a wide grin on his face. Essie's eyes had already brimmed with tears, fearing the worst. All she saw at first was the sparkle in the box and the shine from his countenance. Then she blinked, and her vision cleared enough to see there were two, not one, that it wasn't a ring, but that they were earrings. And that they were beautiful, something Kitty and Ida, even that high society prig Abbie Guthrie, if she ever saw them, would envy. Tears of relief and joy replaced those of dismay. Tuck rounded the table to dry her eyes, place them in her ears, and accept her heartfelt caresses of gratitude. He could not know that a small part of her was disappointed as well.

"You're just one old woman away from being Queen of Alaska Street, Essie," Tuck observed when she returned from dashing off to a mirror to admire the earrings sparkling next to her dark hair. She slipped her hand under his robe to feel the muscles at his side and back. She wished she had thought to wear a robe herself, instead of the camisole. Skin to skin would be so much more satisfying.

"Mmmm," she agreed. "Kitty has the two lots here on Alaska Street, one next to me and one across the street. She's bringing in three cribs and one small brothel, plus the two houses that were here already. She's still Queen. Ida has her house and two small brothels. She's connecting the two places and going to make it the main feature. She said she wanted to rent the old place out and use the bigger place for herself. She'll leave the corner empty for me when I inherit."

"How ill is she?" Tuck asked.

"I don't know," Essie shook her head, worried. "She won't see a doctor. I was surprised she went to a lawyer, to tell you the truth, even more surprised when she said she was giving it all to me. She said she had a son in Kansas City, one who had never come to see her. She didn't want him get her money. She said she worked hard to provide for him after her husband died. She bore six children to the man, but he didn't love her, and he left her nothing. She had to prostitute herself to support them, but they all died in a cholera epidemic but the one son. When he was old enough to care for himself, he ran away, ashamed of his mother. It hardened her heart."

"Why you, Essie? You left her."

Essie smiled at the question. "I'm her success story, Tuck, the replacement for the daughter she lost. Every mentor loves a pupil who makes good. Plus, she worked hard to best Kitty and never could. Kitty has the smarts and natural grace and the looks that Ida never did. Ida just has stamina and grit. She likes the idea that when I inherit her estate, I will at least own half the district. Kitty can no longer claim to be Queen. Mayor Si Tanner and City Hall will have to deal with the both of us on an equal basis, not Kitty first.

"You're telling secrets today, Essie. Does a man get secrets for diamonds? If I'd known, I'd have showered you with jewels from the beginning," Tuck ventured, grinning. Essie almost frowned. He must still remember her wrath when he inadvertently asked her questions about her own past.

Essie realized she had given away Ida's beginnings, an unforgivable betrayal of a woman who would make her dream come true. "You'll keep Ida's secret, won't you, Tuck." It wasn't a question.

"Of course, Darlin'." He raised his eyebrows in surprise that she might think otherwise.

She looked at Tuck, saw the sincerity in his eyes, and knew Ida's past was safe. She also saw the curiosity there, and knew him as just a man. This time it didn't make her angry. She wondered why they all seemed to want to know. She thought the mystery made the women more tempting, more desirable. It ensured that the men kept coming back, hoping they could worm the secret out some day. That's what Ida had told her, that's what she told her girls. Never tell a man your past. Never tell him your real name, where you came from, why you do what you do. It will turn you into an ordinary woman. It will make him pity you. It will give him cause to love you.

Tuck loved her anyway, without the secret, loved her without question. Did she want his pity, too? She didn't think she wanted to dredge up the pain. But then, if she did, maybe he could help her lose it, once and for all. Maybe it was better that he knew.

"Come to bed." Essie took his hand and led him upstairs. She pulled off her camisole and petticoat, leaving the stockings to last. Skin to skin, baring all, it was better that way. In the bed, she pulled him close, drawing the sheets and blankets over them to keep out the chill. As he started to caress her, she stopped his hand and brought it to her mouth instead.

"I was born Augusta Miller. My mother was seventeen and so was my father. He worked for my grandfather, who was a blacksmith in West Virginia. Grandfather didn't run him off because he needed his apprentice, but he wouldn't let him marry Mama, either. He thought Mama could do better. I don't know my daddy's name. They gave me Grandpa's instead."

Tuck simply held her, realizing he heard a story told to no other man.

"My stepfather took me when I was thirteen years old,

then said my stepbrothers should learn about women once I'd been broken in. One of them was only twelve. By then, I had two sisters, one ten and another eight. I knew they would serve Pops and our brothers when they got older. My mother pretended she didn't know what was going on. He was a respectable businessman. He ran a grocery store in Billings, Montana."

Tuck tightened his grip. He knew such things happened, but he still didn't like it. He did not doubt Essie.

"When I was sixteen, I ran away from home, thinking I could go to a big city and make a living as a clerk somewhere. I stole some money from Pops, enough to get me to Seattle. I found a job mopping floors in a dry goods store. It was enough to pay for a room in a boarding house, but not enough for anything else."

Tuck stroked her hair, wanting to comfort her.

"One day the owner said he'd give me a job as a clerk if I had some decent clothes to wear. When I told him all I had was what I wore, he fingered the collar of the dress as if to test its quality. Then he slipped his hand over my breast and suggested that he could advance me the money for a nice dress in return for a favor. He reminded me that a clerk made four times what a mop girl made. He rubbed my nipple, hoping to arouse me, not knowing I'd never felt arousal with a man."

Tuck continued the stroking of her hair, wanting now just to brush it, all desire for her body having fled.

"You know what sort of woman I am, Tuck, and how my stepfather and stepbrothers had ruined me. I considered what the extra money could buy me and the choice was simple. He helped me take off my old dress and under clothing, until I was completed naked, and then he followed me through the store, picking out a new outfit for me. He took me on his desk before dressing me in my new clothing. I got a whole new wardrobe that same way, about one complete outfit, from underwear to overcoat and shoes, each week."

Tuck reached for her hair brush on the small table beside the bed, and then sat her up before him, crossing his legs to give himself a firm base. He began to brush out her long tresses as she continued the story. The gentle pull on her scalp soothed the pain growing inside her, the pain she had hoped she'd forgotten. He loved the silky feel of the dark, heavy mane, it calming his growing rage.

"When the new mop girl started wearing new dresses, too, I realized that I would soon be out the door, looking for another job. I worked as a clerk for only three more stores with similar arrangements before I figured out there was more money doing the same thing in a place like Ida's house. At least there, I didn't have to mop floors or sell dry goods. Lena, on Yesler Street, took me in and taught me what I needed to know to stay healthy and alive. I was lucky, Tuck. I'm pretty, and I didn't have to start out on the streets."

Tuck just brushed, thinking how it was men like him that made Essie what she was. It confused him.

"When the gold rush started, it excited me, as much as it did the men who came to Lena's door. They hardly had time for us, they were so anxious to go north. But they weren't afraid to spend the money because they were sure they'd be rich when they came back. I packed my bags and went north with them."

"The winter of 1899 and 1900, I went to Cleveland with an aging insurance agent and his sadistic, twenty-six year old son. They had been to Dawson with the rush, and they struck it rich. They said I could live with them in luxury. It turns out the sweet old man had a none-too affectionate wife and a daughter. He set me up as a servant in an upstairs bedroom and came to my room every night but Saturday. That night he left me to Ralph and his sick ways while he slept with his wife. The old man paid me handsomely, but in the spring, Ralph's tendencies drove me north again." Tuck's knuckles whitened on the brush handle, but he didn't vary his stroke.

Essie turned to face Tuck. He kept brushing, pulling her hair forward over her shoulders, draping it over her breasts. She smiled at him. "You know the rest, Tuck. You were there. Ida's in the spring and fall, Lena's in the winter, wherever the business was best in the summer. A skinny Irishman from Ohio with a bushy mustache and impish blue eyes worming his way into my heart, doing something no one

like me ever expected, teaching me that the act that had
made me what I was could be good with a man that I loved."

"But I was just like all the others, Essie. I came for the
same reasons. I was just as bad," he protested.

"No, you weren't, Tuck. You always gave everything of
yourself to me, never holding anything back. You were never
selfish, always sharing all of your immeasurable joy of me
and of life. You never asked anything, just accepted it as
given. You took all things as they came and marveled when
those things were good. You treated me as if I was the finest
lady in town, never questioning that you had to buy my time
or my favor. It made me want to give it to you freely so badly
it hurt, Tuck, and still you never thought to even request it.
No other man thought to respect me, a whore, in such a
way."

"I only wanted a woman to make love to."

"You only wanted a woman to love. There's a difference."
She pulled aside her tresses, exposing her breasts again,
laying back on the bed with her arms raised over her head,
inviting him with open arms and open legs. "Love your
woman now, for you've made her yours alone."

As Tuck's body covered hers, Essie suddenly wished the
earrings had been a ring after all. She knew without
reservation what her answer would have been. She was
wedded to him now, whether he knew it or not. It was simply
a matter of time before he and the law knew it, too.

* * *

February 28, 1912 (two years and two months later).
Essie stood in Ida's large, modern kitchen, surveying the
cheerful, lemon-colored walls and the smudged fingerprints
on the creamy white built-in cupboards. Ida rebuilt it when
she moved the house from Seventh Avenue. It just needed a
good cleaning.

No, this wasn't Ida's kitchen, it belonged to Essie, now.
Ida lay in the cemetery along with the other pioneers of
Skagway. Essie was sorry she missed the funeral. Tuck
described it as grand and dignified. Lots of people turned
out, especially businessmen, men he didn't know would even
acknowledge her. Sam Wall had written a dignified death
notice, referring to her as an old resident of Skagway. The

116

town had not ignored her as they did the rest of the demimonde. What a terrible time to be out of town, to not be here during Ida's last days.

Tuck stepped out of the back bedroom, which he had been inspecting with Sarah, Ida's housekeeper. "You've made the room quite cozy, Mrs. Murphy," he complimented her. "I especially like the Roman glass. I didn't know what it was when I read the probate inventory."

"Oh, Mrs. Freidinger had such European tastes," the chubby, white-haired Sarah bubbled. Essie thought her perfect. She charmed the customers with her motherly ways. So many men liked to be mothered before being sent to bed with a naughty girl. The contrast excited them.

"It was her German background. I appreciate Mrs. Miller giving me the glass." She glanced shyly at Essie.

Essie didn't correct her when she used the "Mrs." All the girls had started calling her that, now that Tuck lived at the house with her. While she wasn't Mrs. Flaharty, the "Mrs. Miller" felt right. Tuck never blinked at its use, just grinned from time to time. She thought he liked the sound of it as well, but they never said a word about it.

When Sarah had bustled out of the kitchen with her feather duster, Tuck slipped his arm around Essie's waist. "You've made it, Darlin.' You're Queen."

"Not quite, Tuck, Sweetie. I've still got to build one more place, the one on the corner. Even then, Kitty'll have one more crib than I do."

Tuck flapped a hand, dismissing Kitty's one crib as inconsequential. "You've already got the biggest place, Essie. It's two stories to her one-story places. Your new place will be bigger than anything she has, too. Even Ida's two-woman brothel is bigger than her two woman place. So she has the two cribs to your one. Who's counting?"

"It's the number of girls that counts, not size, you know," she grinned. Men always thought size mattered, when women knew the numbers counted. As long as men demanded numbers of women in Skagway, she and Kitty would find a way to squeeze in the customers. Space wasn't of importance.

"And to think Lyle Speer thought we needed his eight

lots," Essie mused aloud. "Kitty, Ida and I have done it with four, without a man to intervene."

"So I did nothing, huh?" Tuck swung her around for a big, sloppy kiss.

"Oh, all right. I guess the Board of Trade helped out a little," she admitted. The Board of Trade helped out a lot. It had been a long time since the two of them had kept track of what money belonged to whom. They shared a dream. From the day Essie opened a savings account with the money Tuck paid her for her favors, and he came to pay her fines, the two of them had shared a pocketbook.

"My Queen," he sighed, contentedly, releasing her at last. "Let's go inspect your other castle, and then we have to plan the grand palace." He twirled her off towards the door, continuing to help her fulfill her dreams.

Anna Stinebaugh passed the plate of cookies to Grace Zinkan, and then picked up the pot of tea and poured a steaming cup for her guest. She always enjoyed talking to Grace so much. She was like a sister. The two of them thought like soul mates. She wondered why men and women couldn't be like that.

"Well, one less of those horrible women left on Alaska Street," Grace observed. "We only have two left. We are making wonderful progress."

Anna brightened. "Yes, we are reducing our enemies' numbers in both City Hall and the demimonde. John Troy, Chris Shea, Lee Guthrie, Phil Snyder, they have all left. And now Mrs. Freidinger. It won't be long before we have the vote. Then we can take on the saloons. Sarah was so right, Grace. We will have a clean and pure Skagway before the decade is out, I can feel it in my bones."

The two women nibbled on their cookies and sipped their tea, contemplating the glorious vision Anna painted. It seemed so fair, so out of reach, yet so possible.

"I hear a large number of people came out for her funeral," Anna sighed.

"Oh, posh. It was simply curiosity, and mostly men, from what people told me. What women did make an appearance came from the demimonde. No decent woman would have dared show her face."

"Then how do you know?" Anna asked, innocently.

Grace's eyes widened. "Why, Harriet Pullen told me, and I thought she had it on good authority. But now that you mention it, I wonder where she got the information." Both women contemplated the question, knowing that Harriet was not above having gone to the funeral herself.

"I went out to visit Florence just the other day," Anna admitted. "I'm so glad they opened the new cemetery, so that woman is not in the same cemetery with my little girl."

Grace leaned over to pat Anna on the arm, taking the time to let her friend grieve for her lost toddler. When Anna had wiped her tears on her lacy handkerchief, Grace observed kindly, "Charlie Moore's wife, Margaret, told me that Mrs. Freidinger had lost children as well."

"What?" Anna seemed shocked.

"Well, you know that Mr. Moore took the census a couple of years ago, don't you."

Anna nodded.

"And Margaret has lost two children herself. We talked about it, and she told me that Charlie told her that Mrs. Freidinger had borne six children, but only one had survived to become an adult."

"She lied!" Anna asserted. No prostitute could tell such a tale truthfully.

"Charlie said her eyes got misty, with a far away look when she answered his question, and that she wouldn't answer any others for quite some time. Then she told him her one son refused to write or come to see her, despite all she had done to support him after his father had died."

119

Anna stared at the hands in her lap. "Why did she have all those children?" she wondered aloud. "I understand those sorts of women know how to avoid bearing children. They know more than the doctors about such things."

"Perhaps she wasn't a prostitute when she became a mother," Grace suggested.

Anna turned to her in horror. "Was Ida Freidinger the very kind of woman we all talk of saving? Did she turn to her way of life to feed her children, only to lose them after all?" Anna's tears started anew. "I wonder what other sad stories live on Alaska Street?"

"Well, I don't think we can walk up to Mrs. Miller's door and ask her, do you?" Grace demanded, tartly.

Anna chuckled, but sobered immediately, remembering her encounter with Essie in the cemetery. That day had confused her immensely, and the memory would not let her rest easily. She closed her mind to it. "No, I suppose you're right. The best we can do is prevention, work to save the future, and be sympathetic to the past." She sipped some cooling tea. "I do wonder why she started going by the 'Mrs.' Miller."

"Well," Grace hesitated for emphasis, "with 'Mr.' Flaharty coming and going on such a regular basis and no other place to call home, I wonder that she doesn't call herself Mrs. Flaharty."

"She should, and I wonder why she doesn't. I mean, I wonder why they haven't," Anna amended.

"I have ceased to wonder why the people in that world do anything they do," Grace returned, acerbically. "They live for some strange sense of pleasure that we don't understand. They have no awareness of obligation to the future, no need for children. I don't think they know about love or fidelity. When we have closed down Mr. Flaharty's saloon and forced Mrs. Miller out of town, then they will be faced with a decision. Either they will marry or they will go their separate ways. It is my bet that it is the latter."

"You know I don't bet, Grace. But I am indeed curious what Mr. Flaharty and Mrs. Miller will do when we force them to change their evil ways."

Chapter Fifteen

The Old Guard

Tuesday, January 14, 1913 (One year later). Tuck stared at the front page headline. "Chris Shea Dead in Ketchikan; Formerly Mayor of Skagway." Not our Chris! he wanted to shout.

"What was he doing in Ketchikan, Tuck?" Wil Cleveland asked, leaning over the bar at the Board of Trade. "He's the game warden in Seward."

Tuck shook his head, totally bewildered. He felt like the world had just turned upside down. "I dunno' Wil. This is crazy. If Wall hadn't said this Shea had been mayor of Skagway, I'd've said he was talking about another man. But here it says he came up with the rush, got into the saloon business, ran for city council in ought-six and became mayor in oh-eight, with the governor making him game warden the next year. That's our Chris. It doesn't say what happened."

"Maybe that cough of his," Wil suggested.

"That's what it was." Si Tanner stepped up to the bar, materializing out of almost nothing. "I got a telegram from Tad Hillery in Seward. You know Chris had been having trouble with that cough ever since he got there."

Both men nodded. The wetter climate on the Kenai

Peninsula hadn't agreed with Shea's lungs. He'd been diagnosed with tuberculosis just last summer. "Tad said he went up Falls Creek on an outing in November. Caught a bad cold. It just got worse. Helen finally talked him into going to some hot springs in Idaho, a place called Soap Lake. He said he wanted to stay until after the holidays, but he finally let her take him out a few days ago. Apparently they waited too long."

"I heard he tried to resign last August," Tuck volunteered.

Si nodded. "He did. He wanted out of Alaska. With Sarah Shorthill's son, William, in the governor's office, it was getting damn near impossible to get the hunting laws changed like he wanted. Then someone trumped up a bunch of charges against him. Accused him of issuing out-of-territory hunting permits and keeping the money for himself. The governor suspended him, and then he was charged with recommending that his acting warden do exactly the same thing. Governor Clark, in the meantime, was in Seattle all fall, and Shorthill was running the governor's office."

Tuck snorted. "We all know how impartial that investigation was! William Shorthill loved Chris Shea about as much as Anna Stinebaugh loves Essie! The Shorthills believe it is their responsibility to drive every saloon man out of Alaska!"

"In this case, Shorthill wanted Shea to stay in Alaska until Governor Clark came back so that he could fire the game warden personally." Si lit up one of his cigars. "Which he did, as soon as he returned from Seattle in mid-November. Ironically, Governor Clark signed the letter asking for Chris' resignation almost the same day that Chris caught the cold on Falls Creek. By the time he received the letter, he was too ill to respond."

Wil piped up. "You mean, even though Chris wanted to resign all along, he couldn't because he was too sick?"

Si nodded, puffing out a cloud of cigar smoke. "You got it. Tad wrote that Chris received a curt letter of dismissal in December. He'd never been given a chance to defend himself before the governor." Si shook his head. "And now he's dead."

"Those temperance people are winning, Si," Wil

pronounced, after a brief silence. "It's a war, and they're winning."

"Not yet," Si frowned. "I'm still mayor of this town. We finally got permission from the U. S. Congress to elect a territorial legislature. The people of the Southeast made me senator last fall. I'm not going to let those people take over my town without fighting for it." His jaw stood firm.

"You're the fairest man this town has ever had," Tuck assured him. "Everyone knows it. We'll be fine."

"I didn't say you'd be fine, Tuck," Si turned to him. "I'm still a law-abiding man. I'll do my best to see that the laws are good, fair ones. But whatever laws we end up with, I'd advise you to pay attention to them."

Tuck glared at the tall deputy marshal turned judge turned mayor who stood across from his bar. That sounded like a threat, and Tuck didn't like threats. The news about Chris hadn't put any of them in a very good mood.

"Chris," Tuck said, and raised his glass of beer.

"Chris," the others answered, and they each took a swig, remembering what was important at that moment. Tuck launched into a story about the first time he'd played ball with Chris.

* * *

Tuesday, April 7, 1914 (Two years and one month later). Si Tanner pulled his horse, Buck, aside as Harriet Pullen's big coach came to a stop in front of the Fireman's Hall. Securing the reins to the top railing of the coach, the coachman, Alf Baker, swung down onto the step with his left foot, the wheel with his right, and then the ground with both. In two fluid strides, he stood by the door of the coach, pulling the steps out and assisting the bevy of eight ladies down from the coach. Harriet emerged last.

"We'll take you all home after we pick up the next group, Ladies," Si heard her assure them. "Just meet us here when you're done voting. Now, go over to see the nice young man at the table inside the front door of the hall, and he'll tell you what room you need to go to and how to go about marking your ballots. And remember who to vote for!"

After shooing them all along, she turned back to Alf. He waited for her to climb back into the coach so he could set the steps in with her. "Where to next, Mrs. Pullen?" he asked, as she entered the coach. "Let's swing over to State and Eighth this time, Alf," Si overheard her instruct him. "We've covered most of the west and south side of town. We need to start working our way north. Next time we get back, I suspect some ladies will want to go home." He watched Harriet check the sheaf of papers she had in her hand. "Then I think we need to run by the school to see if any of the women there need relief from babysitting."

Harriet appeared to be totally absorbed in her element. Si knew she excelled at organizing these sorts of events and relished being at the center of attention, as if she personally directed this election. He knew all of this effort really belonged to Anna Stinebaugh and Grace Zinkan, but Harriet loved being in the limelight. Anna and Grace often sat by the sidelines and observed, as they did today. He watched as she shut the door behind her, and plopped down on the seat. He shuddered to think what the women would do now that they could vote.

Shaking his head at the coach as it disappeared around the corner of State Street, Si swung off his horse at the side of the Fireman's Hall and tied him up in front of Phil Abraham's office, there not being any room in front of the hall. Si rode that horse every chance he got, especially since his leg had started acting up again. He found it easier to sit on Buck than to walk three blocks. Si liked the extra stature the animal gave him.

Buck had come up with the gold rush, and like Si, got on in years, but didn't act it. Si noticed him one cold January day back in 1898, a frisky young thing, an obvious riding horse being over-packed with gear. Buck didn't take kindly to the pack saddle or the weight, and the man overloading him beat him with a whip before he'd even gotten him to the trail. Si knew some men had started to call that trail the Dead Horse. He paid two hundred and fifty dollars for Buck at a time when a good horse usually cost about a hundred back in Iowa, where Si had raised racing horses.

Buck had been a hard one to break of all his ornery habits. He'd try to nibble on grass while working, or reach back to take a nip out of Si if he wasn't paying attention. He'd toss his head and try to shake the bit if he could. He'd sidle around like the ground was all quicksand and pit vipers when Si tried to mount. The animal always attempted something at first, pushing to see how far Si would let him have his own way. He learned fast that Si had little tolerance for such games, but a great deal of trust, confidence and patience. Now most people in Skagway couldn't remember a time when they hadn't seen the tall man moving around town without the big bay horse.

Now that Si had gotten a limp from that old injury to his leg, he had that much more of an excuse to ride Buck, not that he'd ever needed a reason to ride his horse. He did so in this town where most people walked, thinking a horse too much trouble to tack up every time they wanted to go a few blocks. It took a lot of work to keep a horse warm all winter long. But not for Si. He saw it as a love affair. He'd even ride Buck to work at the courthouse in dead winter, and pay a reliable boy like George Rapuzzi to ride him home to his warm stall before school. Si only trusted his son Fred to saddle him up before George arrived each afternoon, to take him back to Si.

Si Tanner touched his hat as he passed Lena Wurzbacker in the crowded Fireman's Hall. While he had seen women at the polls since 1904, when Alaska decided they could vote for the school board, it frightened him to know they now voted for the city council members. How ironic to know that, as the Southeast's first territorial senator, he had voted for the bill that had given these women their new right to vote. He had done so because he knew it was only fair, because so many women had business interests anymore. Nevertheless, he had known it would not bode well for him.

SIN AND GRACE

"Evening, Si," Oscar Selmer greeted him cordially. He had risen from a helper on the railroad to one of J. D. Stinebaugh's barbers to having his own shop next to Tuck Flaharty's saloon in just a couple of years. The Norwegian claimed five kids at home with no sign of stopping. Oscar also ran for city councilman, on the opposing ticket. Si touched his hat again and smiled wryly.

The polls would be closing soon, and then they'd count the vote. Usually over by nine o'clock, things would take longer with all these women voting. He'd give it until ten tonight. Better just go get a drink. With Chris gone (Si sent a silent prayer for the soul of his friend), that meant only one place to go, the Board of Trade.

At Tuck's saloon, the mood was rowdy, as usual. He didn't see much of the old crowd there. Hell, not much of the old crowd remained in Skagway. Henry Freidenthal, running for councilman on the Taxpayer's ticket with Si, waved him over to a table. Si felt glad to lift a mug of beer with the man. The small crowd of working stiffs with Henry turned familiar faces towards him. Si smiled and sauntered over. He could find far worse groups with which to await election returns.

Tuck hurried over with a half dozen mugs of beer, passing them round the table, including one for Si and saving one for himself. The saloon became quiet. All the boys solemnly raised their mugs and glasses, and Tuck said hoarsely, "To Chris." The men repeated the eulogy. It had become a traditional election night toast, since June 1913. Si knew that toast would remain a Skagway tradition until no Board of Trade or Pack Train or Trail, or any saloon, for that matter, remained in town. Tuck would see to it.

Si looked around the room, seeing a few of the old familiar faces. Besides Tuck and Henry, he recognized only Tuck's brother, Harry Flaharty, along with the old baseball crowd, Martin Itjen, Sut Cotrell, and maybe half a dozen others. Skagway's people drained away from the town. Every year, more folk moved away. Soon it would be a ghost town, a place for tourists, where only the gold rush would matter and the only times people would remember would be the boom days. The tourists would forget good people like

126

Chris Shea, Tuck Flaharty, Lee Guthrie, and – he hated to put him in the same category, but he couldn't deny him – John Troy, and damn it, yeah, even Si Tanner. Josias M. Tanner, a man who had given himself to the law of this town since 1898, first as a U. S. Deputy Marshal, then as city magistrate, and finally as city councilman and mayor, enforcing, interpreting and making the law in Skagway. He'd be forgotten, too. But they all would remember a two-bit con man named Soapy Smith. If they remembered Si at all, it would only be because he helped to round up Soapy's gang. In his own mind, Si counted that as only the beginning.

He shook his head, realizing he wallowed in bitter thoughts. He looked up to see Sam Wall grinning at him. Now there was a man to hate. John Troy could be the very devil, but at least a good government could work with him. Troy understood how it worked. Wall, a complete wild card, actually seemed to like those reform women. Sam had brought Si down as much as – perhaps more than – Anna Stinebaugh and Grace Zinkan put together. Si Tanner wondered if Wall knew how much he had been manipulated by the women of the W. C. T. U.

Si wasn't really surprised when the election results came in at nine-thirty, preceded by a brass band marching down the street. The election board must have brought on extra volunteers to speed things up. The men in the saloon rushed out to the street to hear the music and collect the hastily printed fliers. Just names with numbers beside them, Si had to order the numbers himself. He had received 134 votes. Even with the women not voting, that would have been low. He counted seven names with higher numbers than his. Mild-mannered Oscar Selmer got 138 votes. With only seven seats available, that meant he'd lost his position on Skagway's city council by only four votes after serving five terms in office.

Si folded the small slip of paper in half and put it in his pocket to take home to his wife Juliette and son Fred. As he turned to leave, Sam Wall blocked his way. He had an odd smile on his face.

"I offer you my condolences, Mr. Tanner. This seems to

be the end of an era. I believe the Old Guard has been removed."

Si kept his face impassive. He met the man's gaze squarely and let the silence hang until it was uncomfortable. "Perhaps. Perhaps it is a change. I need a change. We all need a change from time to time. The Skagway city council obviously needs some new blood. I have other plans in mind anyway, Mr. Wall."

"If you are talking about U. S. Marshal, Mr. Tanner, I have it on good authority–"

"Even had I won this election and been chosen mayor, as I have three times before, I would not have stayed in Skagway more than another year. I will be moving to Juneau in less than a month. As a member of the territorial legislature, it will be easier to do my job in the capital city." With that, Si Tanner finally smiled, touched his hat for the last time that evening, and strode into the mild Skagway spring light to find his horse.

* * *

Wednesday, April 8, 1914 (the next day). Not even late afternoon yet, Tuck and Essie had only been awake for half an hour. The newspaper waited on the front porch, as usual, with dim news. They couldn't imagine City Hall without Si Tanner. Essie didn't even know half the new members of the council. Sure, Oscar Selmer had operated the barber shop next door to the Board of Trade for three years now. But they couldn't imagine relying solely on Oscar.

"I remember that this gentleman" and Tuck pointed to one of the councilmen's names "got himself into a heap of trouble a number of years ago over a woman." Tuck wondered if the knowledge would do them any good. "It took place when he worked as a clerk for Behrends' Dry Goods. He and that laundress, Nettie Kelly, had a fling. She called his name out in her sleep. Only it wasn't this young man sleeping with her. It was her husband, a machinist down at the railroad shops. I knew him, worked along side him. We all thought he got cheated because this gentleman worked downtown in a business while Kelly worked in the railroad shops."

"What happened?" Essie prompted. She wanted more

details.

"Nettie came to Behrend's Dry Goods often and insisted that only this particular young man wait on her. As she told the story to her husband later, our councilman came to their house and forced her." Tuck grinned. "She said she didn't cry out because the neighbors were too far away."

"And Mr. Kelly took the villainous store clerk to court, I presume?"

"Well, of course. He had to protect his wife's honor!" Tuck pretended shock that she'd question otherwise.

"John Troy must have had a field day with that one," Essie observed from behind her coffee cup.

"He was furious. Judge Rogers took the deposition in the Kellys' lawyer's private office instead of open court. Somehow Troy got the story anyway. Mrs. Kelly admitted to having encouraged Mr. Store Clerk's attentions, but she said she did not expect him to come to her house, 'beat, wound, ill treat her, then violently and against her will, forcibly and unlawfully and feloniously ravish and carnally know her.'" Tuck remembered Troy's quote of the court documents. He enjoyed their redundancy.

"While Nettie claimed she had not told her husband immediately about the attack because she feared the publicity, and the judge warned that any previous relationship the two might have had should have no bearing on the case, Troy felt no compunction about telling all. Mr. Troy's revelation of the story in his newspaper undid all the careful strategy of judge, lawyers and all parties concerned, except the defense, of course. The business community raised a great hew and cry. Businessmen who didn't even know the store clerk volunteered to put up his bond. The Kellys successfully moved the case to Juneau, but a change of venue didn't work. A Juneau grand jury found insufficient evidence to indict the future councilman and turned him loose."

"Whatever happened to Mrs. Kelly?" Essie asked.

Tuck grinned back at her. "Oh, Mr. and Mrs. Kelly parted company. They divorced within the year, citing irreconcilable differences."

Essie drank her coffee thoughtfully. "Isn't our new

councilman's wife's name Mamie?"

"Why, you do keep up with the social life of this town, my dear," Tuck exclaimed. "But, she used to go by Nettie. It all ended up happily ever after, have no fear."

At that moment, a knock sounded at the front door. Essie raised her eyebrows at Tuck. It was too early for customers. They ignored the knock. The man could go next door to Maybelle's crib. That's why she was there.

The knock sounded again, this time more insistently. Tuck rose from his seat. It wouldn't do to wake the girls. They needed their sleep. Essie didn't like it when they got cranky. He would take care of the man, explain to him that he would have better luck with the crib women this early in the day.

Essie tried not to look surprised when he returned to the kitchen leading Kitty Faith. He pulled out a chair for her, and then hurried to get her a cup of coffee. Kitty thanked him graciously, as if he had just handed her a delicate glass of champagne. Essie still felt clumsy in Kitty's presence.

"To what do we owe this pleasure?" Essie asked. She couldn't remember a time when Kitty had been in her house.

Kitty measured the couple before her, feeling somewhat envious. Tuck stood behind Essie's chair, his left hand settled on her left shoulder. It appeared to be an unconscious gesture, something both of them took totally for granted. They had each other for these difficult times. Kitty had no one, only old friends who came to visit far too seldom. That could have been Chris and me, Kitty thought, with a catch in her throat. Then she remembered a preacher's daughter and knew it could never have been. Chris is dead to me in more ways than one. She closed her eyes. I didn't come here for this.

"In case you haven't seen the newspaper, Si Tanner no longer sits in City Hall," Kitty began. "As Sam Wall so eloquently put it, 'for the past ten years, old Si has had control of the affairs of the town as absolutely as though he owned it in fee simple.' That changed yesterday, thanks to the ladies of the W. C. T. U."

Tuck moved round the table, sliding his hand across

Essie's shoulders, and then taking the chair between the two women. Tuck and Essie's eyes met briefly, and she caught his hand in a quick squeeze before he sat down.

"If Si Tanner owned this town, it was because he loved it, heart and soul," Tuck defended him. "He owns Skagway the way a mother owns a child, or a wife owns her husband. He never did anything that wasn't for the good of Skagway."

"You know that, and I know that. Wall made it sound like he had done something mean and evil with that love," Kitty pointed out.

Essie and Tuck both shook their heads at Sam Wall's incomprehension of what was best for this town.

"We in the district have not known a time when we didn't have a friend in City Hall," she reminded them. "Si has always been there for us in one way or another, as deputy marshal when the feds arrested us, as magistrate, and on the council. Now, the women of the W. C. T. U. have replaced him with a moral reform party. We will not survive much longer."

Essie harrumphed, then followed it with a chuckle. "That's ridiculous, Kitty. Men will always need us. The good women of this city need us. They tire of their husbands pawing at them night after night and tell them to run off to Alaska Street if the men can't leave them in peace. That Anthony Comstock passed a law that forbids them to know how to prevent the conception of children, so they keep their husbands from them to limit the size of their families. Their men find the way to our door. The good people are afraid that the bachelors on the railroad and the wharf will rape their daughters, so they know we must be here for the men to satiate their base lust. That's why they call us the 'Necessary Evil.' They know how basic, how necessary we are to the stability of this town."

"The times are changing, Essie. Not all women think that way anymore. The men on the railroad are no longer strangers. They're the boys next door. They grew up in this town. They want to marry the girls, not rape them. The husbands have grown to respect their wives. The women know more and more about how to prevent children, Comstock law or no Comstock law."

Kitty fiddled with her coffee cup. "You have not been to church lately, have you?" she asked. "I have. Reverend Pederson at the Methodist Church preaches that men must be as pure as their wives, must come to marriage unsullied and stay faithful throughout their lifetime together. He tells his congregation that it's a fallacy to think that men do not have the strength to contain their base lusts."

The three of them sat at the table, stunned by the very thought that men and women could believe such heresy. "Think about it, Tuck. Deep down you know the truth of it. Have you not lain with Essie and held yourself back, not wanting to wake her, knowing you couldn't afford her, waiting to make your pleasure greater later?"

Tuck laughed, as he always did around the whores. They enjoyed talking about sex together. "Yeah, there will always be a later time."

Kitty smiled. "Could you contain yourself if you thought later would be weeks from now? Think of the months when Essie worked in Seattle or Dawson. We all know you didn't wait for her then. You were at my door some of that time, simply because we were the only other choice you had."

"They weren't like Essie," he defended himself, feeling outraged. "They didn't satisfy me."

"So, would you have taken a woman by force rather than take your pleasure by yourself?" Kitty asked, bluntly.

Tuck turned his back on the two women. "'Course not." He hesitated, and then he told them about his long ago conversation with Tad Hillery and the other boys, about how Tad stayed away from Seventh Avenue altogether until he had married Jeannette de Gruyter. Instead he played ball, went bowling, and mastered pool, keeping his mind off women until he had the woman he wanted. "A man just has to put his mind to it," he finished.

Kitty looked at both of them, rather smugly. "My point exactly. And you know these reform women aren't just preaching against us, Tuck. What do you think they will turn to next? If they can't close us down immediately, they'll turn to the saloons. In fact, now that they can vote, the yearly license vote may change dramatically. Have you considered that? Do you think they'll stand for the fact that the political decisions in this town are made in the saloons?"

"Only a third of yesterday's voters were women," Tuck asserted confidently.

"This time around. Si still lost, even if it was only by four votes. Sam Wall attributed Si's loss to the women. They voted together. Only his wife and we women on Alaska Street voted for him. And considering Juliette's friendship with Anna Stinebaugh and Grace Zinkan, I have my doubts about her political support of her own husband's party," Kitty sniffed. "There will be more women voting at each election, as Harriet Pullen bullies them to the polls. I've noticed more men signing their temperance pledges all the time. Some of them won't drink in my place any more. I'm sure you've seen it over here, too."

Tuck and Essie glanced at each other, and Kitty knew they had noticed the men who asked for coffee or tea.

"Emil Korach, one of the first saloon men in Skagway, just closed the Monogram Saloon," Kitty continued. "Those women count his retirement as another victory, Tuck. They'll get you each one at a time or all at once. Only six of you remain in town, and they are determined to vote the town dry."

"It will never happen," Tuck countered. "The men in this town love their beer and whiskey too much. They can't stop drinking, any more than they can stop loving women. It's in their being." He looked at Essie. He would drink his liquor and love her with his body until the day he died, because without those pleasures there would be no reason to go on living.

Kitty recognized that these two refused to see the change coming and would not acknowledge that it already stood on their doorstep. She rose from her chair.

"Thank you for your coffee. It is really quite good."

She smiled at Essie, knowing she had made the coffee, not Tuck. Essie walked with her to the front door, exchanging polite pleasantries along the way. A casual observer would have thought the two friends instead of bitter rivals. Well, in this matter they should be united. They must save the district. Kitty felt nothing but disappointment that she could not rally her only possible ally.

Tuck leaned on the doorway between the parlor and the game room, watching Kitty take her leave. He knew she foretold truly, at least in part. If Essie didn't believe her, he did. He just didn't care, for he trusted his Flaharty luck. It had always worked for him before. He did feel concern for Essie. He hoped he could pull her through with him.

"She's right, you know, Darlin'," he told her as she moved through the gaming room towards the kitchen. "I got notice yesterday. Reverend Pedersen and the W. C. T. U. have protested my application for a license at the new location of the Board of Trade in the old Trail building."

"What?" she rounded on him, shocked and concerned. "Why, those old biddies! They don't have a leg to stand on! The Trail sits well outside the no-saloon zone."

"They're just making trouble," he soothed. "They're protesting the continuance of my existing license on the premise that the existing location is within the zone. They still think I should never have been granted a license in the first place."

Essie paced around the kitchen, skirts flying. Amused, Tuck leaned against the counter in a jaunty pose, with a foot across an ankle. He loved to watch her when she became so fiery.

"I'm going to march up to that Anna Stinebaugh's door and punch her in the eye. Then, I'll wrestle her to the ground and tell her she has no right to interfere in a man's livelihood," Essie hissed. She curled her fists into tight balls of white bone.

"You'll do no such thing. If I lose the fight in court, you'll let me live in the lap of luxury. I'll play baseball all summer and bowl all winter and spend more time smuggling liquor for you. Nothing will change. I'll just be around the house more."

"Oh, no, you won't. Not if I can help it. A man lurking in the halls is bad for business. You have to get your license, and I'll see that you do." Essie banged her fist down on the table. "Damn you, Anna Stinebaugh. I'll see that Tuck Flaharty gets his license." Tuck grinned at the fire in Essie's eyes.

THE TRAIL   SHEA•PATTEN, PROPS.

Chapter Sixteen

The War

Thursday, April 9, 1914 (the next day). Anna Stinebaugh sat in her cozy parlor, finishing off the sweater she had been knitting. True, it was April, but this was Alaska. The family needed sweaters this far north, all year around. This one had a lovely mint color, the latest in fashion. Anna usually didn't care about fashions, but Fay did, and Anna liked to please her daughter.

When the knock came at the door, she was prepared for it. Harriet Pullen had sent a new recruit to her this morning, Jeannette Hillery. Mrs. Hillery saw the need, but did not yet possess the stomach for the cause.

Anna opened the door to a tall, stout woman with sparkling, white hair. A short young woman stood at her side. "Good morning, Mrs. Stinebaugh" the older lady greeted her cheerfully.

"Mrs. Hillery," Anna returned, holding out her hand. Although not circulating in the same social circles, she knew both Melissa Hillery and her daughter-in-law, Jeannette. Skagway was not that large a city and the Hillerys had lived here since 1898. Melissa, the matron of the family, had come up with the gold rush, following her older sons. Anna knew Melissa's otherwise fine, upstanding boys spent far too much time in the Board of Trade Saloon and that both Melissa and Tad Hillery's wife, Jeannette, despaired of getting him out of it.

"You know my daughter-in-law, Jeannette. She is very much interested in the W. C. T. U.," Melissa began.

"Oh, yes, I am," the young woman asserted, without any prompting. Her big, blue eyes appraised Anna Stinebaugh, challenging her to be absolutely honest and forthright, to give her a charge for the future. Anna felt the call. She opened the door widely and invited her guests to tea.

Anna poured the tea and offered the cookies. When all had settled and the appropriate pleasantries had been exchanged, Jeannette, in her almost callow innocence, crassly demanded, "Why must we ruin people's lives in our efforts to save others?"

"Why, whatever do you mean, my dear?" Anna declared, surprised to hear such a deeply thought question from one so young.

Her mother-in-law seemed embarrassed. "Jeannette has been thinking of the men and women whose businesses we seek to close down. My son, Tad, is good friends with Frederick Flaharty, who owns the Board of Trade Saloon. She wonders if it is right to end his livelihood, to make him destitute, with no means of bettering himself."

Jeannette nodded at her mother-in-law's side.

Anna sat quietly, considering her answer. "In a war, a good Christian man knows he must kill. God admonished that he must not take another's life. It was one of his commandments. But the Christian soldier knows that for the greater good, some must die that more may live. If some of the enemy does not die now, then more will die later."

"Is this a war we wage, Mrs. Stinebaugh?" Jeannette asked.

"It is indeed, Mrs. Hillery. We regret that casualties occur in any war, and on either side. Friendly persuasion does not seem to work."

"Did you make overtures of friendship?" the young woman asked.

Anna sighed. "We simply asked our husbands to stop going to the saloons and instead spend their money and their time with the family. We asked them to devote more attention to family issues in city hall, to concern themselves with destitute women and hungry children so they would not have to turn to immoral acts to make a living." Anna glanced at Jeannette. How much about such life did Jeannette know?

Melissa nodded. "You do not need to mince words with my daughter-in-law. She knows that the demimonde exists and that it is far more than just the saloons that you and your organization wish to abolish."

Anna sighed in appreciation. It was so difficult, sometimes, convincing women to help other women, when the knowledge of such ugliness must be shared first, and with uninitiated women. Anna longed for the day when no such knowledge must be conveyed, because no such people existed.

"We thought that for love of us our husbands would grant our simple request. We did not know what hold the people of the demimonde and the saloons had on our husbands. We did not understand how seductive a spell had been placed on them."

"So instead of teaching your husbands to respect you and to love you, you strive to shut those places down?" Jeannette asked.

"Love! This is much more complicated than simply a matter of love. We fight this war on many different fronts, because we know we can't win on only one. We will win through gentle persuasion, but also through the rightness of what we dream. Those we love will understand what we yearn for, and they will eventually help us. We also arm ourselves against those who lure away our men and children. We use any tool we can lay our hands upon, restraining orders, legal protests, and marches. Because we could not persuade our men to do it for us, we wrestled the vote into our own domain, and we will vote people into office that will do it for us. We will make them pass laws to ban places that corrupt our families' souls."

Anna's eyes blazed with righteous fervor. She had warmed to her subject. "The women of the W. C. T. U. will save the children of this town from the evil temptations of the saloon and brothel. We will provide ways for women to earn good livings for themselves and for their children so they do not need to prostitute themselves. We will make sure to provide other entertainments besides the saloons, other places for men to go during their free time, places that don't impoverish a family. They have their sports. They can go to moving picture shows, to our reading rooms, and to our church entertainments."

It seemed so right. Both Melissa and her daughter-in-law wondered how men could resist this change. "What can stop them from going to these places now?"

"Only their old habits and the laws that reinforce them. That's why we worked so hard to get our own vote, to make sure we have men on the city council who will enforce the good laws we have and make new ones to force a change where needed. It's happening, ladies. Why, we even hope that someday, we might have women in public office. Who knows, Jeannette. Perhaps your daughter could be a council woman, or a city magistrate. Think what good she could do for this city if she could aspire to these positions."

Jeannette's eyes glowed at the thought of all the children her unborn daughter could save.

* * *

Friday, April 10, 1914 (the next day). Si Tanner stood in the back of Judge Jennings' courtroom. Si wasn't the U. S. Marshal yet, but with the political winds shifting to the Democrats, he would be soon. He enjoyed courtrooms, having had his own a few years back. He felt comfortable both passing judgment and testifying. Si, the consummate Alaskan lawman, pure and simple, sat here today just to watch the law in practice.

That Juneau lawyer, Zino Cheney, argued for Tuck Flaharty. He did a pretty good job. Tuck, for once in his life, knew that he should keep his own mouth shut. Tuck didn't think well on his feet, and especially so in front of a judge. Tuck had a bit of a temper on him that didn't work well in a court of law. People like Tuck Flaharty created the necessity for lawyers.

A whole horde of petitioners crowded the room, most of them women of the W. C. T. U., who protested Tuck's license. Si noticed that Tuck refused to look at any of them. Wise man. He didn't know who would start the heckling, Tuck's saloon supporters or the biddies, but the hordes didn't look friendly, not on either side. The normally cocky Irishman simply looked grim and kept his eyes on the judge.

This afternoon, federal Judge Jennings had taken the testimony of the protesters. Now, this evening, he recalled the court for the testimony of witnesses, including character witnesses. Si thought it surprised the reform community. Mr. Cheney even asked Father Turnell to come to the stand. The good Catholic priest testified to Tuck's regular attendance at mass and how he had religiously closed down the Board of Trade every Sunday morning, long before the recent order enforcing the blue laws.

Then Cheney called Charles M. Brown, a laborer for the White Pass Railroad, and one of Tuck's best customers. Charlie told the judge how Sunday constituted the men's only day off. Because of the new emphasis on the blue laws, they had to wait until noon to go to their favorite watering hole. He just didn't think that was right.

Then, to everyone's surprise, Tuck's lawyer called Mrs. Louis T. Keller, the dentist's wife, to the stand. She testified that the women of the W. C. T. U. indeed lobbied the railroad for a forty-hour week, so the men could have Saturdays off, too. That way they wouldn't have to spend their Sundays in a saloon. Of course, the women did not agree that the men should spend Saturday in the saloon, either.

When called to testify, White Pass laborer Samuel Popovich said he only wanted one day off a week. He liked his Saturday pay and his Sunday saloon. He didn't know why those women were trying to cut his pay by cutting short his work week. He wanted Tuck's Board of Trade, not stuffy old Herman Grimm's saloon or that dingy Pantheon. He had fun at Tuck's. At Tuck's a man had a chance at a pool table. At Tuck's, he could find his pals. Those women had no right to tell him how much money he could make or what he could spend it on.

Si noted that several working class men in the court room nodded in agreement. A clutch of businessmen's wives near the front grumbled among themselves, and the judge banged his gavel, calling the court to order.

Next, Mr. Cheney called Tony Dortero, the notions, candy and cigar store man who had been in Skagway since the rush. He was well-respected and well-liked by the entire community.

"Mr. Dortero, do you know Mr. Flaharty?"

"I do. Most everyone knows Tuck. He's hard to miss with that jolly grin and bushy mustache."

"How long would you say he's been in Skagway?"

"Oh, Tuck came up with the rush. He and his brother, Harry, they saved a lot of lives on the Chilkoot Pass during the Palm Sunday avalanche. He came back to Skagway in oh-one and went to work for the railroad. About 1905 or so, I'd say, he went to work for Chris Shea at the Pack Train. Chris counted him a good friend." A hum of agreement verified his testimony. The old-timers remembered Chris, and being a friend of Shea didn't hold against Tuck.

"When did he get into the saloon business for himself?"

"Along about 1907, I'd say, he and George Woodburn bought the Board of Trade from Lee Guthrie. George sold out to him a couple of years ago. He's always been a good, reliable business man."

"His saloon sits just across the street from your shop, doesn't it?"

"It does. And his customers behave well, he makes sure of that. I used to have a saloon next door, the old Last Chance. Franz Zwiefehofer always had trouble. Fights and men wandering into my place drunk. Why, I've seen Tuck himself take a man home when he's had more than he should. He doesn't just kick 'em out the door and send 'em on their way, not like some saloon keepers."

Mr. Cheney's last witness was U. S. Deputy Fred Fonzo.

"How long have you been in Skagway, Mr. Fonzo?" was Cheney's first question.

"I came to Skagway in 1908," he replied.

"And you have known Mr. Flaharty during that entire time?"

"Yes, sir."

"What has been your occupation in Skagway, Mr. Fonzo?"

"I was the jailer for the first three years, and have been deputy since."

"So you would be familiar with Mr. Flaharty's criminal record since he became owner of the Board of Trade Saloon?"

"Yes, sir. That's true. 'Ceptin' he doesn't have one. Except for the other time the W. C. T. U. took him into court to try to take away his license, Mr. Flaharty stays away from my jail." The court rumbled with light laughter.

"I believe that will be all, Mr. Fonzo."

With that, Mr. Cheney rested.

The judge called a fifteen minute recess. The bailiff asked the court to rise as Judge Jennings re-entered the room. He brought the court to order and cleared his throat to pass judgment.

"I have found that the protests against the granting of a license have not been sufficiently direct." Mrs. McCann, one of Anna Stinebaugh's newer recruits, gasped in dismay. "As a further reason for dismissing this protest, I find that Mr. Flaharty has been engaged in the saloon business in Skagway for the past several years and the granting of his petition would only entitle him to a continuance under it until the first of July, when the residents of the town would have an opportunity to express their wishes as to a further license. I have decided to grant the license that Mr. Flaharty has asked for until the first of July 1914, the business to be conducted on the southeast corner of Broadway and Fourth Avenue, in the building now known as the Trail, instead of in its present location."

A group of men behind Tuck stood up, cheering and hollering. They had staved off another few days of wandering around, searching for a new place to park their behinds while they quaffed their beer and poured out their stories and souls to their buddies. Essie Miller was the only woman among the cheering crowd, Si noticed. You could never separate Tuck and Essie. He'd known that for a long time. Seeing the two of them together just reminded him they were a couple. The two of them stayed out of trouble so much any more, he'd almost forgotten about them. He tucked that detail away in the ever expanding file of information he kept on the citizens of Skagway.

Mr. and Mrs. Flaherty

Chapter Seventeen

Love and Honor

October 14, 1914 (six months later). Tuck stood with his forearms on the horizontal bands of metal on the gate of the jail cell, looking in. Marshal Hardy wouldn't let him into the cell with Essie, blaming immigration agent Albert H. Joy for the orders. Any other time Nat would have let them be together. This time was different. Nat found the agents tough to get along with, and he didn't want any trouble. Tuck reminded Hardy how many times he'd let him run a tab at the Board of Trade. Nat didn't listen. Tuck had a mind to stop the tabs.

Essie had her back to him, comforting a young slip of a thing sitting on the single bed in the cell. He thought she worked for Essie. What was her name, Gussie? Oh, yeah, Gussie Goldstein. She and the other two women were immigrants. He didn't know why the immigration official thought Essie to be an immigrant, too. Her mother and grandparents had been German, but she was born in West Virginia. Yeah, Essie had that bad habit of telling different people she had different birthplaces, like Virginia or New York. She made it up as she went along. Damn Ida and her silly ideas about keeping a man in suspense about a woman's past. Tuck knew Essie drew her first breath in West Virginia, where she had no daddy and a man and his two sons took their turns sating their lust on his wife's young daughter.

Tuck stood there ready to rescue Essie from jail once again. It would be a little harder than paying a fine and walking her home and letting her sleep it off. With these immigration agents having so much authority, word had it that lawyers couldn't help much. Essie didn't have a birth certificate. The man probably had someone who would swear that Essie told him about her German mother and grandparents.

Well, Tuck had an idea that would work. Not the best time or the best place, he had to do it now or they'd put Essie on a boat to Germany, and he'd never see her again.

"Mornin' Darlin'," he said over the sound of the sobbing women. Essie, the only clear-eyed whore in the room, met her lover's eyes. Confidence replaced the concern that had been there. Everything would be fine now. She rushed to the cell gate and took his hands.

"Oh, Tuck. When they came for Gussie, I had no idea they'd want me, too. What am I doing here?"

"I can't talk to agent Joy, but Nat tells me he thinks you're German without papers. Who'd you tell about your German family? And why wouldn't they believe you were born here in the U. S.?"

"It had to be one of the girls, Tuck. He'd been at our place a couple of weeks ago. He seemed really interested in the foreign girls and asked about them. You know how the girls start chattering. Someone must have given Gussie some booze, probably Joy himself, to get her talking. I may have said something to her myself once, since she's German, about my German family, just to set her at ease. Oh, Tuck, surely Zino can get me out of here."

"I've wired to Juneau for him. He'll be here as soon as he can. Nat said you're here two more nights, then they take you to Seattle for deportation. Essie, I won't let them do that to you. I won't let them take you out of Skagway." He squeezed her hands, wanting to hold her whole body close to his own, shelter her and place himself between her and those who would take her away from him.

She moved to the bars of the cells, so their bodies could touch through the gaps. They pushed their arms through the interwoven strips of metal so they could hold one another about the waist. They could just barely touch lips. Tuck hugged the bars and Essie to him.

"I know this is something you don't want, Darlin' but it's come down to it, and we need to do it now. I've sent for Father Turnell. He can marry us this morning. He said he'd be happy to purge me of my sin," Tuck chuckled. "Do you think you could become a Catholic in order to stay with me?"

Essie joined the other women in the cell with their crying. She couldn't lay her head on Tuck's shoulder, for a band of painted metal lay in the way. She leaned on it instead, tightening her grip on him. "Oh, yes, Tuck. I'll go to mass and confession with you every Sunday and do anything you say. Just tell me what to do."

As they broke from their kiss, Father Turnell cleared his throat at Tuck's side. He had entered, quietly, as they talked. "You must come to believe that our Lord Jesus Christ is your Savior, Miss Miller, and that the Lord above loves you and will redeem you."

Essie turned to the good priest, smiling. "The Lord and I have had an understanding for a very long time, Father. We agreed not to talk to one another. However, of late, Tuck has convinced me that an occasional prayer sent His way would be of no harm, especially of the thankful sort. Tuck does seem to have been right. Tonight I joined my comrades in prayer. God seems to have listened to me this time. I believe I am willing to take up my conversations with Him again."

Tuck looked on with joy on his face. How he had longed to make Essie his wife. He had been sorry it had to happen this way, but at least now it happened.

Only then did Essie notice that Tuck wore his best suit. He had neatly parted his hair down the middle and slicked it down with Florida water. Even his mustache appeared trim and neat. He whirled around to find the large bundle on a hanger he had draped over a chair in the hallway outside the cell. "I brought you one of your prettiest dresses, Essie. I didn't think you'd want to be married in your working clothes."

He brought out the rose-colored, lace evening gown, the one she liked so well for dressing up and going out on the town. Quite modest, covering arms and shoulders, it bared only her throat and long neck, and the lace and fine embroidery made it rich and luxurious. He had even thought of matching shoes and flowers. He slipped the dress through the slot meant for passing food trays.

Tuck, Father Turnell, and, at a glare from Tuck, Nat Hardy all retired to Nat's office at the head of the hallway while the girls helped Essie change. They hollered when they got her ready.

Essie glowed like a vestal virgin at her wedding. Tuck could see neither cell nor bars, nor Essie's cell mates. He only saw the woman of his dreams, the woman he had loved for almost sixteen years, finally to be his and only his. If he ever found another man in her bed, he would kill him, and no one would blame him. Tuck could at last own up to a smoldering jealousy, one that had begun to eat at his soul, one that he had refused to even think about. Now it burst forth in all its ugliness to be banished forever by the knowledge that he would be Essie's husband and could exercise that right, the right to keep his wife to himself.

The ceremony felt awkward with Tuck and the priest on one side of the cell gate and the bride and her attendants on the other. But they could hold hands, and Father Turnell could pass the Eucharist through the bars. The priest called Deputy Fonzo in to act as witness, along with Nat Hardy, thinking the law might not be satisfied with the signatures of three immigrant women who would be deported. He kept to an abbreviated form of the service, skipped a long sermon, and made them promise to come to mass on Sunday. He

146

said he would devote that sermon to speaking of marriage. Tuck brought out not only a gold band, but also a good sized diamond ring to go with it. The couple kissed through the bars again.

Nat, although teary-eyed at the whole affair, eventually made them all leave, even the new groom. He said he couldn't turn his jail into a party room. He especially insisted that Tuck could not run out for champagne. He told them all there would be plenty of time for all of that when Zino Cheney showed up and told Al Joy what he could do with his warrant to keep Mrs. Flaharty in jail. Essie grinned widely when she heard herself called that. Tuck saw the grin, and his heart leapt anew.

Tuck tried to get a little sleep later that morning, but had given it up after a couple of hours. He felt far too excited. He went back to the telegraph office to check on Cheney. His lawyer would be in Skagway later that day, on the Hegg, but he couldn't promise anything, unless Tuck would marry Essie. Tuck wired back, "DONE THE DEED STOP THE MRS AND I AWAITING YOUR ARRIVAL." He worried his bartender at the Board of Trade and bought two rounds on the house to celebrate his wedding. He almost ran down to The Daily Alaskan to gloat in Sam Wall's face, but decided to let him hear however he heard about such things. Wall would find some way to make a snide remark about both Tuck and Essie, and Tuck wouldn't give him the satisfaction.

Tuck met the Hegg at four o'clock that afternoon. His attorney, Zino Cheney, had immigration agent Joy and Essie in U. S. Commissioner Cortez Ford's chambers before five o'clock.

"I understand you want to deport a United States citizen, Mr. Joy," Ford chided the agent.

"Not at all, Mr. Commissioner. Miss Miller is an illegal immigrant. As part of the responsibilities of the Office of Immigration and Naturalization to eliminate white slavery from Alaska, it is our duty to deport as many of these immoral women as we can."

"I beg your pardon, Commissioner Ford," interrupted Mr. Cheney. He knew Ford kept an informal court, especially for

147

these hearings. "I believe the defendant's name is Mrs. Essie Flaharty, nee Essie Miller."

"Really?" Ford beamed at Tuck, who grinned back. "So, you finally did the honorable thing, Tuck. It's about time. Congratulations."

"Thank you, sir," Tuck replied, blushing like a school boy.

Joy looked on in utter bewilderment. "What are you both talking about? You don't mean to tell me that Miss Miller has managed to get herself married in just one evening?"

Ford turned his level gaze back to the immigration agent. "Mr. Joy, Miss Miller and Mr. Flaharty have long enjoyed the sort of personal relationship that most people in this town would have termed a marriage. Most of us have wondered why they have chosen so long to forego the ceremony and sign the papers. It appears they finally found the time."

"Had she not already been one, having married Mr. Flaharty," Mr. Cheney pointed out, "has made Mrs. Flaharty a citizen of the United States. As Mrs. Flaharty has no birth certificate and Mr. Joy has the reputation of being able to deport women on very little evidence, Mr. Flaharty believed he should reinforce Mrs. Flaharty's claim to citizenship. I believe everything is in order." He handed the marriage certificate over to the commissioner.

"Yes, yes. It's all quite regular. Priest – a quite honorable one, too – witnesses, both lawmen. I, myself, can attest to the fact that this wedding constituted no whim, Mr. Joy. The Flahartys have been a couple since they came to Skagway, back in 1901. This is all quite regular. I am afraid you will have to let Mrs. Flaharty go."

Joy glared at the other people in the room, each in turn. Essie gazed innocently at the ceiling.

Cort Ford pushed a piece of paper across his desk and handed a pen to the flustered agent. "If you will sign here, Mr. Joy, you can go about your business. I will see to the release of Mrs. Flaharty."

Joy snatched up the pen, dipped it in the offered well of ink, scribbled in the place indicated, and then stomped from the chamber. Tuck grabbed up his wife and swung her around at least three times, his mouth locked to hers. He had been married to her for thirteen hours and had yet to hold or kiss her in a satisfactory way.

When he could finally bring himself to put her down, he reached into his breast pocket for his checkbook and scribbled out a generous check for his lawyer. "Come, Cheney. We'll get you a room at the Fifth Avenue. We're having a grand reception there tonight, seven o'clock. I've already set it all up. You're invited, too, Cort. Champagne, food, cake, you name it. This will be the celebration to end all celebrations. No one can take my Essie from me."

The arm around her felt possessive. For a moment, Essie quailed, remembering what Kitty said about Si owning Skagway. Did Tuck now think he owned her in fee simple, simply because she said "I do" and signed a piece of paper? But then she remembered Tuck's observation that Si owned Skagway like a mother owned a child or a lover owned his wife. Only love could bind a man and woman to each other in that way. And they had bound themselves that way long ago. Nothing had changed. Nothing would change. They had simply acknowledged those bonds at long last.

Hours later, the two lay sated in one another's arms in their bedroom in Essie's – no their – biggest house. Tuck just remembered that her property had become his when he married her. He suddenly owned a great deal of wealth. He beamed his impish grin at the thought.

"Why did we wait so long, Tuck?" Essie murmured into his neck below his ear.

"I've longed to marry you, Essie. But I saw the panic on your face when I gave you that pair of diamond earrings. You thought they might be a ring. As much as I wanted to make you mine, all mine, I knew I could not frighten you like that again. I feared I would drive you away entirely. I've let the subject lie ever since."

"Oh, Tuck." She leaned on her elbows above him, her hair drifting across her bare shoulders, breasts and onto his chest. "By the end of that evening, I knew I was an ungrateful wretch, wishing the earrings had been a ring instead. I scorned Anna Stinebaugh for not communicating with her husband. I taunted Kitty Faith with how well you and I understood one another. It seems we did not know one another's hearts at all."

Tuck pulled her back to him. "We've known our hearts well enough, my Love. You've known I loved you, greater than anything else I ever loved or wanted. You know I've given up dreams for you."

"What dreams did you sacrifice for me, Tuck?"

"A cottage in an Ohio cornfield, with a plump wife and several children waiting when I came home at sundown each night. My mama down the road to have us all over for chicken dinner on Sunday. My fortune intact to hold us to my old age, when my sons could watch over me and make sure I didn't kill myself trying to patch the roof."

Essie remembered a woman named Minnie Owens who had married and had a child while Tuck sought his fortune in Eagle, after falling under Essie's spell. He took his fortune home and left it there with his parents, returning to Skagway to work on the railroad and visit Essie's bed at Ida's place. Only there did he build his substitute dream of owning the Board of Trade.

"You never said anything about children."

"Every man wants a legacy. And every man knows that children only encumber certain women. Men wanting families do not become enamored of business ladies. If a man falls in love with such a woman and wants to keep her, he forgets about children." Tuck sounded practical, matter of fact. She saw the moisture in his eyes. She had not known about the death of his dream.

"Tuck." She pulled his face towards her. "I would have given you children, if I had only known about that dream!"

To grow up here, in a brothel, among your girls? So our daughters could learn the trade, too, and our sons be taught early what use to make of women? Tuck thought to himself. Instead he said, "Essie, this life is all you know. I couldn't force you into the Ohio cottage. Better to change the dream than the woman I love."

Essie dissolved against him. "All right then. But now that I know, I can try to have those children, for your sake, my love. I am not yet so old nor so tired. Anna Stinebaugh is convinced she will shut us both down. She may be right. If she does and if a child should come, we can return to your original dream, Tuck."

"I'm not sure I can even remember it all, Essie," he admitted, shaken by her willingness to give up her dream for him.

"Then we'll rebuild it from the ground up, if it becomes necessary," she promised.

He settled her comfortably on his shoulder, running a hand down the long length of her naked body. How he loved to feel her beside him. "If you wish to bear me children, then you will ban all other men from your bed," he instructed sternly, his heart racing at his own temerity.

Essie laughed. "Tuck, there has been no other man in my bed since the day I hired two girls to work for me. That's what being a madam is all about. Not having to do it yourself." She snuggled in closer to him. "I have been absolutely faithful to you for at least eight years. Can you say the same?"

Tuck thought about the hollow green-eyed monster had eaten in him of late and smirked in satisfaction at it. "Absolutely," he answered truthfully. "Even in those first couple of years after you left Ida, but still went Outside in the summer and winter, I lost interest in other women. I thought my libido had failed me. Imagine my joy when you returned and my arousal with you. Maybe that's why I grew to love baseball and bowling so much. They kept me occupied when you were gone."

Just thinking of the extra "umph" he had when Tuck struck a home run or slammed down a strike aroused both of them. They had thought themselves sated for the night, ready for sleep, something neither had gotten for well over twenty-four hours. It took another half hour before either of them found that rest.

SIN AND GRACE

BURMAH'S CRIB

Chapter Eighteen

The Queen

January 12, 1916 (one year and three months later). "Oh, and you may be interested to know that I have sold my southern crib to Burmah Belle," Kitty said in an aside, as she turned to walk out Essie's door. "I suspect Mayor Ashley may be more interested in talking to you on matters dealing with Alaska Street than to me." Kitty had paid one of her rare visits to the Flahartys. She smiled her cat-like smile and bowed her head ever so slightly, handing the demimonde's problems over to the new Queen of Alaska Street.

Essie inclined her head in return, acknowledging the hand-over of power. She walked with her to the front door. "Thank you, Kitty, for your concern," Tuck heard Essie say, as he stood in the portiere of the parlor, watching the madam take her leave. She said it like a monarch taking up her scepter. His eyes glowed with pride for her.

Essie turned and leaned against the door after closing it. Her eyes sparkled with joy. "Champagne," she breathed.

Tuck sprang for the ice box and one of the few bottles they kept there for the occasional man who liked to splurge. Too early to drink, neither of them cared. It was the culmination of their dream. How could they worry about those damnable women of the W. C. T. U. when all they had worked for now lay in their hands?

"I'll have a grand party at the Board of Trade tonight," Tuck promised. "Free beer for the first round, half price after that. I'll get them liquored up, then send them to your place to continue the celebration. So what if the spill-over ends up with Kitty? We'll put the lie to her dire predictions."

And it was a grand party at the Board of Trade and at Essie's place and throughout the entire Alaska Street district, with half prices all around. Territorial senator Si Tanner, in town courting his constituency, and the city council scratched their heads and wondered what caused the celebration, at least until they heard word. When Anna Stinebaugh got the news, she sat back grimly and smiled. Those least prepared for the change could least resist it. All went as planned.

Tuck bundled his woman into his arms, warming her against the chill April night. He could hear the celebration continuing downstairs. They had escaped to finish theirs privately. He wanted to do it slowly, luxuriantly, as the occasion deserved. Neither had yet undressed fully. Neither hurried. The champagne chilled in a cooler on the table next to the bed.

He pulled the pins out of Essie's hair to let it cascade around her white shoulders, emphasized by the red camisole. He pulled his fingers through the curls, separating the ringlets as she laid her head back, enjoying the gentle tug on her scalp. He pushed aside the tresses to nibble an ear, taking the diamond eardrop between his teeth, and then sliding it back and forth with his tongue. The pull on her lobe felt delicious. She arched against him, worming a hand under his shirt to feel the bare skin above the firm muscles at his side.

"Suppose Kitty's right," she mused, idly. "How long do you think we have?" Kitty's visit had not been purely social in nature, nor had she come solely to hand over the reins of power. She had spent over an hour trying to convince them that they, like her, should start selling off their Alaska Street properties. Kitty said she would be leaving Skagway soon.

"Oh, a couple of years for me, I suppose," Tuck said nonchalantly, "then I start smuggling liquor for the whole district. I think you have a little more time, three or four years, at the most. Then we go underground. They won't get us down, Essie, not you and me."

He felt under her camisole, his hands doing wonderful things to her nipples. She wished he'd unbutton it and just get rid of the thing. She started doing so to his shirt, hoping he'd get the hint. He did.

That problem solved, she thought about his answer, and found herself relieved. He had a plan, and it sounded like a good one. She sighed with pleasure. She didn't deserve this man. She wasn't a good woman, and he had been meant for a good woman. What had she done by keeping him from a respectable lady? But he made her feel good. She smiled at the thought. Did that make her good? She stopped thinking and gave herself up to feeling. This man was Tuck, her husband, and he was all she needed.

* * *

February 10, 1916 (less than a month later). Tuck sauntered into the kitchen with an amused smile playing around under his bushy mustache and a twinkle in his bright, blue eyes. Essie knew something was up immediately.

"Okay, spit it out," she ordered, not wanting to wait for him to tell her in his own time.

"Kitty sent Sarah over with a request that I get one of my bartenders to fetch a man's luggage for him. He had checked into the Fifth Avenue Hotel."

Essie raised her eyebrows. Tuck grinned. "Yeah, seemed strange to me, too. What guy would want his suitcase at Kitty's? So, when John showed up with the two bags and a carpenter's tool kit, I decided to deliver them myself."

He paused, dragging out the story. Essie swatted him with a cloth she'd been using to polish up some goblets, trying to get him to move along a little faster.

"She has him all fixed up in that nice, quiet room in the back, the one she doesn't use much except in the summer.

He's got an ankle all bandaged up. Older guy, but I suppose a woman would find him good looking enough, especially a woman Kitty's age. He was reading a book in some foreign language, looked like Latin to me."

"Reading, in a whore house?" Essie laughed.

"Yep," Tuck nodded. "Looked like he was settling in to stay a while. So I quizzed Kitty pretty good. She wouldn't answer many of my questions, just said that she had a bunch of carpentry work that needed to be done, and she'd finally found herself a carpenter."

"And she's putting him up in her house?" Essie acted like what Kitty had done went against all the rules.

"Ah, come on, Essie. You've had me in this house since you built it. John Secrest's been with Jane for five years. John Powers has been in Fannie Kiger's house for a good two years, and they're talking about getting married. About time Kitty found herself a man she liked. It's been years since she had anyone steady." Tuck just kept grinning.

"But Kitty always courted powerful men about town, men who could do her some good. Who is this guy? Some carpenter, you say? No one from Skagway? Why would she put up a carpenter?" Essie shook her head, clearly puzzled.

Tuck's grin just grew wider. "I'd say you should pay a call on Kitty and see for yourself, Darlin'. I think you'll figure it out." He gave her a sloppy kiss as he grabbed at her bottom, making her squeal, and then headed for the back stairs so he could finish dressing before he took off for the evening shift at the Board of Trade.

* * *

Tuesday, February 13, 1916 (five days later). It took a while before Essie had the time to go over to Kitty's Place, what with all the work she usually had to do in the winter. Maintenance of the houses, cleaning, trying to spruce up all six places before April when the men started coming back. But her curiosity plagued her. This afternoon, she heard a hammer banging on the porch behind Kitty's main house and thought she might go over and take a look at the carpenter.

As soon as she saw the man, she understood what Tuck had been hinting at, but couldn't say, him being a man and all. Kitty's guest would have made most women swoon with desire. While his weathered skin and calloused hands indicated a life spent outdoors, his deeply set, blue eyes and thick, curly, dark hair, touched with gray on the sides, set off a perfectly formed jaw and generous mouth.

Essie smiled at him as she climbed the back stairs, knowing to enter through the kitchen this time of day. He tipped his hat courteously to her, and then went back to his work without making a joke or ogling her as most men would have done here on Alaska Street. She watched him from the corner of her eye with some amusement, intrigued with this handsome man who seemed unaffected by the aura of sexuality Essie habitually exuded.

In Kitty's kitchen, Essie waited with a cup of excellent coffee while Sarah went to find her mistress. When the lady of the house emerged from the gaming room, she seemed surprised to find the Queen of the District in her kitchen.

"To what do I owe this pleasure?" she asked, curiosity plain on her face. Essie realized that she had never been in Kitty's place before.

"Tuck suggested that I might want to interview your carpenter. We have a few odd jobs we need done, once he's free," Essie extemporized.

Kitty hesitated only a moment and then smiled, smoothly. "I'm sure Mr. Wandsted would appreciate the offer. He came up from San Francisco, thinking he had a job with the railroad. When he got here, they said they changed their mind. I literally ran into him with my sled. He had trouble finding another carpenter's job here in town, but I told him how badly I needed some repairs. I asked him to build a shed for me, as well."

"I see." Essie took a sip of her coffee, nodding into the cup. "He's really very nice looking, isn't he?"

"Oh, is he?" Kitty asked, feigning disinterest. "I really hadn't noticed."

Essie snorted.

Kitty turned to glare at her. Before she could say anything, the subject of their conversation walked in the back door.

"Excuse me, ladies," he said with a deep voice. His accent clearly marked him as an immigrant, probably from

Denmark, Essie thought, the way he emphasized his s's and said his words at the front of his mouth. "I just came in for a glass of water."

"Stay for a cup of coffee, Chris," Kitty invited. "Mrs. Flaharty may have some additional work for you, if you want to try to schedule it in."

Chris, Essie thought. An added allure. All of the sporting world knew of Kitty's one time affair with Chris Shea, and how she had never become close to a man after him.

"Essie," Kitty introduced them. "Please meet Chris Wandsted. Chris, this is Essie Flaharty. She lives across the street. You have already met her husband, Tuck."

The tall, well-proportioned man took Essie's hand and kissed it clumsily, as if he was not accustomed to dealing with women on a regular basis. Essie exchanged a quick smile with Kitty while the man shed his coat at the hooks near the back door, making sure he knocked the last of the snow clods off his boots. By the time he sat down at the table, Kitty had poured another cup of coffee and set some cream and sugar next to it, clearly knowing just what he wanted without having to ask.

The conversation that followed could have taken place in any woman's home in Skagway, as she made arrangements to have the creaks in her floors fixed, the leaks in the roofs plugged, and some stairs checked for soundness. She found him to be a serious businessman with fair rates. Kitty said she was in no hurry to have her own work finished. He could delay the shed until after he had finished Essie's repairs. He said he hated to put off her work, so would do Essie's jobs in the mornings and Kitty's shed in the afternoons when the weather was a little warmer.

He excused himself when he finished his cup of coffee and Essie had come to an agreement with him for his services. The two women watched him don his threadbare coat and wrap his scarf around his throat. He nodded to both of them before exiting through the back door.

"Is he your lover?" Essie asked outright.

Kitty's eyes widened as she pretended shock. Then, her face softened, and she smiled. Essie had never seen such a contented look on her rival's face before.

"Not that it is any of your business, Essie, but yes, he lets me share his bed at night."

Essie raised an eyebrow. "What an odd way to put it, a madam in her own house, begging a man to let her in his bed."

Kitty laughed. "Yes, that's the way it was, almost. He's not the sort of man who would have come to one of our houses on his own. I had to talk him into it, practically beg him, actually. I

find him refreshing, interesting, very different from anyone I've known before." Her eyes glazed over, as if she looked into a long, distant past.

"Anyone?" Essie asked.

Kitty looked at her, rather sharply. "It doesn't matter who or what I knew when I was a girl. What matters is now."

She leaned forward in one, swift movement, leaning on the back of one hand. "Essie. I have tried to warn you and Tuck several times. Our life here in Skagway is ending. Anna Stinebaugh and her women are changing the way the people in this town think about us. And it's not just here. It's in every small town in America. I'm getting too old to fight it anymore. I'm going to leave while I can still make some money off my properties."

She sat back, as abruptly as she had come forward. "If the two of you wait until those women have driven you out of town, you'll lose it all. You won't even get the price of your taxes for your houses."

"Tuck and I don't give up," Essie warned. "You can't scare us with this kind of talk of gloom and doom. We're survivors. If we leave, Anna Stinebaugh will have won for sure. I'm not going to give it up that easily."

"I'm not saying just give up. Me, I'm not selling. I'm just going to rent the places out, but I have to leave. There's nothing here for me anymore. Maybe somewhere else, but not in Skagway." She looked towards the back door, her eyes turning soft, like they had been shortly after the carpenter had gone outside. "Or maybe a whole other kind of life."

Essie stood up, her eyes flashing, her fists planted on the table top. "Go ahead, run off with your carpenter. It will make it just that much easier for me to run this district without you. But Tuck and I stay until the bitter end. No one is running Tuck and Essie Flaharty out of Skagway."

She swirled away from the table, grabbed up the coat she had left hanging by the door, and slammed through it without even thanking Kitty for the coffee.

Kitty sat back in her chair, toying with the empty coffee cup in front of her. The handsome carpenter came back through the door, stomping his feet on the rug, but not entering the kitchen. He looked at her quizzically.

"Oh, Essie's high strung and easily upset. Don't mind her. Tuck will calm her down by evening. They approach life differently than you or I do."

"All of you on Alaska Street approach life differently than I do," he reminded her.

She smiled at him. "Yes, I know. Come, tell me what you would do with our problem." She held out her hand to him as he took off his coat once again. He smiled at her, fondly, and tapped the last of the snow off his boots, before joining her at the table for another cup of coffee.

* * *

Saturday, March 18, 1916 (five weeks later). The floorboards, roof and squeaky steps in all of the houses on Alaska Street now tested sound. Chris had built a solid shed for Kitty, back behind her house on the west side of the street. When she and Essie had found the last squeaky board and the last leaky spot in the last house on the street, and he had pounded the last nail in the shed, he had told Kitty that he would buy the ticket to San Francisco. She had sent for Tuck and made him scour the town for carpentry jobs, but he could find none. The way she told the story to Essie, she begged him to stay, but he insisted he would not be a kept man, especially of a whore. They had a word for such a man in the north, macquereau. In some places, that could also mean a pimp. Chris said he would not be a pimp, even for

160

Kitty.

In anger, she accused him of staying for the free sex. In anger he accused her of holding him hostage, of keeping him to make him fix her roof and give her a shed. She said if he left, she would go with him. He replied in a stream of Danish that she couldn't understand, and then both steamed in silence for half an hour. When he finally remembered his English, he told her she wasn't going with him unless she went as Mrs. Wandsted.

When he did leave town in three days, Kitty would be with him, as Kitty Wandsted. And tonight, Chris would own five whore houses.

Tuck watched Chris straighten his tie, adjust his collar, and thump the silk top hat more securely on his head. He grabbed the gray silk gloves, surveyed himself in the mirror one last time, and then turned towards Tuck, who waited to take him to the Board of Trade. He had closed down the saloon for the biggest wedding the demimonde had ever put on.

Kitty did not mock good women by wearing white on her wedding day. Her peach-colored dress was modest and understated. Anna Stinebaugh would have approved. No veil, but a fanciful hat with feathers and nets and ribbons had set her apart from the other women. All could identify the bride that day. No woman glowed so happily. None, perhaps, until Nora Moore caught the bouquet at the very end, and Danny caught her up and swirled her around in triumph.

Then they all cheered and drank more champagne and jollied the couple into dancing half the night to the ragtime tunes on the big phonograph player Tuck kept in the corner. He'd shoved the pool tables to the side for a dancing floor and everyone took advantage of the unusual occurrence of women at the Board of Trade. Although, technically, the saloon was closed and the party a private one, all of the men in town were Tuck's and Essie's friends, so no one would have been able to tell a customer from a guest that night. Except that all drinks were on the house. Even city marshal, Frank Page, sat in one corner, joking with Si Tanner, who had turned up about eight o'clock that evening, looking a bit forlorn.

Tuck carried a couple of mugs of beer over to the two old lawmen, knowing champagne wouldn't suit either one. Both had empty mugs sitting in front of them.

"Thank you, young man. That's quite thoughtful." Page grinned as he slurped the foam off the top of his draught. He hadn't lived in Skagway all that long, but had already become a regular.

The three men watched Chris Wandsted lead his bride in the first of the dances for the evening. Like most of the men in the room, he appeared more eager than talented.

"That man is the answer to a prayer, Essie told me," Tuck confided.

Both Si and Frank broke out in hearty laughter. "A prayer? I can't imagine Kitty Faith needing to pray for anything," Frank managed to get out.

"Oh, it wasn't Miss Faith who was down on her knees begging God for a man to come along and carry her away," Tuck said with a deadpan face. "Why would he listen to a woman like her?"

"Anna Stinebaugh," the two lawmen chorused. All three of the men burst into hilarious laughter, holding their stomachs, hoping to keep their beer inside. A number of the party guests turned to see what amused them so, and many of them laughed along, just to see them having such a good time.

"I'm going to miss that woman," Si admitted, shaking his head once he caught his breath. "Won't seem like Skagway without her."

"You say that with every pioneer that leaves," Tuck pointed out. Skagwayans took to calling anyone that had come up between July of '97 and the turn of the century a pioneer. It didn't matter if they were sporting or reform or somewhere in between. A pioneer had his or her own special status.

"You turning me into a doddering old man?" Si asked with a tone of indignation in his voice.

"Not me," Tuck answered hastily. Wouldn't do to get the senator from the Southeast upset with him. Not with the liquor laws coming up in the legislative session next spring. Si had been able to keep talk of it sequestered this year. He wasn't sure he could do it again next year.

Si laughed, enjoying being able to tease Tuck like that.

"Well, at least Kitty took my advice," he offered into the general silence that followed.

"What was that?" Frank asked.

"To leave town and cut her losses before the reform women ruined her." Si sat down his beer and brought out three of his favorite cigars. He offered one each to Tuck and Frank. Both grinned and accepted.

"Not you, too, Si," Tuck groaned. "Kitty's been lecturing at Essie and me about leaving town. We're not a-gonna' do it. Anna Stinebaugh's won if she drives us out. We got a right to make a living, and we're staying here. It's the only place we know."

Si exchanged a look with Frank, and both of them shook their heads. Si met Tuck's eyes squarely. "As long as it's legal, Tuck, you're right. I just don't relish the idea of, one day, being the one that has to shut you down."

"Why would you be, Tanner?" Tuck laughed. "You're territorial senator. You don't go around arresting folks. That's Frank's job, here. Sure, he could take out after Essie, but he don't want to. Too many men in town want her here." Tuck just grinned at the ridiculous thought.

Si shook his head. "I'm not going to be able to stay in the legislature forever, man, not with those women voting, and not the way the Republicans are taking over the Southeast. You know what a die-hard Democrat I am."

Tuck nodded at that. He'd never convince Si to change party allegiance, and no one would believe him if he tried.

"And you also know how badly I want to be U. S. Marshal in these parts. Harry Bishop, our current marshal, has messed up pretty badly twice now. He let Hjalmar Rutzebeck escape from the federal prison in Juneau last fall. Then, Commissioner Williams discovered that the marshal had been using a confiscated fishing boat for his personal shrimping trips. He's got one more time to really mess up, and he's out of a job. I have it on very good authority that my name is on the top of the list as replacement."

Si, now that he'd finished his beer, leaned back to enjoy his cigar. "Now, we all know it won't take Harry very long before he makes another mistake, especially considering the way he hires anyone who's ever done a favor for him to run the jails and other facilities here in the Southeast. It's just a matter of time before I'm in charge of the whole coast between Valdez and Ketchikan."

Tuck was privately glad to know that he and Essie would have Si back in the saddle again. In order to stay in office, the old legislator had been focusing far too much on laws that had nothing to do with helping out the business men, trying to distract the women from the reform issues. Sure, they were good, progressive laws, like inheritance laws, ensuring that women had as many rights to a husband's property as a man did to his wife's, and even supporting women's rights to vote. He also made sure they had to pay their taxes, turn about being fair play.

But Tuck also knew that Si Tanner was a lawman above all other things. He believed in the law, and he believed in justice. The moment that Tuck or Essie openly flaunted the law, Si Tanner, friend or no friend, would be the first to see that they ended up in jail for it.

Tuck raised his glass. "To better times."

"To better times," Frank and Si agreed. Then the three of them caught sight of the bride and groom dancing to a jaunty ragtime tune, and they toasted the happy couple, knowing they, at least, had found those times.

Chapter Nineteen

Bootlegging

Thursday, April 6, 1916 (three weeks later).   Tuck Flaharty stared at the numbers, thinking that surely Sam Wall had misprinted them.   But no, the context was clear.   On August 21, Skagway would be a dry town.   Anna Stinebaugh, Grace Zinkan and those women at the W. C. T. U. with their crazy temperance cards, had finally done it.   They had closed him down for the last time.   In yesterday's election, the town had voted itself dry with a ballot of 193 to 153.

Tuck threw the paper to the floor and stomped to the window, muttering curses.   He stared at the top of the Dewey Peaks.   He pictured himself dragging those biddies, one by one, to the top of its western summit and flinging each of them into the ocean from its five thousand foot, barren heights.

"Tuck?"   Essie picked up the paper from the floor and

scrubbed the dusty footprint from the typeface where he had deliberately stamped upon it.

"Oh." She said when she had read the article. She sounded a death knell.

Tuck had four months to close down his business. Skagway would have no more saloons. Ever. Not the way it had been. Not a smoky room full of men – no fear of a woman ever invading their sacred domain – united in the camaraderie of drink, gambling, politics and tall tales. Sharing the stories of where the best women could be found and what to do with them. Talking sports and sharing intimacies that no man could share with his wife. Tuck wondered what would happen to the men's world without their saloons. What would the men do without them?

"Tuck." Essie crossed the room to him and wrapped her arms around his waist, standing at his back so he could lean into her if he wanted. He did. He pulled her arms tighter and covered them with his own, leaning his head back on her shoulder. "You know this means we separate, Darlin'," he sighed heavily, always thinking two or three steps ahead of her. "I can't have a saloon in Skagway anymore, but Juneau still has them. I'll have to go there to open a place and start smuggling liquor up here. There will be plenty of people who will want it. It will get me back here often enough that we won't be missing each other all that much." He desperately hoped he spoke the truth. "If it doesn't work, I guess I start selling cigars. Those biddies haven't made them illegal yet."

He sighed. "You won't be able to start fresh in Juneau. They're running poor like we are in Skagway. They have their own women. You'd have to start from scratch there with a district hanging as close to the edge as Skagway's." He shook his head. "Too late to take up a business like yours in Juneau."

Essie hugged him to her tightly. "How can they do it, Tuck? How can they just shut a man's business down, with no way to make it up to him for all the years of hard work he's put into building his dreams? What gives them the right to destroy a whole way of life?"

"Ya' got me, Darlin'." He felt solid as a rock, solid with tension, true, but still solid. These women had not beat him limp and left him lying like a puddle on the ground. "But Kitty was right. They've been doing it all over the country, not only here in Skagway. Why, in just the last three years, fourteen states have gone completely dry, and I have no idea how many voted that way before that. I don't know what men do for drink – make it at home? Pay twice or three times as much for smuggled liquor?" He shook his head. "I'd think it would defeat all of the purpose of what those women want, making men pay more for their drink instead of less, spending more time away from home looking for it and sneaking around drinking it on the sly."

Tuck swallowed, hard. He wasn't even thinking about the Board of Trade now. He remembered those nights spent in the company of other men, laughing and joking, drinking and gambling, smoking rank cigars, arguing politics, taking pleasure in news and company and a sort of sociability he had never seen women enjoy. "Did they envy us so much that they had to destroy us?"

"I don't think they envied you, Tuck, but feared you. So many men together, night after night, planning for the town without talking to the women, spending the family's money without working it out with their wives. They simply feared, what with the men and women not talking. In the saloon, the men would talk themselves out to the other men, and then forget to talk to their wives when they got home."

"How do you know this, Essie?"

"You've always been different from other men, Tuck. Like any good bartender, you listened at the saloon. Then you talked to me instead and told me what happened at the Board of Trade and what the men said."

She smiled and turned him around to face her, keeping him in her arms. "And I remember a story you told me about writing home one time. You told your mama and papa that you and Flick just needed wives to talk to because you could cook and clean and sew. Flick got mad because your mama wanted you to need a wife to take care of you. But you were right all along. You treat a woman differently than most men do, Tuck. You treat a woman like you do a friend. You love me like you do your brother and your pals at the saloon, and then you come home and make mad, passionate love to me as well. I doubt many women have a man like that."

Tuck looked abashed. "Is that what those old biddies want? They just want their husbands to be friends and to talk to them?"

Essie nodded her head against his shoulder. "I suspect so. I think they really just want a man that will respect them the same way he respects the opinion of his best pal down at the saloon. When they couldn't get that, they decided to destroy the saloon instead."

Tuck leaned back against the window frame, thinking of Chris Shea and how fiercely he had loved his wife. Chris had also loved the men from his saloon, men like Lee Guthrie and Billy Blackmer and himself. Chris had stood by them to the bitter end of a no-win battle with the women of the W. C. T. U., ruining his career and jeopardizing the stability of his family to honor his friendships and the commitments he had made. That's what men did, good men, men who had bonded in the saloon. Would there ever be anything to replace the loyalties that formed in a place like the Board of Trade or the Pack Train?

"Kitty said this would happen, Tuck," Essie said, with a tremble in her voice. "She said Alaska Street would be next. What if she's right?"

Tuck pulled her closer. "I don't know, Darlin'. I thought I did, but now, I don't."

* * *

Friday, November 9, 1917 (one year and seven months later). Tuck lifted the last crate of whiskey bottles onto the table. He and Essie began to transfer them into the liquor cabinet, filling the last empty space. It felt good to have the supply all restocked. He grabbed Essie, kissed her well, and then snatched up the empty crate. "I'll probably be late, Darlin'. I have several more deliveries yet, here on Alaska Street, then around town. Don't look for me before midnight."

"The back door will be open. Watch for Marshal Tanner. I heard he's in town."

Tuck raised his eyebrows at the news, but waved it away while waving goodbye. Then they both went back to making a living in a changing world.

After mentioning Si's name, Essie wasn't all that surprised when Mildred bustled into the parlor at ten that night to tell her that the U. S. Marshal waited in her kitchen, had walked in through the back door, demanding to see her. She smiled at the tall, handsome man whom she hadn't seen for years. "Si Tanner, you old fox. I welcome you to my place. Would you care for some coffee?"

Si, ever the gentleman, tipped his hat and pulled out a warrant. "Thank you, Mrs. Flaharty. I'd appreciate a cup, as long as Tuck didn't make it. But, I'm afraid I have to arrest you."

Essie stared at him for one, two, three heartbeats. She had not been arrested since 1914, by anyone. She had not seen Si Tanner in a court of law since 1908, nor had she been arrested by the man since 1903. "May I ask why you feel obligated to arrest me, Mr. Tanner?"

Si walked through the portiere and into the gaming room that stood between the kitchen and the parlor. Captain Harriman, from the Arctic, Louis Greene, who ran the Dewey Hotel, and Athelia, one of Essie's girls, played cards and drank whiskey at the table. Tanner eyed their drinks. He walked straight to the liquor cabinet and opened the door, revealing row upon row of well-stocked shelves. "Gentlemen, ma'am. Excuse me for interrupting your game. I presume you purchased your drinks from Mrs. Flaharty, here? It looks like high quality whiskey."

"Indeed," Mr. Greene agreed. "Essie Flaharty always sells us the best money can buy."

Essie rolled her eyes. She had such helpful customers.

Si smiled and turned to Essie. "I believe I am arresting you for selling liquor without a license, Mrs. Flaharty. You will come along nicely, won't you? I dislike using handcuffs on a lady."

"Of course, Si. You know me. I'll just go get my coat." She turned to leave the room.

Si reached out and caught her arm. "Perhaps Mildred would get it for you," he suggested. "I would prefer you not leave my sight. In fact, I would rather none of you leave here for some time. I have a number of visits yet to make here on

Alaska Street this evening, and I would rather that my calls remain unannounced. Deputy Hardy will be staying here with all of you until I give him leave. While he's here, he will take the depositions of the gentlemen, and the lady, concerning their purchases of liquor." Then, Si Tanner waited patiently while Mildred, flushed and trembling, found Essie's coat. He held it for her while she put it on, and then he crooked his elbow for her. Essie couldn't help but smile. Si Tanner had always been the perfect gentleman. She accompanied him outside to his wagon.

Hazel, Nora, and Billie, three of the other madams on Alaska Street, excepting only Burmah, had joined her in the cell by the time they let Tuck in to see to her at one thirty in the morning. They also had Birdie Ash, a woman who rented a crib from Essie. The jailer, Nathan Hardy, didn't have a separate room for Tuck and Essie, so they huddled in a corner of the cell, close together, whispering into one another's ears. The other women pretended to ignore them.

"Commissioner Rasmussen is down in Haines. He won't be here until tomorrow. You have to stay the night, Essie. They won't let me bail you out."

Essie's eyes brimmed over. It felt like the old days, only he couldn't rescue her this time. He held her close to him, staring wide-eyed at the ceiling, hoping that would dry his own, over-wet eyes. "I'll be here first thing in the morning with all the cash we have," he added.

"Tuck, I don't think that's a good idea. If they're after us, they're after you, too. They have to know where we're all getting the stuff." She kept her voice low, barely audible in his ear. "You can't be seen here. You should leave Skagway right away."

"I can't leave you, Essie. Who will get you out?"

"Mildred. One of the girls. Leave some bail money with Flick. He'll help if you ask him to. Just leave, Tuck."

"I can't, Essie. I won't leave town not knowing what's happening to you." His lips whispered in her ear, the mustache and stubble from his face scraping her nearby cheek.

"Time's up," Hardy called.

Tuck tightened his grip and kissed her, hard. He'd never felt so helpless, not being able to rescue Essie from the law. He didn't know how he'd be able to let her go. She had to push his arms from her to make him release her. Even then he took her face in his hands and kissed her again. "Tomorrow," he promised.

"No," she whispered back, trying to make him understand that Si would get him, too. But Tuck just touched her lips with his fingers, and then turned to Hardy and nodded that he was ready to leave. He did not look back until he got to the door. Essie saw that his eyes blurred as much as hers.

* * *

Sunday, November 11, 1917 (two days later). The courtroom was crowded. Nothing this exciting had happened for over a year, not since the liquor license vote. Si knew that Commissioner Rasmussen could not remember having such a sensational case in his courtroom before. He had confided that he was afraid they would all plead not guilty, and he'd have to send them on to Juneau. He'd much rather these women would all be cooperative, plead guilty, and let him administer fair justice. With guilty pleas, he could go down in Skagway's history books for closing down the restricted district.

He surveyed the crowd. Anna Stinebaugh and Grace Zinkan had found seats in the gallery on his left, about halfway down the aisle. Si looked around. He noticed Harriet Pullen and Elizabeth Harrison in the crowd as well. They all wore grim, self-satisfied smirks. He knew Rasmussen would cooperate with them, but he would not break the women of Alaska Street. The W. C. T. U. appeared a tad too self-congratulatory this morning.

Up front in the defense attorney's seat sat Steve Regent, a man from Haines, someone hardly anyone knew. As the morning went on, it became obvious that he didn't know Skagway, and his heart wasn't in the job. Si figured that Tuck had done everything in his power to get Zino Cheney to Skagway in time for the hearing, but no ship had come in from Juneau in time.

No sign of Tuck anywhere. Smart man. Si had wondered if he'd be stupid enough to try and sneak in. He caught sight of Tuck's brother, Harry Flaharty, by the back door. And there was Tad Hillery, visiting family from Seward. Of course. One of them knew where the bootlegger was hiding out and would take word to him as soon as Judge Rasmussen finished up this hearing.

As the district attorney called up each of the witnesses, he showed how the whole thing had been carefully planned to bring in the entire demimonde on one night. Si had sent in Captain Harriman as a plant. The district attorney told Essie's Athelia she would not be charged with prostitution if she admitted to drinking liquor with the men. They had promised similar deals to girls at the other houses. With their own employees testifying against them, the madams didn't have much of a self defense. It didn't take long to convince Essie and the other four other women from Alaska Street that it would be a whole lot more expensive to plead not guilty than to plead guilty.

The judge explained the matter to the women before him. "To be found guilty by a jury after pleading not guilty almost certainly will bring each of you a prison sentence," he warned. "While you may have the opportunity to prove yourselves innocent, I suggest you think long and hard about your pleas at this point." He called a half hour recess and let them all go back to their seats to stew a while longer.

Si leaned up against the back wall with his arms folded across his broad chest and watched the crowd in the courtroom. Harry Flaharty engaged in deep conversation with Tad and Max Gutfield, a relative newcomer to town, a baker who was buying up a lot of property as the town emptied out. Si caught Nat Hardy's eye and nodded towards the group. Nat nodded back, getting his drift. He'd have someone tail all three, see if they couldn't find Tuck. One of them surely knew where the bootlegger had to be.

Sweeping his eyes around the crowd, Si locked gazes with Hans Schneider. Brawny, light-haired, starting to go bald on top, the man who used to be a job foreman for the White Pass and Yukon Route had finally out-worn his welcome at the railroad. Now that the union had some power in Skagway, men like him had little use, and White Pass had asked him to leave. He still found work of the kind that took a mean temper. Lately he'd been hanging around the jail too much, and Si didn't like the fact that the temperance folks were offering rewards to anyone who would give information on bootleggers.

What was it about Schneider and Essie Flaharty? Oh, yes, back in '03 he had given Essie some trouble, had attacked her for some teasing at Ida's Place. Ida had used the incident to cut a deal when the city was trying to get the federal courts to let go of the fines, and the U.S. Commissioner had cooperated. Schneider was trouble. Si didn't like the cocky way he turned his right shoulder towards the U. S. Marshal and leered down toward the women awaiting the return of the judge.

At that moment, Rasmussen came back to his seat. Indicating he would hear their pleas, he called on Essie first.

She rose, and he asked, "How do you plead, Mrs. Flaharty?"

Essie hesitated only a moment. "Guilty, your honor."

The others whispered to each other. With that lead, each one of them stood up in turn and admitted her guilt. They obviously just wanted to get this over. They did not want to go to Juneau for the next district court session. There would be no sympathy in either community for any of them. Pay the fine and get back to work, that had always been the way of it in Skagway. They were all thankful they could do it without sitting in a prison cell for a few months first.

"Good," Rasmussen adjudged when they had all entered their pleas. "We'll reconvene on Tuesday at nine o'clock a. m. to pass sentence. Jailer, please escort the women back to their cells."

Si watched in some surprise as the five women from Alaska Street turned confused looks on one another. Their lawyer just stood up and walked away, without a second glance back. Two more days in jail before they even knew what penalty they had to pay? What was happening? Nat Hardy didn't let them wonder for long. Si quickly moved to their rear and in a moment the two of them had the women flanked and headed back for their cells.

It wasn't until he slammed the door shut on Essie that Si realized what Judge Rasmussen meant to do. He wanted to give the newspapers of Southeast Alaska time to send up their representatives. Rasmussen had no mere fine in mind. And he no doubt would have a lot to say on the subject of closing down Skagway's red light district.

The Courthouse

Chapter Twenty

The Final Blow

Monday, November 13, 1917 (the next night). With no drunks or other trouble-makers from the city, Nat Hardy had let the women from Alaska Street spread out among the three jail cells. Only Birdie and Nora had chosen to share. Essie didn't know how she rated one to herself. She guessed as Queen, she had a few perquisites coming her way. She laughed at herself. A private jail cell for the Queen of Alaska Street.

She wanted to holler at Nat Hardy and whoever it was that was making all of that noise out in Nat's office to keep it down, but then she remembered the stories of drunken whores that used to show up in John Troy's newspapers, how he'd make fun of Pop Corn Kate singing in the jail, or Esther Mitchell yelling at the city council while they were trying to hold a meeting. She decided she wouldn't join the ranks of harlots that Skagway's uprighteous citizens laughed at over their morning coffee.

Anyway, it got deadly quiet out in the office, so Essie turned over on her cot and tried to shut out her troubles. One more day, then she'd be out of this place. She could go home, get back to work, and see if she'd ever say anything nice to Si Tanner again.

Essie had just about dropped off to sleep when she heard the rattle of a key in the lock of her cell door. She turned over to see a man she'd almost forgotten existed, Hans Schneider, standing just inside her cell.

"I hear you call yourself Mrs. Flaharty now," he leered.

"What do you want?" she snapped, rising to her feet and meeting him halfway across the cell.

Schneider let the key to the jail cell fall with a clank to its place on the large ring hooked to the belt at his waist. He sauntered over to her and thrust his arm around her waist, pulling her up close to his chest.

"I remember some good times at Ida's Place," he recalled, his whiskey-soaked breath smothering her.

Essie tried to push away from him, without effect. "I don't work for Ida. In fact, I'm not working at all. Remember? I'm in jail."

He loosened his grip, letting her step away from him, but the leer never left his face. "I might be able to do something about that. The jail part. Get you back to work. Wouldn't cost you much."

"I'm not interested. I'm out of this place tomorrow. One more night in here, I can take," she pointed out. She turned her back on him and started to walk towards the cot.

He reached out and grabbed her right arm, twisting hard. Essie cried out at the pain.

"Mrs. Flaharty." His voice suddenly grew cold. "You will do exactly what I tell you, and you will give me what I want for it." He drew an object out of his pocket. Essie startled back as he touched a lever on the side of a slim, black handle, and a shining steel blade sprang for her throat.

The cot had been pushed along the far wall of the cell, leaving a small space between its head and the corner. He forced her into the niche, leaving her no escape. That night fifteen years ago rushed back to her, when she had teased him past the point when he thought she was fun to where he pulled a knife, cut the laces on her corset, and took her by force. Tonight, he had obviously come to her with assault foremost on his mind.

"You don't need the knife, Mr. Schneider," Essie smiled, meaning to disarm him in more ways than one. She started to unbutton her dress, hoping all he wanted was quick relief, and then he'd be gone.

His grin grew broader and the glint in his eyes harder as he watched her quick fingers work at the buttons and snaps and bows. Essie had worn a very pretty dress the night she was arrested, and here, three days later, still wore it, mussed and wrinkled and stained as it had become from being worn in a jail house.

Suddenly he reached over and ripped the dress open, exposing the lace and satin chemise she wore underneath. With a quick upward slice of the jackknife, he split it open to reveal her breasts. Like many modern women, Essie had begun to abandon the uncomfortable corset of the previous decades, letting her natural curves speak for themselves. She didn't flinch, although she felt puzzled. She had clearly indicated her willingness to cooperate with him.

Suddenly his hand darted forward, then down. She felt the sharp sting across her left breast and glanced down in surprise to see the thin trace of blood welling up from the long cut he had given her. Another dash of his hand, and an identical slice appeared across her right breast.

Essie cried out in rage. "Nat! He's—."

"The jailer's taking a nap, "Schneider interrupted. "He's not going to be coming in here any time soon."

"Si!" Essie hollered.

"Save your breath, whore," Schneider chortled. "The marshal's not here, either. I watched him walk onto the Hegg down at the docks this morning. Heard the district attorney tell him he had to go down to Haines for the sentencing of those harlots they arrested last week. You scum are done here in the Southeast."

The knife sliced in and out. The blood welled up in a crisscross on her left breast. Essie had nowhere to go. She cowered in the corner.

"What do you want?" she demanded.

"Where's Tuck?"

Essie felt the blood leave her head, where it had rushed in her rage at his assault. For a moment, panic gripped her. She gulped at the air, grasping at any idea that might work. Nothing came to her. Tuck was always the one with the ideas, not Essie.

"Tuck? Why do you want Tuck?" she asked, bewildered.

The knife flick in again. Slice. Essie groaned, unable to protect herself.

"The temperance people. They've offered a hundred dollars for information leading to the arrest of the bootlegger bringing all of the whiskey into the district. Everyone knows it's Tuck Flaharty. Tell me where he is."

Essie's head suddenly cleared. Send Tuck to jail and enrich this bastard? The answer was clear.

"Tuck's gone back to Juneau." She said, hoping it was true.

Schneider shifted the knife to his left hand, brought back his right hand and swung it wide, landing his flat palm against the left side of her face in a hard blow. Essie made no effort to suppress her cry of pain.

"Don't lie to me. I've been watching all of the steamships and private boats. He's still here in town. I'm not leaving this cell until you've told me where he is."

"I don't know where he's staying!" she snapped as he raised his hand again. It was the truth. He backhanded the right side of her face, sending her head crashing into the plastered wall. Essie cried out again.

She could hear the women down the hall calling out her name, but she couldn't respond. Schneider's questions came one right after the other. Who would Tuck stay with? Where did they live? He didn't wait for answers, as if he knew she wouldn't give him away. Sometimes he hit her, sometimes he used the knife. He never cut deeply, just a scratch across the top of her skin, enough to hurt, enough to bleed, enough to cause a scar.

It seemed to go on and on, Essie saying "I don't know," because she didn't, and telling him to talk to Si, that Si would know more than she did, realizing she'd better not say Flick's name or Tad's or any of the Hillerys. If Schneider didn't know who Tuck hung around with these days, Essie wouldn't tell him. She wouldn't have Tad Hillery or Martin Itjen getting beaten up too.

And then it stopped. Essie blinked open her swollen eyes after a moment or two of silence, hardly comprehending he hadn't said or done anything. Had he gone?

No, he just stood back from her, fumbling with his belt and the buttons at his fly. She watched in horror as he lowered his pants, exposing his arousal. Still grasping the knife firmly in his right hand, he grabbed her arm and pulled her around the side of the cot. Pushing her down onto it, he inserted one of his legs between hers and started to pull her skirt up around her waist.

Essie had not had sex with a man other than Tuck for more than a decade, and she certainly did not want to change that situation now. She kicked at him, aiming for the hand with the knife, her anger overcoming any fear the cuts and blows had instilled in her. Balling up his powerful fist, he delivered two, rapid-fire blows to her abdomen, taking her breath from her. Her breath and something much more.

At thirty-six years of age, Essie had, for only the third time in her life, missed not one, but two menstrual periods. Both previous times had presaged the birth of a child. Unlike the other times, she was euphoric, knowing without question who had fathered the baby, and that the two of them could devote their lives to raising it in an atmosphere of love. She had been waiting until Tuck came up from Juneau and they were alone to give him the good news. With the sudden, aching pain that wracked her lower body, Essie knew that his dream of fatherhood had just been destroyed.

Schneider had no difficulty wrenching apart her legs. "I'll be sure to tell Mr. Flaharty that you've still got what it takes to whip up a real man," he gloated as he thrust himself into her. "Soon as I have him in this cell, he's gonna' hear about everything I got from his wife."

He pumped vigorously, obviously needing no help from either an experienced prostitute or a helpless victim. Essie said and did nothing, now numbed to what had happened to her. She simply closed her eyes and endured, slipping into a state that had helped her once before, a very long time ago, that time that had started it all. Tuck had saved her in the end. He would do it again. She'd just wait for Tuck.

* * *

Tuesday, November 13, 1917 (the next day). Si stood at the back of the federal courtroom again, in his usual spot, scanning the crowd. Damn, he'd hated having to go off to Haines yesterday. The D. A. didn't seem to understand how important it was to stick around Skagway with Tuck on the loose and the madams all in jail like that. The whole setup had made him nervous. He would have been perfectly happy to leave the court appearances in Haines up to Cort Ford, one of his deputies, but the district attorney seemed to think Si needed to be there as the arresting officer. Now Rasmussen was back here in Skagway, holding court again, enjoying his role in shutting down vice in yet another of the Southeast's sinful towns.

He glanced down toward Essie. She still had her back to him. She refused to turn around. He didn't like the way she sagged in her chair. All the women seemed wilted and dejected, unlike any of them, ordinarily a hardy bunch, vivacious and sassy to the last. The lassitude concerned him more than tears would have. Something didn't seem right. He wished the Hegg hadn't gotten delayed by those high winds yesterday evening. As it was, Si was lucky to be here for this sentencing. He knew what would happen. High fines, the women promising to leave town. They'd all be back in a few months and life would go on as usual. Who was fooling who?

Rasmussen obviously enjoyed the full courtroom in front of him. Like Si had predicted, the judge had prolonged the sentencing to give the newspapers from Juneau and other nearby communities time to send reporters. He wanted to make sure all of Alaska knew about the commissioner who had shut down Skagway's notorious Alaska Street. Si narrowed his eyes, watching the judge let the courtroom hum

180

for another minute before he nodded to the bailiff, and only then brought the crowd to order.

After dispensing with preliminaries, Judge Rasmussen called Birdie Ash to the stand. She had been found guilty of selling L. F. Greene two bottles of beer. He fined her twenty-five dollars and costs. Birdie practically bubbled over in gratitude. He then fined Mr. Greene a hundred dollars for buying the beer. Mrs. McCann up in the fourth row sniffed her disdain loudly.

Birdie's case had been different than the others' from the very beginning. She wasn't a madam, just a working girl. She and Greene had shared two quarts of beer in a room at the Golden North Hotel. She wasn't a part of the sting operation Si had set up for the others. He didn't think the rest would get by quite so easily.

Rasmussen called Hazel Crosby up next and fined her a hundred dollars and costs. He did the same for Nora and then Billie, too. Well, a hundred dollars constituted the usual fine for selling liquor without a license. Not cheap, but they'd all managed it somehow. Essie prepared to stand, her ribs aching. The others had made it through their sentencing. She knew she could do the same. She dabbed at the corner of her mouth, bringing the handkerchief away with a stain of blood.

"Mrs. Essie Flaharty," Rasmussen called her name. Essie pushed herself to her feet, glad Tuck had been smart enough to stay away from the sentencing, like he had done for the hearing. She'd caught a glimpse of Flick near the back door, along with Tad. One of them would get word to Tuck, which would be bad enough. Damn the man. If he'd only gone back to Juneau right away, maybe Schneider... Essie shook her head, realizing the bounty hunter would have come for her even with Tuck gone. It was as much Si's fault for leaving town as Tuck's for staying. This never would have happened if Si had been in Skagway.

Once Essie stood, Judge Rasmussen paused, no doubt for some sort of effect. He let the courtroom hang in silence for a good sixty seconds. Essie trembled at her table, grateful she could lean on it and wasn't forced to stand in the middle of the room, alone.

"Mrs. Flaharty," the judge finally began. "I understand that you have enjoyed the sobriquet of 'Queen of Alaska Street' for some time now. As such, it is my responsibility to make a particular example of you, so that women in your position in other communities will take heed and learn what can happen if they do not mend their ways. I, therefore, feel obligated to make your fine somewhat more severe than that of the others."

He paused, again for effect. "However, before I assess your fine, I want to make it very clear to all of you assembled here. At the district attorney's orders, Marshal Tanner has assured me that this is not the first time that he will invade your places of business with the express purpose of searching for contraband liquor. Nor will he stop at the prosecution of that sort of criminal activity. We all know that the way in which you and the women on Alaska Street earn your living is illegal. Mr. Tanner informs me that the district judge has ordered the prosecution of federal prostitution laws in the First District to the full extent of the law. If the city of Skagway chooses to ignore you women, then the U. S. Marshal will be arresting you on a regular, frequent and punitive schedule, and I assure you, my fines will not be low ones."

Essie supported herself on her left arm. When Schneider had twisted the right one behind her back last night, she had pulled a muscle. She could not lean against it. She could barely stand because of the beating he had given her ribs and abdomen. Long after he'd left, she had lain there, hoping that she was wrong about the baby, but she knew now that it no longer existed. The blood had oozed from her steadily since the beating. She only needed to get home. As a madam, she knew what to take to staunch the flow and to save her own life. She didn't know what she would say to Tuck. She only wanted this nightmare to end, to go home, and to rest, and to save Tuck.

"Therefore, Mrs. Flaharty," Judge Rasmussen jerked Essie back to the courtroom, "it is in the best interests of you and your confederates on Alaska Street to close your doors and leave Skagway entirely. The people of Skagway no

longer welcome you. I suggest you board up all your houses
and seek to sell them in any way that you can. They will no
longer be used for immoral purposes. Before I assess you
your fine, I want your solemn word that you will adhere to this
condition."

Essie nodded her head. Yes, anything. Please, let's just
get this over with. Sam Wall scribbled on his paper pad
frantically. The women of the W. C. T. U., especially Anna
Stinebaugh, looked about with smug, self-satisfied smirks.
Essie heard a muttering from Flick and Tad's direction. She
knew they wondered at her lack of spirit. She didn't have it in
her to even pretend.

"That settled, then, Mrs. Essie Flaharty, I assess you a
two hundred dollar fine and costs." Rasmussen slammed
down his gavel. "Court recessed until four o'clock." He stood
and left the room.

Essie collapsed in her chair, her lawyer finally deciding
that he might lend her a hand, at least until her fine had been
paid and his fee had been collected.

Si Tanner marched directly for Flick, taking his forearm in
his hand. He spoke very softly. "Mr. Flaharty. For the sake
of your sister-in-law, I will give Tuck two days with her. She
appears to need them. I suggest he not leave town. I will
personally be watching their house. Tell him I have no
knowledge of what happened, but I promise I'll take care of it.
On my word. He will be avenged."

He let go of Flick abruptly. The visibly shaken man
stared at him for only a moment, and then raced for the
defense table on the floor of the courtroom. Tad Hillery, who
stood nearby, having heard every word, disappeared outside
the door.

Essie shuddered as Tuck bathed the cuts and bruises on
her ribs. It looked as if the man had taken a knife to her.
Essie didn't tell Tuck much, but she didn't need to. He
understood immediately as soon as he saw her. Someone
wanting that reward knew Tuck was in town and Si wasn't.
None of the women could betray him, because none of them
knew where he hid. Si now promised him he would be safe.
Tuck trusted Si. Although he didn't trust Si to take his

vengeance for him, he did trust him to keep him safe until Essie started mending.

Tuck gently dabbed at each cut with the antiseptic solution on his rags, even as she flinched at each touch. Neither of them considered sending for a doctor, not at first. Essie knew far more than the doctors anyway. What had to be done must be done just between them, not with doctors or nurses. The healing would start with their private efforts to make her well.

When he found the blood-soaked rags between her legs, he sat on the edge of the bed completely baffled. She still didn't explain, but told him what herbs and solutions and medicines to bring. She measured and mixed and gave him strict instructions on what to heat and what not to and for how long, and then she mixed some more. Later, she drank some of what they made and bottled the rest.

Then, and only then, did she tell him to go get Dr. Brawand. He dashed out the door, forgetting his coat. Si made him go back for it.

She told Doc Brawand everything that happened, and Tuck heard it there for the first time. He knew she could only say the words to the doctor, not to him. He sat and held her hand, rage kept barely under control, staying in the room only because he needed to hear it all before he went to kill the bastard.

"I tell you all of this, Dr. Brawand, only because I mean to bring charges against him. I want you as a witness to the things he did to me." So the doctor got out his notebook and did a thorough examination, complementing them both on the care they had given her afterwards.

"How far along were you with child, do you think?" he asked gently, when he saw the brightness of the blood on her menstrual rags.

"I had just missed two cycles," she replied. Try as she might, she couldn't stop the tears. With a cry of agony, she buried her face in Tuck's lap.

Tuck clutched her to him, as fiercely and as gently as he could, while staring at the doctor in utter disbelief and horror. Doc Brawand had never seen a man's love for his wife and desire for her children so plainly written as in the agony on this man's face. "Women are wonderfully strong and resilient, Tuck. There will be other children. Give her time."

Tuck closed his eyes, rejecting all the calm and reason and comfort. He wanted only to rage, to vent his fury, and to kill. With a very great effort, he brought all his passions under control and focused all his desire on Essie. "You'll help us, then, Dr. Brawand? When Essie needs you to testify, you'll help her?"

"Yes, of course, of course," he assented gruffly, sensing a change in Tuck. He shuffled around in his bag a little, and then brought up a bottle of laudanum. He handed it to Tuck. "Give her a tablespoon of this every two hours if she has trouble sleeping. She should sleep for a couple of days. Lots of fluids, too. Change the rags often. Keep the other wounds uncovered so they won't fester. Nothing looks like it needs stitching. Call me if anything gets red or she develops a fever."

Tuck kept nodding. He knew all of this.

"You'd better check the other houses. I think most of them went through much the same thing. They'll all know how to deal with it, but some may also want to press charges."

The doctor nodded.

"Can you see yourself out? I'd like to stay with Essie."

Again, Dr. Brawand nodded. Then he left. Essie laid nude, half on Tuck's lap, half off, her battered and bruised body more red and purple than milky flesh. She fell asleep, clutching his thighs tightly. He pulled the blanket up over her, covering the damage the craven man had done to her in the name of cornering a smuggler. Tuck stroked the hair of his beloved and let the tears fall unabated.

Two hours later, Tuck appeared in the back doorway. "Come in, Si. You'll need some coffee if you're going to stand out there all night."

Si Tanner materialized out of the shadows with his cheap Arabe cigar. "Did you make the coffee, Tuck?"

"It's left over from what Mildred made for the girls earlier this evening. I just warmed it up."

"All right, then. I guess a cup would be good." He

hunkered up the walkway.

"Where is he, Si?" Tuck asked as he handed the marshal a steaming cup of coffee.

Tanner saw the barely contained rage. "I told you I'd take care of him, Tuck. Trust me."

"It won't do, Marshal. I gotta' watch the bastard squirm for myself. I gotta' see the agony in his eyes. I gotta' watch the man knowing he's gonna' die and – ."

Si cut him off. "Why, man? So that Essie can watch you hang? You think that will solve anything? You think that will bring her any satisfaction? Do you think she lived through that so you can get yourself killed in a stupid game of revenge?"

Tuck crossed his arms over his chest. He thought another man would understand. Tanner was married, too. Everyone knew how he doted on his wife. "She was pregnant, Marshal. He beat the child from her. Will you add murder to his list of atrocities? He beat her, he raped her, and he killed our child. God knows if she'll ever let me in her bed again. You cannot begin to know the horrors that woman has known in her life. He's just added a heap more. I will have my vengeance."

Si took two deep breaths before he could find a way to talk to Tuck. "I have Schneider in a cell at the jail. I'd have Nat Hardy in there with him if I thought for one second he had even a whiff of what was happening in those cells. Turns out Hardy was out cold, drugged. Nat's taken it personally, and I'm having to work at keeping him from taking his own kind of revenge. Schneider's not going anywhere. I'll see he spends years in the federal prison at McNeil's Island over this, years to stew about what he's done."

"Essie wants to press charges. Doc Brawand will testify to her injuries. She wants to give a deposition. She told Doc to go round to the other houses. We won't let the bastard get away with it, Si."

"That's good, Tuck. It's a lot better than you killing him and me having to take you in for murder. Send word to that fancy lawyer of yours. Get him up here to help you out of your own scrape, and then he'll help you come up with a legal way to wreck your vengeance on Hans Schneider. But don't do yourself anymore harm along the way."

The two men sat at the table, sipping the stale coffee. It tasted pretty good to both of them.

"No woman should have to take that from a man, Si. How could she just endure it? Why didn't she just tell him where I was?" Tuck felt miserable now that Si had stolen his ability to strike back.

"How do you know she didn't tell? The bastard was bent on doing what he did. It wasn't information he wanted. He wanted to torture your wife and the other women of Alaska Street. He thought he could get away with it because of what they are. You were only an excuse. You could have been in Juneau the first night, before I even set foot in your door, and he still would have done what he did. At least you were here to pick up the pieces when he finished."

Si stretched out his long legs, and finished off his coffee. He climbed to his feet. "I think I'll head on home, now. I'm thinking you're not going anywhere with that sick woman upstairs, so I'll lay low for a couple of days. Be assured I'll be watching to see how she's getting along, though." With that, Si Tanner adjusted his hat, ducked his head and walked out the back door.

Tuck locked it behind him, switched off the lights, and headed up the stairs to keep a vigil over Essie. He felt totally helpless, as if the entire world had changed, leaving Essie and him stranded on a barren island with no food, water, clothing or signs of sustenance. With him unarmed and her lying huddled and broken at his feet, the future seemed utterly hopeless.

In their bedroom, he took off his clothes and lay beside his wife, fearful she would cringe from him. Still, with indomitable, Tuck-like optimism, he gathered her into his arms and cupped his body around hers. In her sleep she snuggled against him, pulling his arms more comfortably into place, nuzzling against his chest. "Tuck," she breathed quietly.

It was all he needed, one small ray of hope that love and life would go on. He sighed contentedly, closed his eyes, and went to sleep.

Sin and Grace

Chapter Twenty-One

Vengeance

Wednesday, November 14, 1917 (the next day). "Come on, Si. Arrest me now, today. I just need fifteen minutes with the bastard. Let me beat the crap out of him, then Max will bail me out, then I'll ask for a deferment until Zino can get up here. Please. I'm begging you."

Tanner sized up Tuck. Schneider was a lot bigger man than Flaharty. But then, the bounty hunter didn't have Tuck's passion. The man sitting in Nat Hardy's jail leaned towards beating women more than taking on enraged husbands.

"I swear to you, I'm on the City of Seattle this afternoon if

189

you don't arrest me, now, Si."

"How's Essie doing, Tuck?"

"She's resting. She let me sleep with her last night. She needs me to stay," he admitted.

"So stay. I'll arrest you next week."

"The ship leaves at two o'clock. I'm on it if I'm not in jail."

At one thirty, Si Tanner pulled Tuck Flaharty from the queue of people boarding the City of Seattle bound for Juneau. He made a great show of arresting the old time Skagway saloon man for bootlegging, putting him in handcuffs and marching him off to jail. Tuck looked fierce and belligerent. Wil Cleveland stood in the crowd to see him off.

"Find someone to bail me out," Tuck barked at him. "Max Gutfield. Find Max."

Nat Hardy put him in the cell with Schneider. He shoved Tuck against the right wall before removing his cuffs. Tuck didn't look at Nat the whole time. Instead, he glared at Schneider, naked hatred in his eyes. Hardy stared long and hard at both of them before he left. Both prisoners ignored him.

"You know me, buddy?" Schneider asked.

"I do," Tuck replied, spitting.

"Well, I don't know you. And I don't like your attitude."

"I heard you came looking for me, just three nights ago. Wanted me so bad, you beat up some women to get at me. So, I've come to you. Name's Flaharty. I have a score to settle." Tuck kept his voice low and steady.

Schneider laughed, a mean, mocking guffaw. He shut his eyes and turned his head when he did it, indicating what he thought of Tuck and his threats. Tuck knew the arrogant bastard would do just that and was prepared. He moved in like lightning and, swinging a baseball bat, hit Schneider on the left temple. The bastard fell like an ox.

Tuck moved quickly. He pulled Schneider's shirt open. He toyed with the idea of ripping up the shirt, tying his hands, and waiting until Schneider regained consciousness, but decided that would take too many risks. The bastard might just get out of the make-shift bonds. He took out the small knife he had concealed in his pocket and went to work on Schneider's chest, cut for cut imitating the wounds given Essie, especially the ones across her nipples.

Then he jerked down Schneider's pants, struggling with the belt for a minute, but pulling apart the buttons as easily as he had done those on the shirt.

Then he sat back on his heels. He could castrate the man in thirty seconds, quickly and neatly. He'd worked on a farm with his uncle when a young man, so he knew how to do it. He'd made sure he had a good, sharp knife so it wouldn't hang up on anything. The bleeding would be minimal. Schneider wouldn't die. Schneider would spend the rest of his life cursing Tuck Flaharty and what he, himself, had done to Flaharty's wife.

Tuck shook his head, realizing he couldn't lower himself to become the sick animal Schneider was, much as he'd enjoy the momentary feeling of triumph it would bring him. He considered another message. Schneider had left his initials sliced in Essie's abdomen. Tuck's name on the man's privates, a visual reminder every time he had to take a pee? The knowledge that Tuck could have done more, but didn't?

Tuck hesitated only one more moment, and then leaned forward. With a light touch, he quickly cut a single letter, a "T," onto the bounty hunter's glans. That would do the trick. Small enough payment for the loss of a child. It should hurt like hell, and the scar wouldn't last more than a couple of years, but long enough to remind him what a vengeful husband with friends in a small community could do.

Tuck sat back on his heels once again. He used Schneider's ripped shirt to wipe the blood from his blade, folded it back up, and stuck it in his pocket. He let the shirt fall back over Schneider's chest and the open wounds at his groin. He spit again, this time on Schneider's face. Then he stood and called for Nat Hardy.

"I think this guy needs a doctor, Nat. He doesn't seem to be feeling too good."

Nat glanced at Schneider when he came into the cell. He had to have seen the blood soaking through the shirt, but didn't say a word. Nat knew some of what Schneider had done to Essie. Some of the details had leaked out.

"Yeah, he does look a might poorly at that. I'll give Doc Brawand a call in a little while. In the meantime, Max is here to bail you out, Tuck. I'm to take you over to Rasmussen's office."

They both left the cell without a backwards look, Tuck swinging the bat nonchalantly.

* * *

Thursday, November 15, 1917 (the next day). "Why give me a subpoena, Mr. Tanner? I know nothing about this case," Anna Stinebaugh protested.

"I'm just the delivery boy, Ma'am." Si smiled, tipped his hat and said good-day. Zino Cheney had thought he had a good reason to call Mrs. Stinebaugh as a material witness to this hearing, but Si wasn't sure what it was. He did want her to observe this hearing, so he had certainly cooperated with Cheney and encouraged the lawyer. He knew Sam Wall would not write a word of it in his newspaper. The day was gone when John Troy would reveal Nettie Kelly's secret deposition to all of Skagway. This topic was too shocking to be told. However, Si believed the ladies of the W. C. T. U. needed to know what had come of their good intentions.

At eight twenty-five, Si Tanner settled in to watch from his post at the back of the room, near the door. He preferred to stand. He could keep an eye on everyone this way. Tanner had a hundred eyes, and he knew how to use them all. He looked around to find those who most interested him.

Tuck Flaharty sat in the front row, his arm wrapped protectively around Essie. A society that eschewed outward displays of affection would ordinarily have frowned on this gesture. Here, the court understood it exactly for what it was – a husband attempting to shield his wife from the hostile masses.

Hans Schneider did not attend the court. Si smiled grimly. Letting Tuck at him had not been a very smart thing to do, but the justice of it appealed to him. Knowing that Schneider might well get away with what he had done had prompted Si to help out Tuck. Knowing that Schneider had a good chance of getting out of the territory before the smuggler could catch up with him had been the deciding factor. Si Tanner was a good lawman. He'd been marshal, judge and legislator. Now he guessed he played God, too. Well, maybe this once. Just this once.

Anna Stinebaugh sat near the back, still totally baffled about why she was there. She didn't know anything about the case. Well, she'd soon find out. As long as Si felt in a Godly mood, he thought he'd teach a lesson or two.

All four other madams sat with Tuck and Essie. Si made sure the judge called them all as witnesses. He found Dr. Brawand sitting halfway back on the right. Nat Hardy stood at his place by the front entrance. He knew Cheney had some character witnesses lined up to attest to Essie's reliability and honesty. They all seemed to be in the room.

When U. S. Commissioner Edward Rasmussen walked into his courtroom at precisely eight thirty, Si watched him look upon it with satisfaction. The room had filled to capacity. The marshal knew the judge had received the most incredible cases these days. Too bad this one was so terribly sensational, so much so that it could not even be printed. However, word of mouth would be sufficient publicity. Outside Skagway, in the less respectable press, the story would get quite the attention.

He called the court to order, and then went through the preliminaries, explaining briefly, and in as neutral a way as possible, the outline of the case. Hans Schneider, a bounty hunter, had been charged with five counts of assault and one of rape, purportedly to have taken place on the night of November 12, against five female prisoners being held in the federal jail at the time. This hearing would determine whether the charges merited serious consideration or whether the commissioner would dismiss them. The commissioner looked up when a woman gasped near the back of the hall. Si glanced at Anna Stinebaugh, knowing the judge probably wondered who in the room had come to the hearing unaware of its nature.

The judge shuffled through a few papers, and next announced that Mr. Schneider, the defendant, could not personally attend the hearing. Schneider lay in the White Pass Hospital, recovering from a serious stomach indisposition. Dr. Brawand said he should not be forced to give a deposition just yet. His council, Steve Regent, the man who had done so poorly for Essie and the other madams on Alaska Street, indicated that Mr. Schneider wanted Regent to represent him in his absence.

Each madam took the stand and told her story. This wasn't a trial, not yet, so they did not recount each blow. But whores did not believe in sugar-coating a story to make it palatable.

"They exaggerate, Mr. Tanner," a whisper came from his side.

"You only hope they exaggerate, Mrs. Stinebaugh." He turned to watch her eyes. She looked at the dead expression on the madams' faces.

"They have no souls. They're used to being treated in this manner." Anna Stinebaugh sounded outraged. "I don't have to be subjected to this sick, sadistic display."

She turned to leave, and Tanner stared her back down into her seat.

When Essie's turn came to testify, she explained the excuse for the beating and the torture, how Schneider said he wanted Tuck. None of the other women had mentioned that fact. Perhaps Schneider had neglected to ask them. She described her wounds in detail, including the initials carved on her abdomen. The others had not been cut, only beaten.

Anna held a handkerchief to her mouth, wondering if her stomach would rebel before the testimony ended. Her eyes pleaded with Si Tanner to let her go. He sternly forbade her from moving.

Essie said she remembered little of the beating, other than the sick feeling in her womb after one particularly harsh blow.

"I had not had my menses for two months," she said to the floor. "Since marrying, I had hoped for a child. I thought that perhaps now, we could raise a family. But that's not to be. I have bled ever since he struck that blow." Essie dissolved into tears.

Si glanced at Anna and noticed that her eyes would not meet his.

Zino Cheney gave Essie a few moments to compose

herself, handing her another handkerchief. Then he asked her. "Is that your deposition, Mrs. Flaharty?"

"No," she managed to say. "I have something else." She took three deep breaths, and then looked the judge straight in the eye. "Some people in this room, Your Honor, without a doubt, believe the crime committed against me and these other women is somehow less terrible because of who I am and what I do for a living. They believe that I am so accustomed to use by men that such ravages upon my body is tolerable to me where they would be unendurable to a woman who had known only her husband. I can assure you that the sort of act that brought me into the life I have led for the past twenty years began in just this way. It appears that Mr. Schneider thought it his duty to usher each of the women of Alaska Street from their professions with similar acts of violence. I found it just as loathsome, as horrible, as unendurable as I did when I was thirteen years old."

Essie buried her face in her hands, sobbing. Her strength had left her. She didn't know if she could do this again for a trial. She wanted Tuck beside her, but the judge allowed her only the bailiff. He, at least, handled her gently and helped her to where Tuck could gather her into his arms.

Anna sat frozen in her chair through the remaining depositions. Dr. Brawand testified to the extent and degree of the injuries suffered by each of the women. He verified that Essie had indeed lost a child.

Nat Hardy, the jailer, when called to the stand, swore how he believed Schneider drugged him with a cup of coffee that he brought by half an hour before he fell asleep at his post. He had never done that before. He said that his neighbor, Ed Wallace, would testify that he had come over to the house earlier that afternoon to borrow a tool and had trouble waking him, he had slept so soundly during the day. He couldn't have slept at his post from exhaustion because he had had such a good rest before his shift. It had to be a drug.

Judge Rasmussen asked Mr. Cheney if he wished to call forth any more witnesses to make depositions. Zino said he thought he had presented enough evidence to make a case. Rasmussen concurred. He then asked Mr. Regent if he would like to call anyone forward to make statements on the behalf of the defense. Regent asked Dr. Brawand to take the stand again.

"Dr. Brawand, I would like you to describe the condition of Mr. Schneider when you checked him into your hospital yesterday afternoon at about four o'clock in the afternoon."

"Mr. Schneider was delirious, raving about killing someone, I'm not sure who. He appeared to be suffering from severe cramps. He had a high fever. I have been treating him for stomach distress. I have also been considering ordering a mental examination."

"Objection, Your Honor. Move to strike the last."

"Sustained," Rasmussen agreed. "Please continue."

"Dr. Brawand," Regent continued, struggling to bring himself back under control after the flurry of excitement. It had, perhaps, been his greatest moment. "Was that all that seemed to be out of order with Mr. Schneider? Did you see no wounds or bruises?"

"Objection." Zino Cheney interjected. "Leading the witness."

"Sustained," again Rasmussen agreed.

"You observed nothing else about Mr. Schneider that required your medical attention, Dr. Brawand? May I remind you that you are under oath and that I can subpoena your medical records?"

"I doubt you can subpoena my records, Mr. Regent. However, I will tell you truthfully that Mr. Schneider appeared to have been in a brawl fairly recently. I do not believe he had sustained his knife wounds from the ladies he allegedly attacked on November 12, as these wounds appeared to be more recent than that. I would say he had acquired them within thirty-six hours of arriving at my hospital," the doctor answered truthfully. More like two hours, but two hours lay within the thirty-six hour margin Si had allowed to find someone with whom Schneider had picked a fight before landing in jail. Brawand said he'd seen two or three other wounds that looked about that old.

Regent contemptuously dismissed the well-respected doctor. Si heard Anna gasp at the arrogance of the young man.

Regent then recalled Nat Hardy to the stand. "Can you

tell the court who you incarcerated at about two o'clock yesterday afternoon, Mr. Hardy?"

"Tuck Flaharty, sir. Si Tanner arrested him for bootlegging."

Regent nodded, sagely. "That's Frederick Flaharty, isn't it, Mrs. Flaharty's husband?"

Nat nodded. "Yes, sir."

"Did you put Mr. Flaharty in the same cell with Mr. Schneider?"

Nat hesitated only a heartbeat. "Yes, sir. We had a brawl at the Pantheon Saloon the night before. The other cell was full."

"And then you left the two of them alone?"

"Yes, sir," Nat replied, succinctly.

"For how long, would you say?" Regent acted like he was pulling teeth.

"Ten minutes. Tuck had sent for a friend to bail him out."

"And when you returned to take Mr. Flaharty to the bail officer, did Mr. Schneider seem all right to you, then?" Regent asked.

"I really didn't notice," Nat replied, vaguely. "I was busy with Tuck. Tuck's slippery sometimes. I wanted to make sure I had the cuffs on good. I didn't notice Mr. Schneider wasn't feeling good until I came back from the bail office."

Regent snorted, and then said he had finished with his witness.

The judge asked Mr. Cheney if he wanted to redirect.

"I think, upon further reflection, that a couple of more witnesses might be appropriate, Mr. Rasmussen."

The judge rolled his eyes, but waved his hand in permission. Zino Cheney called Jack McCabe, a laborer for the railroad, and one of Tuck's old customers. After establishing Mr. McCabe's identity and occupation, Mr. Cheney asked him what he did with himself the evening of Tuesday, November 13.

"I had me a bottle of whiskey some friends had gotten, can't tell you where." McCabe shifted his eyes around the room. They landed on Tanner. Si nodded, ever so slightly. Don't worry, Jack. Tell it straight. You have nothing to worry about.

"Sitting out on Moore's Wharf, watching the moon. This big guy comes up to me, built like a steam engine, real friendly like. Tells me his name is Hans Schneider. I sorta' remember him from ought-one or so. A foreman on one of the railroad gangs. He sees the bottle and watches it a lot. I'm thinking he just wants some, so I offer to share. He won't take any. Keeps talking about it, though. Wants to know where I got it. I keep tellin' him it came from a friend, just gave it to me, like friends do, you know? He wants to know the friend's name. Hey, these are bad times. I'm not givin' out names to a man I hardly know, and I tell him so. The guy comes at me punchin'."

McCabe looked around the courtroom. He warmed to his story. He'd probably had some of that whiskey before he'd come into Rasmussen's court and felt better already. "Well, I got sorta' mad when that happened. I keep a switchblade in my pocket, like most men. That Schneider guy got a few tastes of my knife, and then just took off. That's why I keep it. Better than duking it out 'til one of you'se out."

Zino Cheney thanked Mr. McCabe for his account and dismissed him. With these depositions, cross examination became unnecessary.

Mr. Cheney then surprised the entire courtroom by calling for Mrs. Anna Stinebaugh. Anna sat stunned. She glared at Si Tanner, who smiled and tipped his hat. She thought he had merely meant to force her to beg forgiveness of God, knowing that Hans Schneider'd probably been after that reward money the Anti-Saloon League had put up for information on the identity of the bootleggers. Anna had never much liked that plan, and didn't feel responsible for it. It was something the ladies of the W. C. T. U. had stated publicly that they had nothing to do with. She couldn't imagine what new horrors Tanner could subject her to.

"Mrs. Stinebaugh," Cheney began, once he finished all the preliminaries, "do you know Mr. Frederick C. Flaharty?"

"I know of Mr. Flaharty. I know him by sight. I do not know that I have ever spoken to him," she replied.

"Would you say that you know Mr. Flaharty by reputation, Mrs. Stinebaugh?"

Anna sensed a trap. She couldn't see where it led. She had sworn to tell the truth, so tell the truth she would. "Yes, I would say I know Mr. Flaharty's reputation."

"You and Mr. Flaharty have not always seen eye to eye on issues in this community, have you, Mrs. Stinebaugh?"

Anna harrumphed, a very unladylike thing to do, but he caught her quite by surprise. She answered his question, though. "No. I would say that Mr. Flaharty and I disagree on quite a number of issues in this community."

Tuck grinned at her. She refused to look in his direction.

"Did you join an effort to block his acquisition of a liquor license in the fall of 1908?" Anna assented to his question. She allowed she had done the same in April of 1914. She also admitted she led the movement to close down all of the saloons in Skagway in 1916.

"Mrs. Stinebaugh, you are the Vice President of the Woman's Christian Temperance Union, are you not?"

"Yes, I am." Anna held her head high as she proudly admitted to the title.

"Were you not a member in 1901?"

Anna paused. "Yes, I was a member of the W. C. T. U. in 1901."

"Did you assist in the effort to district the prostitutes in September of that year?"

Anna lifted her chin. She answered smugly, "I did indeed."

"Didn't the W. C. T. U. initiate the effort to move the restricted district in April 1909?"

"Yes, we were involved in that effort," Anna admitted, still satisfied with the results of that fight.

"And did the W. C. T. U. not complain to the First District court on November 2, 1917 that someone smuggled liquor into the restricted district of Skagway?"

"Of course, we made that complaint," Anna allowed.

"Mrs. Stinebaugh, you have systematically pursued and hunted this man and his wife over the course of sixteen years. In the process, you have destroyed their livelihood. Do you think Mr. Flaharty may have reason to hate you?"

"Objection," Regent shouted. Anna blessed him.

"Sustained," Rasmussen sighed.

"You admitted that you know Mr. Flaharty's reputation, Mrs. Stinebaugh," Zino redirected his questioning. "Does he have a reputation for violence? Has he ever threatened you or anyone in your family – perhaps your husband – because of your activities against his and his wife's livelihoods?"

Cheney waited for an answer. Anna sat there quietly, her hands in her lap. "No," she finally answered quietly. "Mr. Flaharty has always defended himself in a court of law. When he lost, he behaved honorably."

"Thank you, Mrs. Stinebaugh. That will be all."

Judge Rasmussen did not want any more testimony, by anyone. "It is my judgment that there is sufficient evidence to hold Hans Schneider as charged for the assault of Olive Hazel Crosby, Nora Moore, Billie Morris, Birdie Ash and Essie Flaharty. In addition, he is charged with the rape of Essie Flaharty. What is Mr. Schneider's plea, Mr. Regent?"

"Not guilty to all charges, of course."

"Bail is set at ten thousand dollars. He is to be returned to the jail as soon as Dr. Brawand can release him, unless, of course, he can make bail. The next district court session is in Juneau beginning December 15. You will receive notice when to appear. Court dismissed. Reconvene at one o'clock this afternoon." Rasmussen banged his gavel, rose and left his courtroom, satisfied that he didn't have to have anything further to do with this messy case.

Tuck met Si's eyes. Tanner touched his hat. Tuck nodded, grimly. It didn't feel as good as he hoped, but he considered it a whole lot better than doing it Si's way. And Si had given him Anna Stinebaugh, too. That added some sweetness to a bitter dish. Tuck gathered Essie into his arms to take her home and explain it all to her.

Chapter Twenty-Two

The City of Seattle

Wednesday, November 21, 1917 (six days later).   Tuck stood at the stern of The City of Seattle, leaning against the rail, watching Skagway recede into the gray curtain of falling snow.   Essie had gone down to their cabin to unpack, she said.   Neither of them had any reason to come back to this town.   He didn't think he'd see the place again.   Even Flick said he'd be coming out soon.   Tuck wasn't sure how he felt about it.   Maybe someday he'd be sorry for leaving.   Right now he felt glad to be rid of the place.   Still, he looked at the way the cliff plunged into the sea and remembered the exaltation of the first time he'd seen it.   For a moment, he recaptured the joy of being that young and that excited. He wondered if he and Essie could ever go back to that feeling again.

He settled in a seat by the window to watch the rocky shore along the base of the mountains slip by. He hadn't been there long before Marshal Tanner materialized in front of him.

"Si," Tuck acknowledged. "Sit down."

"Don't mind if I do," Tanner admitted. He eased his pants up a hitch before taking the seat opposite Tuck, measuring the ex-smuggler evenly.

"You got yourself a good lawyer," Si shook his head. "I thought we had you, dead to rights. I was sorry about it, I really was, but I was sure you would end up at McNeil's for at least a year, maybe two. We had witnesses, men seeing you unload the whiskey, folks who didn't want to admit it but would be forced to testify you had sold them liquor. Hell, they did admit to buying liquor from you. It was all tight, Tuck. Cheney got you off on a simple technicality."

"That's why I pay him very good money, Si. He earns every penny and then some. It's why other people lose when they're up against him." Tuck chuckled, some of his indomitable spirit returning.

"Also, that bastard Schneider helped me win this one. There wasn't a man on that jury that would convict me after what he did to Essie. Not that I wouldn't have gladly gone to McNeil prison to spare her that. But they weren't going to lock me up with that man facing a trial in Juneau, where who knows what could happen, with the chance that he could go free, and Essie out there alone. A lot of those men remember having a good time at Essie's place. Some of them can remember as far back as Ida's place. I'll bet there's not a one of them hasn't lifted more than a few beers at the Board of Trade. That jury had a different idea of justice than Judge Rasmussen did."

"I figure you're right," Si admitted. He cleared his thoughts. "I'm a great believer in the American way of justice, with its system of checks and balances. Good lawyers, bad lawyers, good laws, bad laws. Sometimes the juries make all the difference. Sometimes, it's the lawman.

We all play our part."

He took a deep breath, breathing in the clean air. "That's why I've always done what I've done. I'm not a lawman because it makes me any money, you know that."

They both chuckled. After the W. C. T. U. shut down the Reception Saloon back in 1899, Si Tanner had gone into the hardware business. He, his wife and son, Fred, had struggled along with it ever since. Si's heart had never been in the hardware business, but always in the law. But he couldn't support a family on the salary of a deputy marshal, a magistrate, a city councilman, a mayor, or a territorial legislator, most of which paid nothing at all. He'd always kept that hardware store, as well, showing up at the counter and keeping the books and making sure the inventory met demand. Tuck Flaharty had only known one other man to work as hard as Si Tanner, his good friend Chris Shea. And he had known no man so dedicated to the law.

"So why did you help me out, if you're such a stickler for the law?" Tuck wanted to know, with the business now done and over, now that he didn't need to beg any more.

Si grinned at Tuck's impertinence. "Because I'm interested in justice, perhaps. I, like you, do not always trust that the Lady will prevail. Take your own smuggling case as a prime example. I trusted all the lawyers to be equally well qualified and all the jurors to be fair-minded and honest. I should have been as distrusting of them as I am of those in Juneau at Mr. Schneider's trial."

Tuck smirked. "Thank you, Si, for your selective trust."

Si leaned back in his seat. "It is dangerous for a U. S. Marshal to have ever been a judge. I should not have been magistrate for so many years, especially in a town where I later have to come and arrest the good people I know so well. I have judged them, have made decisions on their guilt and innocence, far too long. I know who is capable of redemption, and who is not. I have come to love some and hate others. My neutrality is largely suspect. I am a far better legislator than I am a lawman, Tuck. But I love what I do now better than what I ever did before, or what I will ever do again. As much as it has frightened me that I could do it, that I would do it, it's perhaps the best thing I have done, to help you and Essie. And it gave me great satisfaction to chastise the good Anna Stinebaugh."

Tuck grinned widely at the memory. "You have turned Essie around with that gambit, Si. She has been a new woman since you made Mrs. Stinebaugh eat humble pie at that hearing. Essie's spirit returned when she heard Anna tell the court what an honorable man I am. It was all I could do to keep her from flouncing down the aisle and stuffing it down Mrs. Stinebaugh's throat."

Si smiled his slow half smile. He had caught a glimpse of Essie Flaharty at that moment, face alive with pride in her man. Si's tactic had worked, far better than he planned. Anna had come through like a trooper. He had not seen her around much since. She hadn't gone to Tuck's smuggling trial. Her vindictive spirit had taken a crushing.

"So the Mrs. is recovering?"

"Nicely. She said she would be up here soon, so you can see for yourself. The wounds heal, I believe all of them. I catch her staring off into space far less often each day. She needs me in her bed, saying she doesn't feel safe without me. My smuggling days in Alaska are over, unless I take her with me."

"Did I trust correctly then? Are you and the Mrs. redeemable?"

"If by that, you wonder if we know when we are beaten, the answer is yes. You've proven you're more than a match for the two of us. Good friend that you are, you will still hold with higher principles when it comes to doing your job." Tuck admired the man. No one he knew held a stronger sense of right and wrong. "We will do nothing more illegal in the First District of Alaska."

"We all must stand true to our beliefs, Tuck," Si reminded him.

"We all must do what we know, Si. We all have to do what's in our hearts and in our souls. Sarah Shorthill has prevailed upon the legislature of this territory to pass the 'Bone Dry Law.' They will be closing down my Juneau saloon – Tuck's Place – on December 31. Essie and I will leave for Seattle in January. We've already bought another saloon on Yesler Street, in the heart of the tenderloin." Tuck beamed his impish Flaharty grin. "It has three floors, one for the drinking and gaming, one for the girls and one for Essie and me."

Tanner shook his head. "There's word there will be a constitutional amendment banning the manufacture and sale of liquor all over the country. What will you do, then?"

The sparkle never left Tuck's eyes. "But we'll be out of Alaska's First District, Si. Seattle's a big place. I hear they call them 'speak-easies.' Essie's an expert at running places that aren't entirely legal. Seattle never has honored its own vice laws. No, we belong in Seattle, now. Essie knows the place, and it's big enough to get lost in. We'll be comfortable there." Tuck stared at the shoreline, wondering if he'd ever see this craggy coast again.

"I should wire Seattle, warn them you're coming," Tanner chuckled. Tuck's blue eyes twinkled back at him, daring him to do just that. Both knew the emptiness of Si's threat.

The well-dressed Essie sashayed into the room, her clothing rich and of the latest fashion, not gauche or immodest. With understated furs and her elaborate, but not too colorful hat, making an entrance no man missed, she vibrated with energy. Both men scrambled to their feet as she neared them.

"Si Tanner, you old fox," she purred, after accepting Tuck's possessive kiss on her cheek. She extended a hand to the marshal, which he calmly accepted and, without so much as a look of permission from Tuck, brought to his lips. Essie pretended to blush. The gesture seemed greatly daring for the old lawman, the nearest he had ever come to an overture. Tuck grinned and captured his wife's hand for himself.

"That will be enough, you two," he scolded. "We're all respectable, now. We're to act it. Sit, Darlin', so Mr. Tanner and I can, too." And so they settled for a nice, long, pleasant conversation between old friends, as The City of Seattle steamed its way to Juneau in the falling snow.

In Skagway, Anna Stinebaugh sat on an unpadded pew in the Presbyterian Church. She had tried to start many conversations with God, lately, with very little success. God didn't seem to be paying much attention to her. Perhaps here, in the church, she might get a better hearing.

Why, Dear Lord? she begged. It seemed to be going so well. It all went according to plan. We curried favor with the businessmen of this town. We cleaned up the cemetery, built reading rooms and rest rooms for the tourists, and put in drinking fountains for the horses and the dogs. We've worked for eight hour work days and forty hour work weeks for the laboring men. We've helped destitute women find work. We got the men to sign their temperance pledges. You helped us get the vote, so that women could put the right men in City Hall. We moved the prostitutes from Seventh Avenue to Alaska Street, out of the sight of children and ladies shopping downtown. We shut down the saloons, just like you wanted us to. We've done everything we've known to be Good and Right to Do, all for the sake of our men and our children and for the women who will follow us.

Anna fell on her knees and laid her forehead on her folded hands. Dear Lord, why did you send that evil man to so abuse those poor women? They promised to leave. We had defeated them.

Anna's tears ran down her face unabated when her Lord would not answer her. Then, with sudden insight, she understood why He had been mute. Anna Stinebaugh, in great humbleness of spirit, began to beg her Lord for forgiveness for her long list of sins of pride and bigotry and elitism and the other transgressions she hadn't even known she possessed. Before she prayed for the souls of Hans Schneider, Kitty Wandsted, Essie Flaharty, the madams of Alaska Street, Frederick C. Flaharty and Josias M. Tanner, she prayed deeply and fervently for her own, for she seriously doubted whether she had any place reserved in heaven. She first thanked her Lord, and then begged His forgiveness for her role in the attacks on those women, the rape of Essie and in the change of Skagway.

When Anna emerged from the church, she saw three little girls wending their way home on this cold afternoon. Rosy-cheeked, alive with fun, they skipped through the falling snow, tossing handfuls of snow towards each other. She recognized them as Jeannette and Tad Hillery's girls, Helen, Jean and little Virginia. Anna smiled at their play, and then

stopped dead. Knowing her soul was damned, Anna's heart swelled with pride to know these little girls would grow up in a world without saloons and brothels, having the right to vote, to find a paying job outside the demimonde. With her help, they would yet be able to have healthy families at their own choosing.

With a surge of returning pride, Anna Stinebaugh decided it was a fair trade, the souls of a few women of the W. C. T. U. for the lives of all the women to follow. Such were the casualties of war. She walked home through the falling snow, still at peace with her God.

Sin and Grace

Epilogue

Hans Schneider, convicted of the assault of Nora Moore, Billie Morris, Hazel Crosby, Birdie Ashe and Essie Flaharty on January 12, 1918, received a sentence of a year in prison for each assault. The jury of Juneau men also convicted him of the rape of Essie Flaharty, for which he received an additional year in the federal prison at McNeil Island. Tuck thought six years too light a sentence, but then he remembered that men died in the cold and damp of McNeil's. In six years, Schneider would not know where to find them. Essie was the last woman Schneider had. He did not remember her fondly. He cursed Tuck daily. He didn't make it for six years. The ex-bounty hunter died of pneumonia on February 23, 1922. Si Tanner wrote to let the Flahartys know the man's fate.

Harry Burton Flaharty and his wife, Ellen, moved to Seattle shortly after Tuck and Essie did. Mother Flaharty joined the boys after Papa Flaharty died so they could have fried chicken dinners on Sunday. Content at last that her sons had wives to care for them, she wondered how they had managed all those years. During the Great Depression, when he lost Tuck, Harry left Seattle for California, where he died in 1945.

Jeannette deGruyter and Albert "Tad" Hillery, after they married, had their first child, Helen, in Skagway, then briefly moved to Lovelock, Nevada, where they had a second girl, Jean. Their third daughter, Virginia, was born in Charleston, West Virginia, where Jeannette's parents had moved after the gold rush. Tad spent a year in California in the early 1920s, but for the most part, they always came back to Skagway, where Tad worked for the White Pass and Yukon Route. They had a fourth daughter, Beatrice, in Skagway. The Hillerys separated in the 1940s. Tad died in Tenakee, Alaska in 1961, at age 77. Jeannette lived another six years, dying in Juneau in 1967. They left a wealth of descendants, and many still live in Skagway. Virginia would become one of Alaska's first female magistrates.

Anna and J. D. Stinebaugh returned to Grants Pass, Oregon once they could wring no more living or salvation from Skagway. James died on March 6, 1921, at fifty-nine years of age. Anna lived to the ripe old age of eighty-five in Grants Pass. Until her death on September 23, 1952, she remained convinced she had made life better for Virginia Hillery and women like her, but knew she had lost her soul in the process.

Kitty and Chris Wandsted moved to San Francisco where they lived in his mortgaged house. In 1929, the couple bought a farm near Hildebrand, Oregon, in Klamath County. Kitty died in the Hillside Hospital in Klamath Falls, Oregon on January 21, 1937 at the age of 71, still married to her Danish carpenter with the deep-set blue eyes.

Josias M. "Si" Tanner did not retire from his job as U. S. Marshal until he was seventy-one years old, in 1921 when Woodrow Wilson became president of the United States. At that time, he returned to Skagway to sit behind the counter of his hardware store and trade stories with the old-timers of Skagway. On the evening of September 20, 1927, he sat down to play cards with Fred and his daughter-in-law, Frances. An hour later, his heart failed him. He was seventy-seven years of age, still strong, still hale, still handsome to the end. His son took him to Tacoma to be buried next to his beloved Juliette.

Tuck and Essie Flaharty left Juneau upon the completion of Hans Schneider's trial in January 1918. They opened their saloon at First and Yesler Street in the Tenderloin of Seattle, turning it into a speak-easy after National Prohibition went into effect on January 1, 1919. When the census enumerator came knocking on their door morning after morning in June 1920, they ignored him. They and the girls worked nights, and they had no reason to answer the door during the day.

By 1930, the Great Depression had hit America. The Flaharty luck did not abandon Tuck. He found a job with the Great Northern Railroad as a special agent, giving the bum's rush to the men who boarded the freight cars and tried to hitch a ride across the country. Tuck lived for the day Prohibition would end so he could buy another bar. His heart didn't make it, though. It failed him on July 20, 1930. He held Essie in his arms and was laughing when the pain first came. It didn't last long. He was fifty-six years old.

Essie gave up her working name and went by her childhood name Augusta. She never had the child Tuck wanted, and he never said a word about it, but to console her in her grief and assure her that he found nothing wrong with the dream they had first built together. He still called her Essie. She never called him Fred. She did not stay a widow long. She died of a stroke on June 15, 1932. She was fifty-two years old. She had mourned Tuck every day since he had left her.

Essie and Tuck

Author's Notes

The Change and Women's Rights

The first two decades of the twentieth century fascinate me. In my view, at no time during the last two hundred years has the nation endured and survived such dramatic social change in such a short period of time. Freed from the cares of housework by the burgeoning wealth of their husbands and the increased mechanization of household chores, middle class women began to engage in political action. They chose social reform as their cause. To this dedication beyond self, women today owe their freedoms, freedoms they often take all too much for granted.

It seems ironic to me that if not for the curbing of some men's liberties, I would not have the freedoms I enjoy today. Working-class bachelor men sacrificed their rights to drink with their comrades in gregarious companionship and to relax in the company of women unrestrained by matrimonial bounds. If they had fought back harder, women today might still lack a voice, might still be forced to work at half wages, when they could find work at all, and might still be selling their bodies because that was the best money they could make. Women could still be without birth control, because a conservative government forbade research on contraception until women's votes in the 1930's overturned the laws that banned it as pornography. What a thought. My vote was bought at the expense of men's licentious behavior.

The social upheaval between 1900 and 1920 can only be matched by that experienced by Southerners in the wake of the Civil War. During the Progressive Era, our nation fought political graft and corruption, but it also struggled to find its social identity. Would it be a moral society? And at what expense to the freedoms of its citizens? And to what citizens?

As I researched this period, I came to respect the women who doggedly fought against what seemed to be overwhelming odds, but I also understood the men – and the women who loved them – who could not change who they were and what they had always known. As an anthropologist, I understand how difficult culture change can be.

That the middle class women of the early twentieth century could change their world in twenty years seems miraculous. That my grandparents, all now dead, lived through that period and never spoke of it, also seems astounding. They simply accepted the change as The Way It Was, just as we today accept women's (virtual) equality to men as The Way It Is.

I am sorry that men had to give up so much so that we women could have so much. We modern women owe as great a debt to the working class bachelor as we do to the middle class woman who won us our freedoms.

Why Skagway?

I admit to a love-hate relationship with Skagway. I once tried mightily to live there. My husband thinks I'm crazy. He did live there. He ought to know. As an archaeologist who had done quite a bit of work in Skagway, newly divorced and free to do whatever I pleased, I begged and pleaded with my employers at the National Park Service to be transferred to Klondike Gold Rush National Historic Park and from there be allowed to work as the Regional Historical Archaeologist. I thought it was the perfect arrangement. I made the mistake of asking for too much money, a failing uppity folk often have. They called my bluff. So I went to graduate school instead.

There, in retribution, I gathered together all I had dug up on Skagway and turned it into a PhD dissertation. Along the way, I started reading the turn-of-the-century Skagway newspapers. They opened up a whole new world to me. Newspaper editor John Troy's charm and acid wit brought the city alive in a way the mute artifacts and rich earth had only suggested. I learned of a world of decent people struggling against greedy souls amidst an atmosphere of unbounded hope and enthusiasm.

Throughout the years that followed, I continued to read those newspapers, and I came to know the people of Skagway between 1900 and 1920 better than I do the people who live in my own city today. All the while, I returned to

Skagway for a few weeks each summer (occasionally in the winter, too) to dig in her sandy, rocky soil and find more shattered fragments of her people's lives. When Uncle Sam decided I had spent enough time digging in Skagway's ground, I started spending my own money and continued digging in Alaska's archives, hungry to continue my relationship with the now dead people I had met there.

In all those summers (and a few weeks in the winter), I hated the rain and the wind. I am a Southwesterner at heart. I love the warmth and the sunshine and blue skies. The last time I did any digging in Skagway was in September 1991. I had a bad cold for the entire three weeks I spent in the town, and I swear, it rained every day, all day long. I lived at the Golden North Hotel, before they renovated it. I could have sworn the windows had not been caulked since 1908. They put me in a room on the south side, and the wind constantly howled through them. I paid extra to have a bathtub in my room, one of those old-fashioned kinds, the ones with feet in the shape of a lion's paw, deep enough you could fill it to your shoulders. I'd come out of the rain each night as it turned dark, strip off my wet, sandy clothes, and sink into the hot bath, nursing my aching hands. You may not know it, but they don't make a shovel handle small enough around for a woman's hands, and, when it's cold and wet like that, mine always ached by the end of the day. I vowed I'd never again excavate in a place where I couldn't come in when it was raining outside. I've kept my vow. I moved to Santa Fe and work only in the Southwest. You can't buy Rite-in-Rain paper here.

That's when I decided that if I wanted to continue to do research on Skagway, I would have to become a historian. I told my husband I wanted to go back to school for another PhD, this one in history. Again, he called me a crazy woman. He told me to just do the research and write and don't worry if the academic types wanted credentials. I said I needed to know how to do it. He said I already knew how to do it, I'd been doing it all along.

I've written my histories of Skagway, in several different places. This novel is a different, joyful way of telling you its history. Skagway has so much more in it than just its gold rush history. To me, what happened between 1897 and 1900 was just the beginning. We have all forgotten what happened afterwards, and that excites me even more than the city's boom years. Because Harriet Pullen told the stories, and because Harriet wanted to entertain her visitors with embroidered tales of the gold rush days, Skagway seems to have forgotten the glorious times that followed. They must have seemed ordinary to most of Skagway's citizens, just the day-to-day business of trying to make a living, of making a life. My God, those days beat with energy, with life, with hope. With change.

And twenty years is a long enough time that you don't notice the drama taking place around you. When it's over, the men stand around in shock and wonder what happened, and the women are amazed that they pulled it off. And they all move on, trying desperately to adapt to the situation they have created, wanting to forget as quickly as possible all of the ugliness – the messiness and casualties of the sporting war – they saw along the way. They certainly don't want the children to know anything about the bad old times. Both Mom and Dad had created a new world for the kids. That was the whole point.

And so the people of Skagway forgot about the enormous changes that took place right under their noses. I mean to help us all remember that they did it for us. We shouldn't forget those casualties of war.

Truth and Fiction

This book is a novel, but most of the people in it really lived. Most of the events really happened. However, I invented the way they happened and the personalities of the people involved. The historic documents fall mute on how Essie looked – I have no photograph of her – about her personality or what she said. I can guess some and imagine a lot because I have immersed myself in the culture of the prostitutes of the time and the men who patronized them. I think I know what a woman who did what she did must have been like in order to succeed the way she did.

I know quite a bit more about Tuck's personality, thanks to the way his family kept his letters and his nephew Charles

J. Roehr reprinted them in a book, Klondike Gold Rush Letters (New York: Vantage Press, 1976). John Troy also kept the town aware of his pranks and sports exploits. Because of Troy's gift with the pen, it is almost impossible not to know Tuck by reading Troy's newspaper. All I had to do was invent his dialogue.

I really don't know if Tuck and Essie loved each other for so long. An alternative scenario is that they didn't establish a personal relationship until he began to smuggle liquor for her in 1917. Being a romantic, I like to think they loved long and well. I don't want to believe they each lived their youth without love. There is no evidence that Tuck courted a woman until he married Essie.

Both John Troy and Harriet Pullen were extremely influential in keeping and developing the history of Skagway. Besides being Skagway's first historian, Harriet was instrumental in getting women out to vote. Troy epitomized the gifted writer, and, although he often made my blood boil – there was no such thing as an unbiased press in those days – he more often made me laugh or left me in awe of his ability to evoke the sights, the smells, and the sounds of Skagway in the first decade of its existence.

As to Anna Stinebaugh, I hope I have not portrayed her as the villain of this story. She really is the hero. Today's women owe the Anna Stinebaughs of America their right to vote, their right to work, their right to divorce the men who treat them badly. Generals make hard choices, and casualties come of every war. Anna deserves our utmost respect. I made efforts to find and contact descendants of Anna and James D. Stinebaugh, but failed. Perhaps this book will find its way to one or more of them. If so, I hope they will try to contact me through this publisher.

The only person of any note in the novel that I invented was Hans Schneider. That said, I have several reasons for believing someone like him existed. The assault on Essie in 1903 did happen, although to another prostitute and perpetrated by a prominent businessman. One of the madams – not Ida Freidinger – did indeed work a deal to change her testimony in exchange for "losing the paperwork," on a charge of keeping a house of ill-fame, at about the same time the federal and local courts were fighting over who got to keep the fines from the prostitutes.

I strongly suspect that something highly illegal happened to Essie and the other madams of Alaska Street on the nights of November 9 through 13, 1917. The authorities needed Tuck, and only these women, most probably Essie, knew where he was. The court did not grant bail, a standard practice at the time, forcing the women to stay in jail. The women left Skagway, without protest, after twenty years of fighting off all efforts to make them leave. Something happened during those five nights to frighten them so. Something happened to keep Tuck from leaving Skagway immediately, the moment Essie was arrested. The story I tell in this novel, I believe, is a likely scenario.

If You Want to Know More

If you want to know the true stories of the people I've written about in these pages, I have written an annotated history on vice and reform in Skagway entitled Behind the Red Curtains: Prostitution, Politics and Reform in Skagway, Alaska, 1897-1917. It is now at a university press undergoing professional review. It is my fond hope that it will be published soon. There you can find what I truly know about these people and these events, complete with hundreds of footnotes and scholarly discussions.

If you want a good book on the working class saloon in the late nineteenth century and early twentieth century, try Madelon Powers' Faces Along the Bar: Lore and Order in the Workingman's Saloon, 1870-1920 (Chicago: University of Chicago, 1998). To learn more about the history of liquor, gambling and saloons in Alaska, you will have to watch for my next academic book. I intend to call it something like The Life and Death of the Bachelor Culture in Alaska.

To understand the life of the bachelor at the end of the nineteenth century and the beginning of the twentieth century, I relied heavily on Howard P. Chudacoff's The Age of the Bachelor: Creating an American Subculture (Princeton: Princeton University, 1999). The women's reform movement has been discussed in some detail in a number of texts. I found James A. Morone's recent Hellfire Nation: The Politics of Sin in American History (New Haven, Connecticut: Yale University, 2003) to be a thought-provoking treatment of the subject, especially his section entitled "The Victorian Quest for Virtue." Sandra Haarsanger has a chapter on the Woman's Christian Temperance Union in Organized Womanhood: Cultural Politics in the Pacific Northwest, 1840-1920 (Norman, Oklahoma: University of Oklahoma Press, 1997).

Finally, if you want the real scoop on Si Tanner, I have published a biography on his life that I called "Josiah M. 'Si' Tanner: Southeast Alaska's Favorite Lawman," in the Quarterly of the National Organization for Outlaw and Lawman History, Inc. , Volume XXX, No. 1, January-March 2006, pages 29-37. Another of my articles about the man will be appearing very soon in True West magazine, entitled "Si Tanner, Con Man's Curse." You'll find I haven't exaggerated a thing about the man. Si is Skagway's real hero. They don't come any better.

Acknowledgments

Speaking of Si, his great granddaughter, Susan Tanner Schimling, and her family have kindly given their blessing to the naming of this first of what I hope to be a series of historical novels about the early days of Skagway after her great grandfather. I very much appreciate their confidence in my ability to do right by my hero.

Chuck Roehr and his sister, Paula Roehr Mahle, the grand nephew and grand niece of Tuck Flaharty, grew up in Skagway. Paula raised three children in Skagway and still lives there. I am very grateful that Chuck chose to share dozens of photographs of his great uncle with me (unfortunately, too late for me to use as a model for my drawings!) and gave me his blessing for this story, which must surely have come as a bit of a surprise, given Tuck's, Essie's and Flick's evident efforts to keep it all a secret. I hope that I have not betrayed them, as I have come to care so deeply for all of them.

I cannot thank my publisher and editor, Jeff Brady, enough. He believed in me and this book. We both hope you, the reader, will come to know Skagway much better through its pages. Also thanks to Jeff's wife, Dorothy, a Hillery descendant, who helped proofread.

Every author needs readers to help her see what she's missing. My friends Doreen Cooper, Karl Gurcke, Ted Birkedal, and Rachel Mason all pointed out weaknesses, the facts I had flubbed and helped make it easier for you to read what we all think is a fascinating story.

I could not have written this book without the love and support of Kinsey and Bob. While she complained that Mom spent far too much time monopolizing the computer, my daughter, the budding artist who will be far better than me, did like the sketches and offered helpful criticisms. My husband, Bob, the real historian, suffered many hours of reading and listening to chapters over and over again. He knows these stories by heart, but still patiently offered insightful critique. I love them both madly.